Sherman's Fifth Corps

A Civil War Novel

By J. A. Barnes

Sherman's Fifth Corps

ISBN 978-0-9840050-4-8

Brown Tones Publishing

Tacoma, WA, USA

253-581-1954

Thanks, Justy

.

Contents

THE CHARACTERS

William Tecumseh Sherman, 44, Union Army Major General, commander of the Great March from Atlanta to the Sea.
Virginia "Jennie" Lewis, 18, newly-free Georgia woman hired by the Union army as an assistant to General Sherman's cook.
Ellen Sherman, Lancaster, Ohio, Sherman's wife

General Sherman's Staff & Union Officials
L. M. Dayton, Aide-de-Camp; Major Henry Hitchcock, Assistant Adjutant General; Capt. George W. Pepper, Aide-de-Camp; Brigadier General Jefferson C. Davis, Commander, 14th Corps; Brevet Major George Ward Nichols, Aide-de-Camp; Major General Thomas, Union Commander; Daniel P. Conyngham, War Correspondent, *New York Herald*; Henry W. Halleck, Army Chief of Staff; Ulysses S. Grant, Commander of Union Forces;

Abraham Lincoln, President of the United States

Union Soldiers
Major James A. Connolly, 123rd Illinois Infantry; Capt. James Laughlin Orr, 42nd Indiana Regiment; Pvt. Charles W. Wills, 8th Illinois Infantry; Captain R. Cruikshank, 123rd New York Infantry Regiment; Lt. Colonel S. Merrill, 70th Regiment, Indiana Volunteers; Cornelius C. Platter, 81st Ohio Infantry Volunteers; Captain James M. Randall, 21st Wisconsin; Theodore Upson, 100th Indiana Infantry; Rev. G. S. Bradley, Chaplain, 22nd Wisconsin; Harvey Reid, 22nd Wisconsin; and others

Confederate Officers & Officials
Brig. Gen Pierre Gustave Toutant Beauregard, General John Bell Hood, Maj. General Joseph Wheeler; General Braxton Bragg; General William Hardee, Commanders of Confederate Forces; George Wm. Brent, Asst. to Beauregard;

General Howell Cobb, Robert Toombs, slave-holders, Commanders of Georgia Troops;
Joseph E. Brown, Governor of Georgia;
R. D. Arnold, Mayor of Savannah;
General Robert E. Lee, Commander, Army of Northern Virginia;
Jefferson Davis, President, Confederate States of America

Jennie's Family& Friends
George Lewis, Jennie's father, seaman in the Union navy;
Isabella Lewis, Atlanta, Jennie's mother; Caroline Lewis, Jennie's sister; Aleck Jones, Jennie's cousin, servant to Maj. Hitchcock;
Rev. Gaston C. Quarles, Atlanta, newly-free minister;
Fortune Bell, newly-free Muslim from the Georgia Sea Islands; Rev. James Lynch,

Savannah; N. I. Houston, Pastor-Third African Church, Savannah

Southern Whites
Mary Ann Hale, slave-holder;
Mrs. Louise Neal, Mary's Aunt;
Lizzie Perkerson, Fulton County sheriff's daughter;
Anna Marie Cook, friend of Mary; Carrie Berry, 8-year-old cousin to Mary; Dolly S. L. Burge, slave-holder;
Mrs. Ella Gertrude Clanton Thomas, educated Southern woman;
Other Southern Mistresses: Miss A. C. Cooper; Ella Mitchell;
Mrs. L.F.J.; Sue Sample; Nora M. Canning;
Ella Wilson;
Frances Howard;
Fanny Cohen Taylor

And many others…

"...all persons held as slaves within any State or designated part of a State, the people whereof shall then be in rebellion against the United States, shall be then, thenceforward, and forever free; and the Executive Government of the United States, including the military and naval authority thereof, will recognize and maintain the freedom of such persons, and will do no act or acts to repress such persons, or any of them, in any efforts they may make *for their actual freedom.*"

Abraham Lincoln, *The Emancipation Proclamation*, January 1, 1863

PART ONE: NOVEMBER 1864

Tuesday, November 8

<u>L.M. DAYTON</u>, Aide-de-Camp,

By order of <u>GENERAL WILLIAM T. SHERMAN</u>

SPECIAL FIELD ORDERS No. 119, Headquarters Military Division of the Mississippi, In the Field, Kingston, Georgia

The general commanding deems it proper at this time to inform the officers and men of the Fourteenth, Fifteenth, Seventeenth, and Twentieth Corps, that he has organized them into an army for a special purpose, well known to the War Department and to General Grant. It is sufficient for you to know that it involves a departure from our present base, and a long and difficult march to a new one. All the chances of war have been considered and provided for, as far as human sagacity can. All he asks of you is to maintain that discipline, patience, and courage, which have characterized you in the past; and he hopes, through you, to strike a blow at our enemy that will have a material effect in producing what we all so much desire, his complete overthrow.

Of all things, the most important is, that the men, during marches and in camp, keep their places and do not scatter about as stragglers or foragers, to be picked up by a hostile people in detail. It is also of the utmost importance that our wagons should not be loaded with anything but provisions and ammunition. All surplus servants, non-combatants, and refugees, should now go to the rear, and none should be encouraged to encumber us on the march. At some future time we will be able to provide for the poor whites and blacks who seek to escape the bondage under which they are now suffering. With these few simple cautions, he hopes to lead you to achievements equal in importance to those of the past.

MARY ANN HALE, Hale Farm, Decatur, Georgia

Aunt Louisa,

I have had another crisis with my negroes. Jennie has for a long time been perversely and uncontrollably sulky and sullen whenever I have spoken to her. Her conduct was most insufferable, and to have submitted to it would have been in effect to have resigned my position as the head of this family, and have reduced myself to a plaything in the hands of my slaves. I saw that strong measures were necessary, or else I must resign the rule of my household and be ruled myself by my slaves.

Last week I had Billy up here to whip Jennie until she humbled herself a little, which was not till she was well punished, for she tried very hard to 'stout it out'. It was a very bitter pill, and I would not go through it all again for the worth of the whole of them in gold. But I did my duty; I can see it in no other light; and the effect on my other negroes seems so far and will I have no doubt continue to be very good. But with Jennie, the effect is only temporary. So I have hired her out in Atlanta where she can be closer to her mother. Let Isabella look after her for I tire of it.

MRS. LOUISA NEAL, Boarding House, Atlanta, Georgia

Mary,

What difference does it make where one negro is or another? To-day will no doubt decide the fate of the Confederacy, and if Lincoln is re-elected I think our fate is a hard one. But we are in the hands of a merciful God, and if He sees that we are in the wrong, I trust that He will show it unto us.

I have never felt that slavery was altogether right, for it is abused by men, and I have often heard Captain Neal say that if he could see that it was sinful for him to own slaves, if he felt that it was wrong, he would take them where he could free them. He would not sin for his right hand. The purest and holiest men have owned them, and I can see nothing in the scriptures which forbids it. I have never bought or sold slaves and I have tried to make life easy and pleasant to those that have been bequeathed me by the dead. I have never ceased to work until now. Now I am evicted from my home!

Many a Northern housekeeper has a much easier time than a Southern matron with her hundred negroes.

LIZZIE PERKERSON, Sheriff Perkerson's Farm,

Fulton County, Georgia

Dearest Mary,

The negroes are flocking to the Yankee Army. Ed Taliaferro went down to Henry County and all his negro men ran away from him and this last move the Yankees made they got all his horses and mules and destroyed pretty near all his household goods and came so near getting him they shot him in the back. But he says he escaped by good running. He is now fixing to move back with his women and children and nothing else. Joe and Emma are gone up North. Every negro Terry had went but Kit. Ours are all at home and they are all the negroes left in the neighborhood.

ANNA MARIE COOK, Cook House, Milledgeville,

The Capital of Georgia

Oh, Dear Mary,

Like your own dear Thomas, my precious brother left us today to return to the hardships and dangers of the soldier's life. He left some days sooner than the expiration of his furlough by an order through the newspapers from Gen. Young. It was a bitter trial to give him up, to bid him goodbye, but necessity called him and yield we must. God only knows how I love that brother, how I cling to him, but we all love him. He is so good, so gentle and kind.

Heavenly Father bless and comfort our brothers tonight, and be with us all forevermore for our Redeemer's sake.

[5]

CARRIE BERRY, Berry House, Atlanta, Georgia

Cousin Mary!

Every boddie seems to be in confusion. The black wimmen are running around trying to get up north for fear that the Rebels will come in and take them. This is Zuie's birthday and she has been very smart. We lost our last hog this morning early. Soldiers took him out of the pen. Me and Buddie went around to hunt for him and every where that we inquired they would say that they saw two soldiers driving off to kill him. We will have to live on bread.

MARY ANN HALE, Hale Farm, Decatur, Georgia

We must all look to the blessed day when General Sherman, the fiend in human form, finally leaves us to continue his destruction elsewhere. I have heard he issued another order for all men, women and children, white and black, to leave Atlanta and go North, thus forcing the few families left out of their houses and homes to the colder charity of the Northern world. Emperor Alexander of Russia sent the rebellious Poles as exiles to Siberia, and Lincoln through his tool Sherman exiles "freemen from their Republican home."

Civilization is going backwards and enlightened religion is a mockery, nothing but humbug as practiced in Yankee Land. When enlightened millions of souls, raised and educated in freedom of speech and action have tamely to submit to such outrages—Liberty is gone indeed!

JENNIE LEWIS, Neal House, Atlanta, Georgia

Dere Papa,

She thinks she had me beten--but she did not. Billy never hit me but told me to screme for dere life and I did so. Now I am in Atlanta and the Union solders are all arond. Miss Mary can not toch me any more. Thats how it is now Papa. Now Sherman come-- slavery is played out.

Your dauter,

Wednesday, November 9

W. T. SHERMAN, Headquarters, In the Field, Kingston, GA

Dear Ellie:

I got Uncle Charley to write you a letter today because my arm pains me so much if I attempt to write on a table. I have caught cold in it by sleeping on the ground. I hate to confess to Rheumatism or Neuralgia, but it is one or the other, but by putting a book on my knee I can write with less pain. I did not get your letters sent by the Priest Father till tonight and I was so glad to hear you were not homesick, but so very happy at school that I determined to write you a short letter although every motion of my hand was as painful as a toothache.

It is now raining but as soon as the storm clears up I am going to make another campaign that I hope will prove as successful as that of Atlanta and after it is over I will try to come & see you. I want to See you very much, indeed I cannot Say how much, and then I can tell you all about the things of which you hear so much but can know so little. War is something about which you should not concern yourself and I am now fighting that you may live in peace. I am not fighting for myself but for you and the little children, who have more to live than us older People. But if I do lose my life I know there will be some people still living who will take care of you. Mama tells me the baby is quite sick, and she is afraid he will not get well. I hope that he will live long and take poor Willy's place in our Love. Mama also tells me how smart Minnie and Lizzie are, but I am like you and wonder why they aint smart when we are at home.

You may not hear from me for some time but I will turn up if alive. Give my love to all, and believe me always thinking of you, no matter how great the danger.

Yr. father,

Dear Tommy,

I have not had a letter from you for a long time, but Mama writes me often and tells me how good a boy you are, and how you like to go to the farm in the time of gathering grapes and apples. That is right, get your share of fruit now, and be careful not to eat too many at any one time. Do you remember the time you and Willy & I gathered the Chestnuts on that tree by the Rock, and afterwards the walnuts in the tiller wagon. In a short time you will be able to drive Old Sara in a wagon & gather your own walnuts & hickory nuts. I well remember our taking Willy out by Mount Pleasant where we gathered a bag of hickory nuts and poor little fellow, not as big as you now are, he was so happy and so proud to carry his own bag of hickory nuts.

People write to me that I am now a Great General, and if I were to come home they would gather round me in crowds & play music and all such things. That is what the People call fame & Glory, but I tell you that I would rather come home quietly and have you & Willy meet me at the cars than to hear the Shouts of the People. Willy will never meet us again in this world and you and I must take care of the family as long as I live and then will be your turn. So you See you have a good deal to do. You have much to learn, but while your body is growing up strong as a man you will have time to learn all I know & more too.

Mama tells me that the baby is very sick but I hope he is now well and that he too will grow up and help you. I am told you are all very fond of the baby, and am glad of it. I have not Seen him yet, and expect he will be a big fellow before I do.

Give my love to your sisters & all our little Cousins, and believe me always thinking of you, no matter how great the danger.

Yr. loving father

ELLEN SHERMAN, Lancaster, Ohio

Dearest Cump:

Dear Willy's picture has just been brought and now stands framed in my room. I will have it hung in the parlor until I keep house somewhere. All think it excellent. I am sure you will like it but should you suggest any alterations or slight changes they can be made at any time. We need this to keep him fresh in the minds and hearts of all the children for all must love and know and talk of their holy brother until by God's grace we join him in his heavenly home.

The baby has such a severe cold which has taken such firm hold on his lungs that I greatly fear he will never get over it but that it will end in consumption. The Doctor thinks that if hereditary tendency to asthma has anything to do with its persistency that a change of climate will be of service to him. I expect to get off next week or at latest the first of the week following. As soon as I get there I will put Tommy at school and keep him there, He has had a fine time all Summer and Fall, at the farm and now he is eight years old it is time for him to begin to Study in earnest. Lizzie is fat and hearty & happy. I think she will be ready to go to the New York school when Minnie goes. Henceforth I shall devote myself to the education of the children and not allow their studies to be interrupted for any cause but to See you when they can have that happiness.

I am anxious about you dear Cump but I trust in the Mercy of God and the prayers of Willy --

Ever your truly affectionate wife,

ELLIE SHERMAN, Lancaster, Ohio

Dear Papa,

It's a very long time since you felt us and we all miss you dearly. In your last letter which we received with warmest welcome you speak of your neglecting writing to us but indeed it is that you should be ashamed. I know well that you have business to attend to and it is in this way I have always accounted for your silence.

You affectionate daughter,

ALECK JONES, In camp, Kingston, Georgia

My Dear Wife,

I write these few lines to inform you that I am well, and hope they may find you and the children well, and my cousins Isabella and Jennie, and all the friends. My dear wife, I long to see you and the children one time more in this world. I hope to see you all soon. Don't get out of heart, for I will come as soon as I can. I hope it will not be long, for God will be my helper, and I feel he will help me. Tell John he must be a good boy till I see him. Dear wife, you may look for me in Atlanta soon. I will arrive with the returning General in a few days from now. You must try and do the best you can till I come.

I remain, your dear husband, till death,

P.S. Tell Isabella her George is not with me but he is with the Union.

ISABELLA LEWIS, Medical College, Atlanta, Georgia

My Husband,

I would be mitey glad to see you and I wish you would rite here and let me no how you are getting on. I am doing tolerable well and have enjoyed very good helth since you left. I haven't forgot you nor I never will forget you as long as the world stands. My love is just as grate as it was the first night I married you, and I hope it will be so with you. My hart and love is pinned to your brest, and I hope

[12]

yours is to mine. There is no time nite or day but that I am studying about you. I havent had a letter from you since you left. I am very anxus to here from you. I herd that you had left Master Thomie and gone over to the Union Army, but I herd afterwards that you were dead. I cannot beleve that is true. If it is, Jennie is my only hope in this world now, with our dere Caroline seemingly lost to us forever.

I long to see you, husband. I wish I new where to send this.

Your loving wife till death

JENNIE LEWIS, Neal House, Atlanta, Georgia

Dearest Papa,

You can not no how much you are missed by us here in this place. Miss Mary said that you had run off to join the yankeys and that you were probably caut and are now dead but I no you are yet alive and so dose Mama and that you did not run anywhere but walked away as a Man. Mama said she would have felt the hole in her heart if you were no longer living, and she dose not feel so. So we all have fathe that you are alive and will come back to get us one day but we have not herd one word from you.

I now stay in Atlanta in the Neal famlys house but they are all gone cept old Mistis Neal. She stays in the bording house. General Sherman and his army stay every were else. I help Lena the cook. She is a mad woman but she lets me see Mama at the Medical Hospital any time I want so I dont mind her. Lena hates general Sherman more than Miss Mary dose. He is the devil, she says. Hes on his way back here and hes going to burn Atlanta to the grond, she says. But the colored folks in town say hes Moses leeding an army of the Lord. Leeding the colored slaves out of Atlanta and to the promised land of Freedom. So is he Moses or the devil?

Mama nurses the solders nite and day. It keeps such an awful smell at that Hospital, Papa. But she never leves. I do not have her spirit. You have said I was more like you who likes to be out and about with folks and I am "not the kind of chicken to sit in a coop and hatch eggs."

Mama says we must rite to you every day even if we dont know were to send our letters. I have told Tobias to check the mails for a letter from you every day and not to let Miss Mary no a thing. I pray to God you are safe and will send word soon or better yet, that you will come home and then we will truley be as free as you must be now and we can leve here. The colored folks say we are alredy free, but I swere the wite folks dont no it.

Your loveing dauter

Thursday, November 10

JAS. COOPER, Acting Assistant Adjutant- General,
Headquarters, near Florence, Alabama

Major-General Cheatham, Commanding Corps:

General Hood directs that you will cook to-morrow morning three days' bread from day after to-morrow morning, and that to-morrow evening you will move your command to the river and go into camp on this side, just opposite to Florence. The army will resume its march on Saturday morning next.

JAS. COOPER, Acting Assistant Adjutant- General,
Headquarters, near Florence, Alabama —7.30 p. m.

Major-General Cheatham, Commanding Corps:

General Hood directs that you will not move to-morrow evening as previously directed; that, instead of cooking three days' rations, as ordered, you will have two days' rations cooked and kept on hand till further orders. The wagons will be sent out for forage, as ordered.

GEORGE WM. BRENT, Colonel and Assistant Adjutant-General, Headquarters, Military Div. Of The West, Tuscumbia, Ala.

General J. B. Hood, Commanding Army of Tennessee:

GENERAL: General Beauregard directed me to acknowledge the receipt of your communication of the 3d instant. He, however, expresses the hope that you will soon be able to comply with the request contained in his communication of the 30th ultimo. A brief report of your plan of operations from this point for the information of the Government he deems important, and requests that you will forward the same as early as practicable.

I am, general, very respectfully, your obedient servant

J. B. HOOD, General, Headquarters, near Florence, Ala.

Col. George Wm. Brent, Assistant Adjutant- General:

I have just received your letter of this morning. It is not possible for me to furnish any plan of my operations for the future, as so much must depend upon the movements of the enemy. It is more prudent that we remain at this place so as not to provide intelligence to the enemy. The matter has been fully discussed between General Beauregard and myself.

GEORGE WM. BRENT, Colonel and Assistant Adjutant-General, Headquarters, Military Div Of The West, Tuscumbia, Ala.

General J. B. Hood, Commanding, &c.:

GENERAL: General Beauregard thinks you must have a low estimate of the intelligence and judgment of your wily adversary, if you suppose at this late day that he is ignorant of the position of your army and the strength of your corps.

I am, general, respectfully, your obedient servant

GEG. H. THOMAS, Major General, U. S. Volunteers, Commanding, Headquarters, Dept. Of The Cumberland, Nashville, Tenn., 5 p. m.

Major-General Sherman:

Your dispatch of 6.30 p. m. yesterday just received. My dispatch of last night contained all the information I could get up to that time. General Hatch confirms that the greater part of the enemy's infantry is at Tuscumbia and Florence. Granger reports the river rising; if so, I hardly think Hood will venture to throw a very large force across the river, nor can he molest you much, as the streams between you have doubtless been as much affected by the rain as those in Tennessee.

W. T. SHERMAN, Major-General, Kingston—8.30 p. m.

Major-General Thomas:

Your dispatch of 5 p. m. is received. All will be ready to start from here the day after to-morrow. It is now raining hard, and when it clears away we must be off. Keep me well advised. Think you will find Hood marching off, and you should be ready to follow him. Decatur, Tuscaloosa, Columbus, and Selma are all good points to forage and feed an army. Let us keep Beauregard busy, and the people of the South will realize his inability to protect them.

Friday, November 11

<u>MARY ANN HALE</u>, Hale Plantation, Decatur Georgia

Toby has developed an uncanny ability to predict the contents of the day's mail. He woke me early this morning, declaring, "It is most time to go to the post-office, ain't it, Miss Mary? We are going to get a letter from Marse Thomie today."

"What makes you so certain of it, Toby?" I asked him.

"I don't know'm, but I am; and every time I feels this way, I gets one; so I'll just take my two little black calves and trot off to the office and get it;" and suiting the action to the word he struck a pretty brisk gait and was soon around the corner and out of sight.

The team of which Toby was the proud possessor did its work rather more leisurely than I expected, but in due time he returned from the post office—one hand clasping a package of papers and letters, and the other, raised high above his head, holding a letter. I could not wait, and ran to meet him.

"I've got a whole lot of letters, and every one of them is from Dalton, and this one is from Marse Thomie!"

Toby had "read" the Dalton post-mark, and had made a correct statement. The well-known chirography of my brother had become so familiar to him that he never mistook it for another, and was unerring in his declarations regarding it. On this occasion Thomie's letter thus read:

[18]

Nov 7, 1864.

"My Dear Sister—As there is a probability of the mail courier leaving here early in the morning, I hastily scratch you a few lines that you may know that under the blessings of a kind Providence I am yet alive, and, though somewhat wearied, enjoying good health. There has been but one opportunity of writing to you since leaving Atlanta, and then had just finished one to Texas, and was fixing to write to you, when the order came to 'fall in.'

I have heard George made it into the Federal lines. Well, if so, he will have a hard time of it if he is captured by our boys for they pledge to take no quarter when it comes to niggers in blue.

Tomorrow we cross the Lookout Mountain, and will, I suppose, make directly for the Tennessee river, though of this I'm not certain. Hood has shown himself a general in strategy, and has secured the confidence of the troops. Wherever we go, may God's blessing attend us. Pray for me. In haste.

Your affectionate brother, Thomas Hale

We are so grateful he is still alive. We retain our confidence in the ability and judgment of General Hood.

Tobias came to-nite with a letter from Papa!

Onboard the Planter

Dear Wife and Daughter,

I have enlisted in the Navy and am now onboard a steamer called the Planter. The ship i am on is captined by a colored man by the name of Robert Smalls. He is a brave and galant man who spirited a ship past the confederates and has been rewarded in his daring. we are all, colored and white, prod to serve him. I am a soldier endeavring to strike at the rebellion that so long has kept us in chains. Though grate is the present national difficulties yet i look forward to a brighter day when i shall have the opertunity of seeing you in the full enjoyment of freedom.

It will not be long before we shall have crushed the system that now opreses you for in the course of three months you shall be free and we will be together, all of us. Master Thomie let it slip where Caroline now lives. Once we are reunited in freedom, we will go get her. Dear wife i can not reveal much about my location in this letter but a post to the above will get to me. Write back and say you will make your way with the army now ocupying Atlanta on whatever course that army may take. Trust that i will meet you in December, and that is all i can say.

Grate is the outpouring of the colored people that is now rallying with the hearts of lions against that very curse that has

[20]

separated you and me. Yet we shall meet again and oh what happy
time that will be when this ungodly rebellion shall be put down and
the curse of our land is trampled under our feet.

 Tell me you have left that place of cruel slavery and are on
the road to freedom with our precious daughter Jennie, who is with
you now.

 i send my best to Jennie and my love likewise.
  i must close now but remain your own afectionate husband
    until death,
    Seaman George Lewis

 His words took are breth away. We all three cride and
hugged until doctor sent Tobias and me away. But we left Mama
with joy in her hart. Papa said we will meet in December! He said
we shold rite him back to say we are comeing. I want to send him
every letters I rote but Mama said one note will do. So she rote 'We
will come, George! We will follow the Sherman army wherever it
goes for we no they are on the road to Freedom and you are wating
for us there!' She folded it and adressed the envelope then she gave it
to me with shakeing hands. 'You male this to Papa first thing to-
morrow.'

 I will be at the postal office when they open the door. But
how will I ever sleep to-nite with Papas words burned into my hart?

LOUISA NEAL, Atlanta, Georgia

Mary,

You put too much trust in your negroes. I saw your Toby and Jennie in close conversation right on the public street. The two of them with their heads together did not even look up as I passed.

There is so much commotion and activity in Atlanta and the colored move about as they please. Mary, stop sending them into town. Toby yes ma'ams with the best of manners but he is fresh and could board one of those northbound trains and be gone before you know it. Then what will you do, Mary, you dote on him so.

W. T. SHERMAN, Major-General, Kingston, Ga., midnight

Major-General Halleck, Chief of Staff:

My arrangements are now all complete, and the railroad cars are being sent to the rear. Last night we burned all foundries, mills, and shops of every kind in Rome, and to-morrow I leave Kingston with the rear guard for Atlanta, which I propose to dispose of in a similar manner, and to start on the 16th on the projected grand raid. All appearances still indicate that Beauregard has got back to his old hole at Corinth, and I hope he will enjoy it. My army prefers to enjoy the fresh sweet-potato fields of the Ocmulgee. I have balanced all the figures well, and am satisfied that General Thomas has in Tennessee a force sufficient for all probabilities, and I have urged him the moment Beauregard turns south to cross the Tennessee at Decatur and push straight for Selma. To-morrow our wires will be broken, and this is probably my last dispatch. I would like to have General Foster to break the Savannah and Charleston road about Pocotaligo about December 1. All other preparations are to my entire satisfaction.

Saturday, November 12

W. T. SHERMAN, Headquarters, Military Division of the
Mississippi, In the Field Kingston, Georgia
Dearest Ellen,
We start today. Write no more till you hear of me. Goodbye.

MAJOR JAMES A. CONNOLLY, 123rd Illinois Infantry,
Headquarters, Kingston, Georgia
Dear Sarah,
We received orders to march today at 6 ½ o'clock; so, I
suppose, begins our part of the great campaign through Georgia. We
can't exactly see our way through now, but I guess it will all come
out right.

CAPT. JAMES LAUGHLIN ORR, 42nd Indiana Regiment,
In the Field, Cartersville, Georgia
Father,
This day about 8 o'clock the last train north on the Georgia
R. R. left for Chattanooga and R. R. connection with U. S. was thus
severed. The telegraph operator took out his instruments & left early
in the a.m. At 12 Gen. Sherman arrived—hitched on his pocket
instrument & probably that may be the last link binding us to the
north. We are now adrift for a great raid. But whither? *Quien sabe?*

[24]

MAJOR HENRY HITCHCOCK, Assistant Adjutant
General, Headquarters, Military Division of the Mississippi,
Kingston, Georgia

Dear Elizabeth,

Today we set out on a campaign which will be remembered. God grant it aid to bring to a speedy end this terrible and lamentable war!

Hired a negro servant Aleck last P.M.—seems simple, honest fellow. Has wife, Laura, mother, Amy, and three children, to whom devoted. : Gave him time to arrange for them to go North in the last cars from Atlanta. Told him if he served faithfully would try to help them hereafter. What a lie his anxious care shows it, that "negroes have no family affection." --Poor fellow—"One touch of nature makes the whole world kin."

PVT. CHARLES W. WILLS, 8th Illinois Infantry, In the
field, Vinings Station, Georgia

Dear Friends,

The Rubicon is passed, the die is cast, and all that sort of thing. We to-day severed our own cracker line. At 11 a.m. ours and the 17th Corps were let loose on the railroad, the men worked with a will and before dark the 12 miles of track between here and Marietta were destroyed. The ties were piled and burned and the rails, after being heated red hot in the middle were looped around trees or telegraph poles. Old destruction himself could not have done the work better. The way the Rebels destroyed our road on their raid was not even a fair parody on our style. The 20th Corps is at it between Atlanta and the river, and the 14th and 23rd in Decatur. We have orders to-night to move at 7 a.m.

LT. COLONEL S. MERRILL, 70th Regiment, Indiana
Volunteers, In camp, Atlanta
My Darling,

Don't send me any more newspapers till I request it, or until at least you hear from the newspapers that we have emerged.

Oh my dear Emma I can never tell you how much I love you and the children. If you all pray with faith for me God will permit me to return safely. To His care I commit you with the firm assurance that no evil will befall you.

I send this by hand as all mails have ceased to go North.

We have no idea where we are going.

PVT. THEODORE UPSON, 100th Indiana, In Camp,
Atlanta

We are back at Atlanta again and have been drawing pay and some much needed supplies. Most of the boys have sent a good part of their money home. We have been tearing up some more Rail Road and utterly destroying evry thing in the City that can be of any use to the Armies of the South. There are rumors that we are to cut

[26]

loose and march South to the Ocean. We are in fine shape and I think could go anywhere Uncle Billy would lead. We are told we are going on a great campaign.

BRIGADIER GENERAL JEFFERSON C. DAVIS,
Commander, 14th Corps. Atlanta, Georgia
My Dear Marietta,

The last train for the north left here this morning. Our soldiers were scattered along the railroad a hundred miles north, and as soon as that train passed, the work of destruction commenced. The railroad will be completely destroyed and every bridge burned. Then both armies (the armies of the Tennessee and Georgia) will assemble here, and after destroying the city will commence the march. I fear their track will be one of desolation.

I have been to the railroad depot for the past three days several times and have witnessed many sad and some ludicrous scenes. All citizens (white and black) begin to apprehend that something is about to happen. The few white people remaining after their families were sent away are alarmed and many are leaving the city, giving up horses, lands, furnitures, negroes and all. The black want to go North, and the Car House is surrounded by them. Hundreds of cars are literally packed with them and their dirty bundles, inside and outside. Old toothless hags, little pickaninnies, fat wenches of all shades, from light brown to jet black, are piled up together with their old bags, bundles, broken chairs, etc. Some are gnawing old bones, some squatted by the cars making hoecakes, some crying for food which we cannot supply. Many of the white people are as anxious to get north as the darks, and gladly accept a place in a car reeking with the odor peculiar to the 'American of African descent.' It is a sad sight and I anticipate seeing many such before spring.

CAPT. DAVID P. CONYNGHAM, War Correspondent,
Atlanta, Georgia

The depot presented a scene of confusion and suffering seldom witnessed. Women and children were huddled together, while men, who had lately been millionaires, were now frantically rushing about, trying to procure transportation, and forced to give their last dollar to some exacting conductor or railway official. An order had been issued by General Easton providing all these people with free transportation; but several of his employees and railroad officials could not see it in that light. They saw that the thing could be made to pay, and they did make it pay.... In some cases they managed to divide families, so that they could extort the more from those remaining.

I wanted myself to get a poor soldier, who was going home to die, inside on one of the cars. Though they were full of strapping, healthy negroes, who were either servants to the extortioners, or had the almighty dollars to pay their way, I could not gain admittance for the poor fellow. A few dollars in a conductor's pocket were of more importance than his comfort or safety. I gave him my blanket and oil-cloth, but I have since learned he never reached home, for when taken off the top of the cars at Chattanooga he was found dead.

<u>JENNIE LEWIS</u>, Neal House, Atlanta

Oh Papa!

The post office is shut down and the last train from Atlanta left with out our letter. Now Mama says we must stay here. 'Your father will look for us here. He nos he can find us here.' No amont of crying and pleeding on my part will change her mind. She says when the army leves we must go back to Decatur. Papa, I cant go back to live with Miss Mary. I just cant.

Your hartbroken ~~dauter~~ daughter,

Sunday, November 13

CAPT. GEORGE W. PEPPER, Headquarters Staff, In Camp, Atlanta, Georgia

Some of the boys strayed with me to an African church tonight. As we entered, a row of colored brethren took up a monotonous tune, keeping time by the swaying of their bodies, and thus for nearly an hour one song after another was sung in the same dismal, weary strain. About half of the time in the meeting was taken up with singing. The leader repeated large portions of Bible history, or religious sentiment, and the congregation sang it after him. If the meter was short, or excessive in any part, it made no difference. At regular intervals they tacked on a chorus, which, at first, was pertinent to the subject, but which very soon was entirely foreign to the sense, yet the chorus must be had at all events. The excitement gradually grew intense. The women stood up and swayed to and fro to the sound of the music. The young men stood, and at each repetition of the chorus, rose up on tiptoe, and had it not been for the restraining influence of three or four delegates in attendance, they would very likely have had more or less dancing. But it was all the natural expression of deep, religious enthusiasm to those untutored minds, even as it might have been with David, who "danced before the Lord with all his might."

Their prayers were the best part of the meeting, full of strong faith, earnest feeling and deep humility. One brother prayed for the army, for the Christian Commission, for the sick in the hospital, for the President and his own colored brethren; "and now Lord," said he, "when you's 'membered all the rest, then come down and 'member poor, unworthy me, who am less than the least of all saints, if I am anything at all!" Another; "Lord, get on your Great White Horse of Salvation, and ride through every impenitent heart in Atlanta," to which a response was duly made: "Yes, Lord, get on to de fastest!"

Then arose a thin, wiry, emaciated, old man, whose gray locks, wrinkled features, sunken eyes, were almost spectral, and leaning on the desk, seemed almost on the very verge of dissolution. In a weak and tremulous voice, he addressed his audience after this manner: "My children, the Master will, I fear, allow me only this opportunity of addressing you again this side of the grave. I am old and feeble, and near the border land, but I want to tell you of Jesus." Then for nearly half an hour he spoke in a strain of impassioned eloquence, such as I have seldom heard surpassed. His frame expanded, and his voice was shrill and clear, while those deep set, cavernous eyes, gleamed and glistened and glared like coals of fire, and the listeners were held spell bound by the fiery eloquence and burning words of the patriarch. Said he: "My brethren, take up the cross and bear it manfully, take it up and hold it before you; do not attempt to drag it on the ground, for if you do, the devil will get on to the other end, and you will have to drag him too!" This was acted out by the representation of dragging the cross, so masterly, that one almost expected to see his Satanic Majesty rising up before him.

Again, said he, "The Bible no where tells us that we walk through the valley of death; it says we only pass through the shadows of it."

After all, that is not very different from a good white prayer. The image only differs, and is somewhat bolder.

At the end of the services, prayer was duly offered for the leader, a Reverend Gaston C. Quarles (remarkable man, having been a slave!) that God would please to douse his head in wisdom. Their imaginations were certainly more developed than their theology, but even in their most erroneous conceptions, they evidently showed strong faith. Said he: "We serve that Master who always is awake when every body else is asleep. Just as he sent Moses to free the Jews in the Old Time, so he sends General Sherman to deliver us from our bondage. The Day of Jubilee has come!"

I will only add that the more we become acquainted with negro character, both as men and Christians, the more we are compelled to respect them.

P.S. Talked with some honey-colored congregants (of the female variety) after the service. The general has told us no "surplus Negroes" should be taken along, but the history of this Army shows otherwise. The boys tried to coax some of the bronzed beauties into taking "the Grand Tour." Seems there is a keen interest in marrying with the boys and coming along, except for one (she said her name was Virginia Lewis but people call her Jennie). Said she was staying put. "Don't you know Atlanta will burn," I asked. She did not answer, but looked at me, alarmed. I explained to her some of the benefits of taking up with the Federal Government, but she would not be moved. Pity. She seems an intelligent soul. And surely a pretty negress. Told me she can read and write. Doubtful. Possibly my first student? Must speak to her again. G.P.

JENNIE LEWIS, Neal House, Atlanta

Dear Papa,

We met to-nite at Friendship Baptist. The question on everyones lips, 'Is you going?' Rev. Woods from Marietta said colored folks should not follow a Yankee solder past the front gate. 'The northern people are not frends of the negro and many a time from my pulpit have I warned niggers about going North. No, sir, the colored man dosent belong in the North—and you may tell the world that the Reverend Joseph Wood makes no bones about saying that!'

Rev. Quarles preeched next. He said 'I lerned to pray when very yung and kept it up even in my unsaved days. My wite masters new me to be a praying boy, and asked me to pray to God to hold the Yankeys back! Of course, I didnt have any love for any Yankeys— and havent now, for that matter—but I told my wite folks strate from the sholder that I cold not pray along those lines. I told them flatfootedly that wile I loved them, I cold not pray aginst my conshus: that I not only wanted to be free, but that I wanted to see all the negroes freed!'

'Yes Lord!' the peeple said.

'I told them that God was using the Yankeys to scurage the slave-holders just as He had, sentrees before used heethens to scold His chosen peeple. If we are going to end slavery for all colored peeple, we must take up with the Union Army and work with them. Never mind what the Yankey solders will do for us. What will we do for ourselves and our country?'

Just then some wite solders came into the church. Rev. Quarles stopped preeching and told us to sing. 'Didnt my Lord deliver Daniel? Then why not every man?' and 'Whose that out there dressed in red, must be the people that Moses led.' I looked at Mama. She looked back at me and shook her hed.

After a long time Uncle Ned stood up. He is an elder of our church so we had to be quite and lissen to him. He said 'My children, I am old and feeble, and nere the border land, but I want to tell you my brothers and sisters to take up the cross and bare it. The Bible dose not say we walk throu the valley of death it says we only pass thru the shadows of it.' Uncle Ned is going away to be Free and he has been a slave for 75 yeres!

To-nite I asked Mama, 'If Uncle Ned is going why cant we? You can nurse solders along the way. I can wash clothes. Them solders at the church to-nite said the Army will pay the colored folks to do work. Cousin Aleck is alredy going. Pleese Mama lets leve with the Sherman Army.'

[34]

'Jennie! You are all I have left. Your sister sold away. Your father in harms way. I wont let you out of my site. When the solders leve we going back to Decatur. Your Papa will look for us there.'

This is the state of things Papa. It seems I am not free after all. How can that be Papa?

Monday, November 14

<u>CARRIE BERRY</u>, Berry House, Atlanta, Georgia

Dear Cousin Mary,

They came burning Atlanta to day! We all dread it because they say that they will burn the last house before they stop. We will dread it.

<u>MAJ. HENRY HITCHCOCK</u>, Assistant Adjutant General, Headquarters, Neal House, Atlanta, Georgia

Rome was abandoned last night and today by our forces, and all buildings in it of use to the enemy were destroyed. No private residences were burned nor was there any violence done to the people. Probably Hood will begin now to understand Sherman's plans—in part. The rebel papers will claim, of course, that Sherman is being forced to evacuate this, and that, etc., etc. Southerners should pay no attention to any of these things, and have no concern for Sherman. He never was further from defeat nor were J.D.'s predictions and promises ever further from fulfillment. Our men are in the finest condition and spirits; everything useless and cumbersome has gone back, and early in the morning we are off. The weather is cool, bright and beautiful and the moonlight tonight lovely.

I am in perfect health, and so far as we are concerned here, in the fullest confidence and good spirits, as are all....

[36]

CORNELIUS C. PLATTER, 81st Ohio Infantry Volunteers,

In Camp, Kennesaw, Georgia

We marched today in two ranks on each side of the train. Went into camp at the foot of Kennesaw Mt on the South side. About 1 mile from Marietta. Genl Kilpatricks Cavalry was reviewed by Genl Sherman at Marietta today and it is said they presented a fine appearance. Did not go up on Kennesaw Mt. those who did. say they can see burning buildings in every direction - even see Atlanta burning - . Marietta is all a "blaze" - We had a fine days march. - the country was entirely cut up with fortifications of every description - Seen graves of many a brave hero who fell in the defense of his country.

CAPTAIN JAMES M. RANDALL, 21st Wisconsin, On the

March, Marietta, Georgia

Marietta shared the same fate as Ackworth and as other towns through which we passed. All public buildings were burned and many other buildings also.

JOS. WHEELER, Jonesborough, Ga., 9.25 p. m.

General Braxton Bragg, Richmond, Va.:

Prisoners taken yesterday report Sherman with three corps in and about Atlanta. Scouts and prisoners report enemy destroying railroad between Atlanta and Marietta. Yankee camp rumors say Sherman will move forward.

DANIEL P. CONYNGHAM, War Correspondent,

Observations In Camp, Atlanta, Georgia

"Look around, boys; I reckon 'Old Billy' has set the world on fire."

"Why, darn it, 'Old Billy' has nothing to do with it; it's ourselves that are making the bonfires."

Specks so; guess it's all right, anyhow."

"Why wouldn't it be right? Old Billy wouldn't have done it otherwise."

"True."

"But any of ye reckon, boys, where we are going to?

"Yes. I had a private talk with Old Billy himself, and he told me that we were going, going—would ye guess it?

"To hell!"

"O, no. I have no doubt but that will be the end of your journey; but we are going—somewhere."

"I tell ye, boys, we should never ask where we are going, or what are we going to do. Obedience is the duty of a soldier; and whatever Old Billy says or does is right. He does the plotting and flanking; let us do the fighting, and things will go on well."

"Bully for Old Billy! We'll follow him!"

Tuesday, November 15

MAJOR HENRY HITCHCOCK, Assistant Adjutant

General, Headquarters, Neal House, Atlanta, Georgia

Tonight, the grandest and most awful scene. Our
Headquarters are on high ground: From our rear and E. windows, 1/3
of horizon shows immense and raging fires, lighting up whole
heavens—probably, says Sherman, visible at Griffin, fifty miles off.
First bursts of smoke, dense, black volumes, then tongues of flame,
then huge waves of fire roll up into the sky: presently the skeletons
of great warehouses stand out in relief against and amidst sheets of
roaring, blazing, furious flames,--then the angry waves roll less high,
and are of deeper color, then sink and cease, and only the fierce glow
from the bare and blackened walls, etc.

Went down to the corner and looked out over where the R.R.
depots were—all covered with smoking and still blazing ruins. But
was rejoiced to find on the way that sentries were posted in front of
the two churches near our Headquarters, with orders so strict that on
returning with other officers he would not let us go by it on the
sidewalk, but ordered us out into the street: and soon after did same
to two or three others going down cross street along west side of
church. This is right. I note these and preceding facts because Gen.
S. will hereafter be charged with indiscriminate burning, which is
not true. His orders are to destroy only such buildings as are used or
useful for war purposes, whether for producing, storing, or

transporting materials, etc., of war: but all others are to be spared, and no dwelling touched. He talked about this again today, apparently because of the evidently painful impressions from Rome and Marietta. Said nothing like excuse, but simply explained the facts. At table he remarked—"this city has done and contributed probably more to carry on and sustain the war than any other, save perhaps Richmond. We have been fighting Atlanta all the time, in the past: have been capturing guns, wagons, etc., etc., marked 'Atlanta' and made here, all the time: and now since they have been doing so much to destroy us and our Government we have to destroy them, at least enough to prevent any more of that."

CAPT. DANIEL P. CONYNGHAM, War Correspondent,
Headquarters, Neal House, Atlanta, Georgia

The heart is burning out of beautiful Atlanta. The few people that have remained in the city flee, scared by the conflagration and the dread of violence. It is hard to restrain the soldiers. The Atlanta Hotel, Washington Hall and all the squares around the railroad depot are in one sheet of flame. Drug stores, dry goods stores, hotels, Negro marts, theaters and grog shops are all now feeding the fiery element. Worn-out wagons and camp equipage are piled up in the depot and added to the flames. The men plunge into the houses, break windows and doors with their muskets, drag out armfuls of clothes, tobacco and whiskey. The men dress themselves in new clothes and then fling the rest into the fire. The streets are now in

[40]

one fierce sheet of flame. Houses are falling on all sides and fiery flakes of cinders are whirled about. Occasionally shells explode and excited men rush through the choking atmosphere and hurry away from the city of ruins. At a distance, the city seems overshadowed by a cloud of black smoke, through which now and then gets a gushing flame of fire or projectiles hurled from the burning ruin. The sun looks, through the hazy cloud, like a blood-red ball of fire, and the air, for miles around, feels oppressive and intolerable.

A new campaign is about to start. Sherman issued a special field order, November 8th, in which he exhorted the men to maintain discipline. On the following day he issued another order: "The army will forage liberally on the country during the march. To regular foraging parties must be intrusted the gathering of provisions and forage at any distance from the roads traveled. The cavalry and artillery may appropriate horses, mules, wagons, &c. freely and without limit. Foraging parties may also take mules or horses." He also noted that Negroes "who are able-bodied and can be of service to the several columns" may be taken along.

I wonder if he has any particular "able body" in mind.

CAPT. GEORGE W. PEPPER, Headquarters Staff,
Headquarters, Neal House, Atlanta, Georgia
At General Sherman's head-quarters tonight, there were gathered together in consultation, a noble set of men: That one armed man, is the saintly Howard, the Havelock of our army. He is

slender, quiet, exceedingly, in his aspect, with nothing whatever of personal bravado or vanity. There was not a glance that would betray the lurking ambition that would say, "I am the man who rode through a storm of shot and shell at Antietam, for which I received my second star." His face is almost feminine, his features small. He is full of courage, quiet and impassable, yet when occasion demands, he would spring into the saddle, at the summons of danger, and ride without one moment's hesitation into the very thickest of the fight. He is a shining example of the Christian religion. Long may he remain in command of this Department!

The man leaning against the wall, is Jeff. C. Davis, the hero of Pea Ridge. He has a keen eye, a cadaverous face, sunken cheeks, and looks care-worn. Were we to meet him in the dark, we would take him to be a vitalized ghost. He commands the 14th Corps, and has infused his own energy into the splendid battalions of that historic legion.

The fine, manly, sandy-haired man, is Schofield, commanding the Department of the Ohio. He has a West-Pointish carriage, and is nearly six feet high, possessing a piercing eye, looking right through a fellow. His popularity is of an enduring character.

There, too, is the noble Sherman. He towers above them all. General Sherman is very striking in his physiognomy, which is of the Corsair character. He is straight as an arrow, complexion fair, eyes dark.

[42]

Thus were gathered with the gentlemen of Atlanta this Last Supper in Atlanta. And what American now has not heard of Atlanta? and who does not feel his pulse beat high, his brow elevate, and his soul expand with conscious pride and exultation at the recollection of the glorious struggles which took place in front of this renowned city, when, after desperate battles the gallant army of patriots drove back the fierce legions of Hood? Perhaps there is no city in the South of the same population, that affords so many evidences of wealth. Here are luxurious homes, now the scenes of no domestic joys; stately warehouses, where no wealthy merchants congregate; beautiful temples where resound no more the organ's swell or the notes of praise. All is afire. Whole buildings are shattered. Clouds of smoke, as we passed through, were bursting from several princely mansions. Railroad depots, rebel factories, foundries and mills—destroyed. This is the penalty of rebellion. Heaven and earth both agree in decreeing a terrible punishment to those perfidious wretches who concocted this wasting and desolating war.

Hundreds of able-bodied negroes have been collected, and armed with pick and shovel, will now do Uncle Samuel good service. I have procured my first student, Miss Jennie Lewis, after I persuaded her mother she would do well to seize this opportunity. She is a bright girl. Oberlin College would do well to welcome her into their midst, a genuine slave uplifted by God's humble servant.

And so, with pity and hope, we will pass the Gate City, breathing a prayer that the All-powerful will grant forgiveness to the miserable ingrates, whose love of slavery inaugurated this terrible rebellion. Once more to the march.

JENNIE LEWIS, Neal House, Atlanta

Dear Papa,

Slavery is burning to the grond! Tomorrow, it will all be ashes. And I have been delivered into Freedom. All because of General William Tecumseh Sherman.

He rode along a canal of fire into this place. This house is his Hed kworters. People come and go all day and nite and he sees them all. He is no devil. His is the Deliverer. Oh, Papa, who wold think Miss Mary sending me here wold turn out to be such a miracle. For now, I will truely be free.

I served supper to General Sherman and his officers to-nite. Men from town came with there hats in hand. I helped his cook Manual becose Lena said she wold not lift a finger. 'Dont mind me. I lerned to cook in' – she said some place that sonded like Pares Frares-- 'but I guess I aint good enuff for these gentlemens from Ohio.' Lena said she would not lower herself to be a common servant. 'You on your own this evening Jennie.'

I peeked into the dineing room after they all took there seets. General Sherman sat at one end. Officers filled in around him and hanging on his ever word.

[44]

I walked in carrying the hot soup, my legs just shakeing and my ears pricked. I did not let on that I too lissened to every word he said threw the blue gray smoke around his head. 'War is cruell,' he said. 'Those who brot war into our country deserve all the curses and maladishes a people can pore out.' I do not no what that word maladishes menes but it sonded like the rite thing to say. "We have been fiteing Atlanta all the time. Ah, here is the soup! Gentlemen, lets enjoy our last mele as enemees and all look to the day when this cruell war is over!'

I hardly took a breth but I did not spill a drop. I worked with a stedy hand like you have taut me to do Papa. Manual called me a good helper. After supper General Sherman thanked me himself and asked my name.

'Virginia Lewis, Master General Sherman. Jennie.' My voce was merely a whisper.

'Well, Miss Jennie' General Sherman said, 'What do you think about your city burning to the grond?'

Before I cold stop myself, I said, 'I think you make a lot of sense.' The officers laffed but the general looked me strate in the eyes. 'How so Jennie?'

I was scared, Papa, I had spoken my mind to wite people. The men of Atlanta were not laffing. I did not no what wold happen next. But General Sherman looked at me as if—I don't know Papa. Its as if he rely wanted to no what I thot. So I said, bolder now 'About Atlanta and the maladishes. I hope you burn Atlanta to a crisp!' No one laffed now. And I added in a whisper 'Master…General…Master Sherman.'

The generals face under the firey hare cresed ubti a smile. He took my hand. 'I am not your Master Jennie. No man is. You are no longer a slave. You are free. You are all free.'

For a long time after that I thot I cold not brethe. I no I cold not speke. I wanted to run out into the burning streets and shot to the hole town. 'We're free! General Sherman said it. You have to listen to him. Hes in charge of everything now. We're free. Body and soul.' I thot I wold drop to the grond in prayer and jubilation. But I just stood there, not brething until I herd Captin Pepper spekeing beside me.

'She shold come along with us General. She wold make an excellent cook's assistant.' I asked Captin Pepper later to rite the words for me and he rote 'excellent cook's assistant' so I copeed it here. Papa I have never heard those words before but that is what I am to be! I have joined the army!

And the best thing of all, Papa, is that I am going with Mamas blessings. After supper, Captin Pepper came with me to the Medical College. He talked to Mama for a long time. 'You need not worry about her safety' he said. 'She will be with the United States Army, under the Command of General Sherman. He is a smart man. He has thot this all out. She will be under the best protection. I personally promise you that.'

'And Captin Pepper will teech me how to spell!' I told her, 'and rede papers and hole books.'

'Jennie will have lessons every day. And when this cruell war is over, she may come to Ohio and attend school, become a teecher herself.'

Mamas eyes filled up with teres. She held me and cride until Captin Pepper slipped out. Then we went to the Neal House and got my things. We packed and cride some more but Mama talked to me the hole time about how I must be. 'Look to Cousin Aleck and Rev. Quartles for protection. Do not get taken away by a solder—Jennie. Your father will want to meet the same girl he left here.'

'Yes, Mama,' I said.

'Magdelena is going along. She can help you in any way you need—in womanly ways. Do you understand Jennie.

I nodded. Then she handed me the locket from around her neck. Inside is the picture of Caroline and me as little girls. A man came once to make pictures of Miss Mary and he saw Mama and asked to make her picture too. She told him he must make one of her daughters, and he did. Now she folded the locket into my hands. 'Most of all, find your Papa! And tell him to come back for me so that I can leve this God Forsaken place and be free.'

We cride more and then Mama fell asleep.

'I no how she feels Papa. Once the Sherman Army leves, the wite people will act like nothing has changed. Even tho I know it to be true in fact, I cant feel free in this place. Not in Atlanta or Decatur or maybe the hole south. Maybe I have to go up North. To a place called Ohio where General Sherman came here from and Captin Pepper too. Surly this Ohio is a grate place to be free.

Now, Papa, I rite this last letter before I leve this place and get on the rode to Freedom. Oh, Papa, to-morrow I bid ado to slavery. I will not miss it!

Your loveing and grateful daughter,

THEODORE UPSON, 100th Indiana Infantry, In Camp, Atlanta, Georgia, 2:00 a.m.

We have utterly destroyed Atlanta. I dont think any people will want to try and live here now. It is pretty tough to rout people out of their homes in this way, but it is war, and General Sherman is credited with saying that "War Is Hell." I think that it is.

Wednesday, November 16

<u>CAPTAIN JAMES M. RANDALL</u>, 21st Wisconsin, In
Camp, Lithonia, Georgia

The left wing of our army moved out from Atlanta between seven and eight o'clock A.M. today. Our course was nearly due east along the Augusta Railroad. We passed through Decatur, seven miles from Atlanta, and made a march for the day of 20 miles and came into camp at Lathonia.

Decatur was a pretty place of over 1,000 inhabitants, but now many people have fled. Witnessed a row from one of the Secesh women at the Hale farm. Captain Pepper had to order her back into her home, all in defense of a pretty Negress he's hired to assist the General's cook. My boy knows her. Says she is a "good girl." Good luck to her. Good luck to all of the Negroes.

<u>MARY ANN HALE</u>, Hale Farm, Decatur, Georgia
Dear Aunt Louisa,

The Negroes have everything in their hands and they know it! Surrounded and protected as they are by the Federal soldiers. As many as see proper can walk off and there is no remedy. What a race of ungrateful creatures.

JENNIE LEWIS, On the Road to Freedom, Stone Mountain, Georgia

Miss Mary showed out when I left Decatur this morning. She called me everything but a child of God. She said I was ungrateful and a hore. 'The Yankees have no more use for you than as a bed warmer!' she yelled.

Mama told her to hush. Then she relly got mad. 'Isabella' she said. 'You can not talk to me that way. ' You dont pick on my Mama. I jumped out of the kitchen wagon and ran rite up to her face. "Shame on you, Mistress. Shame! You sold my sister. You sold Caroline. What did you bye with that money, Mistress?"

"Wool for our solders!' she said.

"Shame on you and slavery too."

Miss Mary rased her arm to hit me but Mama stoped her and Captin Pepper had to carry her back into her house. Mama noded for me to get on back on the wagon and I did. We did not cry any teres, becase we new there was only time to pass before we would be together again. Along with Papa and Caroline. When this cruell war is over, we will be joned as a family again.

Now I am in an army tent with three other girls. We are in the Union camp at the big stone mountin. All around us are rows and rows of white army tens just like this one, and in them sleep all the solders of General Shermans Army. We are solders too. The girls are named Savanda, Nora, and Ilene. They are older than me but they are just like me. We all just want to be free. They will lauder the solders clothes and I will be an excellent cook's assistant to General Shermans cook Manual. I no I shold sleep now, but I look across the camp and see General Sherman is seated before a fire, the sleeve of his rite arm rolled up almost to his sholder. It is cold now, but the fires warm and sweeten the air. He wears his hat still, and that cigar smokeing. He is writeing to. I wonder what is on the mind of that grate man to-nite.

W.T. SHERMAN, In the field, Stone Mountain, Georgia
Dearest Ellen,

This morning we rode out of Atlanta by the Decatur road, filled by the marching troops and wagons of the Fourteenth Corps; and reaching the hill, just outside of the old rebel works, we naturally paused to look back upon the scenes of our past battles. We stood upon the very ground whereon was fought the bloody battle of July 22d, and could see the copse of wood where McPherson fell. Behind us lay Atlanta, smoldering and in ruins, the black smoke rising high in the air, and hanging like a pall over the ruined city. Away off in the distance, on the McDonough road, was the rear of Howard's column, the gun-barrels glistening in the sun, the white-topped wagons stretching away to the south; and right before us the Fourteenth Corps, marching steadily and rapidly, with a cheery look and swinging pace, that made light of the thousand miles that lay between us and Richmond. Some band, by accident, struck up the anthem of "John Brown's soul goes marching on;" the men caught

[51]

up the strain, and never before or since have I heard the chorus of "Glory, glory, hallelujah!" done with more spirit, or in better harmony of time and place.

Then we turned our horses' heads to the east; Atlanta was soon lost behind the screen of trees, and became a thing of the past. Today was extremely beautiful, clear sunlight, with bracing air, and an unusual feeling of exhilaration seemed to pervade all minds—a feeling of something to come, vague and undefined, still full of venture and intense interest.

There is a "devil-may-care" feeling pervading officers and men, that makes me feel the full load of responsibility, for success will be accepted as a matter of course, whereas, should we fail, this "march" will be adjudged the wild adventure of a crazy fool.

PART TWO: NOVEMBER 1864

Wednesday, November 16

BRIG. GEN. PIERRE GUSTAVE TOUTANT BEAUREGARD, Confederate States Army, Alabama

To The People of Georgia

Arise for the defense of your native soil! Rally around your patriotic Governor and gallant soldiers. Obstruct and destroy all the roads in Sherman's front, flank, and rear, and his army will soon starve in your midst.

Adopt Fabian system. Don't run risk of losing your active forces and guns, available for the field, to hold any one place or position, but harass at all points. Hannibal held the heart of Italy for sixteen years, and then was defeated. Be cool and confident, and all will yet be right. I will join you soon as possible.

Be confident. Be resolute. Trust in an over-ruling Providence, and success will soon crown your efforts.

I hasten to join you in the defense of your homes and firesides.

LOUISA NEAL, Boarding House, Atlanta

This is a dark hour in our country's history. Lincoln has been elected by a 300,000 majority. President Davis in his message says that we are better off than we were this time last year, but when President Davis advocates the training of Negroes to aid us in fighting—promising them, as an inducement to do so, their freedom, and in the same message intimates that rather than yield we would place every Negro in the Army—he so clearly betrays the weakness of our force that I candidly confess I am disheartened.

I take a woman's view of the subject but it does seem strangely inconsistent, the idea of our offering to a Negro the rich boon—the priceless reward of freedom to aid us in keeping in bondage a large portion of his brethren, when by joining the Yankees he will instantly gain the very reward which Mr. Davis offers to him after a certain amount of labor rendered and danger incurred. Mr. Davis to the contrary, the Negro has had a great deal to do with this war.

ROBERT TOOMBS, Macon, Georgia

Dear Governor:

Things are very bad here. Sherman in person is leading, say, 30,000 men against us. We are retreating as rapidly as possible consistent with order and efficiency. The militia are retreating in admirable order and good discipline, as General Cobb reports. I will meet them between this and Forsyth this evening. I believe the

Legislature will grant you large and liberal powers. Tell them the country is in danger. Let all of her sons come to the rescue.

Yours, faithfully,

P.S.—We have called for the troops in Wilmington, Charleston, and Savannah. If we do defend here they will be on us by Monday. Cavalry force said to be about 6,000. Send all the troops you can. If we do not get help we must abandon this place.

GENERAL HOWELL COBB, Confederate States Army,

Camp near Griffin, Georgia

My Dear Wife,

I have time only to write you a hurried note. When I reached the camp at Lovejoy's station on yesterday evening I found everything in motion to fall back. The enemy has burned Atlanta, destroyed the railroad from Atlanta to Chattahoochee and burnt the railroad bridge over the Chattahoochee. How much has been destroyed the other side of the Chattahoochee is not known, but the rumor is they destroyed the road to Marietta--(all very strange and unaccountable to me). The enemy commenced his movement in this direction with an army estimated by Genl. Wheeler to be not less than thirty thousand, including six thousand cavalry under Kilpatrick. Sherman is believed to be with this army. Our cavalry was driven out of Jonesboro and was last night at Lovejoy's station occupying our old camp, whilst the infantry and artillery are here.

That Sherman intends to move with this large army upon some point in Georgia I have no doubt, but where it will be is not yet so certain though my opinion is that Macon is the point. With our small force we can do but little to impede his progress, but I hope we shall be reinforced in time to defeat this formidable invasion.

It would be well as soon as you see that the movement is in direction of Macon--of which I will try to give you notice--to move down with the family to Americus, for though I have no serious fears now that Macon can be taken, still it will not be so comfortable to be there with a Yankee army around it.

THOMAS MAGUIRE, Promised Land Plantation,
Rockbridge

Up last night nearly all night. News that Yankees were coming this way after burning Atlanta, Decatur and some houses at Stone Mountain. Hid our box tools, horse, buggy and other things. We are now waiting for the worst to come, still hoping they will not come this way. If they are coming they will be here at nine o-clock. It is now 7.

Later: I went to see Mr. Anderson and while I was gone the Yankees came sure enough. I did not like to go back home so I stayed with David. A little after ten the Yankees were here and coming. Slocum's corps came and camped all around the house. At every side hogs and sheep are being shot down and skinned to regale the Yankee palates. Mr. Anderson and I slept in the woods all night,

[56]

not very pleasant for either body or mind not knowing what was going on at home.

DOLLY S. L. BURGE, Burg Plantation, Near Covington
I have been uneasy all day. At night some of the neighbors who had been to town called. They said it was a large force moving very slowly. What shall I do? Where go?

Thursday, November 17

CAPT. GEORGE W. PEPPER, Headquarters Staff, In the Field, Conyers, Georgia

A wonderful march is being made, and most substantial successes will be achieved. This great and unexampled expedition will add another laurel to the brilliant record of the armies of the Military Division of the Mississippi, and justify the hopes of its most ardent friends. The conception and execution of this stupendous military movement will be the crowning glory of Sherman's brilliant career, and will place his name high on the roll of fame, as the most consummate General of the nation. The immense army of 62,000 men is composed of the following Corps: the 14th, 15th, 17th, and 20th, commanded severally by Gens. Davis, Osterhaus, Blair, and Slocum, with Judson Kilpatrick leading a cavalry of some 6,000 and now!—a growing civil crowd of Sherman's Fifth Corps, the former slaves throwing down their plows and joining the Army of the Lord, as they call us--the whole Corps D'Armee under the immediate supervision of Gen. Sherman. We have sixty-five cannons with two hundred rounds for each, six hundred ambulances, pontoon bridges for river crossings, supply wagons with 1.2 million rations, enough for 20 days for each man. Gen. Sherman has directed our mails to be delivered in December to the blockade off Savannah. Until then, all communications are cut off. It is as if we are going into a hole and pulling the hole in after us.

Well, then, we are ready. Monsieur le General, we follow you cheerfully.

MAJ. HENRY HITCHCOCK, Assistant Adjutant General,
On the Railroad 1 Mile We. of Yellow River

Up at 4 A.M.—marched fourteen or fifteen miles—in camp at 4 P.M. in a field 150 to 200 yards from railroad, and 1 mile from Y. River.

From Lithonia followed railroad—partly on the track, partly over roads, seven miles to Conyers: halted 1 1/2 hours at Mrs. Scott's—widow, say thirty-five, civil and disposed to talk. She told Audenried that at Atlanta we had shot, burned and drowned negroes, old and young, drove men into houses and burned them, etc. etc.: first said she believed it, then admitted she did not, but said they wanted negroes to believe it.

Here and hereabouts "liberally foraged" as per order: got potatoes (sweet), fodder, chickens, etc.

Very jolly to send train ahead and find tents pitched and dinner nearly ready on reaching camp. Ordered Aleck never to unpack cot in fine weather—prefer bed of blankets on pine boughs on dry ground: cot very well when it rains. Plenty of forage along road, corn, fodder, finest sweet potatoes, pigs, chickens, etc. Passed troops all day, some on march, some destroying railroad thoroughly. Two cotton gins on roadside burned, and pile of cotton with one, also burned. Houses in Conyers look comfortable for Georgia village, and sundry good ones along road. Soldiers foraging all along, but only for forage—no violence so far as I saw or hear.... Saw some few men—almost all women and children, at front door or gate. Whites look sullen—darkies pleased. At Conyers, Mrs. S. told me "The niggers are the only free ones now—whites all slaves, in our country and yours too."

General sent for negro resident to inquire about roads and bridges. "Don't want white man," says Sherman. Very intelligent old fellow came, long talk with General at camp fire. "When the Yanks far off, our white people very brave—women and children whip 'em—but come close and den how dey does git up and dust."

"Many a dark population has worked on dat railroad— contractor for dis section whipped some of 'em to death—buried over in dose woods." Evidently the negro knew what lies the reb stories about us are.

JENNIE LEWIS, On the Freedom Road

Dear Papa,

The colored people line up along the road with there famlees and wagons. The solders sing 'Glory glory hallelujah!' as they fall into line, and the people on the road jone in. They shout to us, "How the Yanks treeting you?" and we call back, "Fine and well."

So when the wagons pass, they sweep onto the road in waves, falling in line, singing

Bye, bye, don't greve after me, wont give you my place, not for yours

Bye bye, don't greve after me, cause, you be here and I'll be gone.

Rev. Quarles says its the duty of every one to put down the hoe and walk away from slavery. "If we are gone, who will do all the work? The South will fall apart without our labor and the North will win the war with our help." If they ask me I say they cant no what its like to be free unless they leve. General Sherman tells them they shold stay in there homes and wate until this cruel war is over. But we say, Come along and in the end they lissen to us.

Captain Pepper gave me a book called 'The American Spelling Book' ritten written by a man named 'Noah Webster. Esq.' Papa it has so many pages and words in it you wold not beleve. I think more than the bible. Captain Pepper says any word I want to rite write or spell is in this book. And so far Papa, its true.

Ilene saw me with the book and asked me to tee teach her to read. 'Come to my lessons with Captain Pepper,' I said. But Ilene said she is afrade to learn in front of a wite white man. Her Old Master used to spell out rele fast anything he did not want her to no. "I would pack them letters up in my hed all the time. As soons I finished dishes, I rush down to my father and say them to him. Father always new what they ment. And he told me never to let on that he new." Sevanda and Nora have never even held a book.

Sevanda and Ilene are from Ten o see. Oh Papa I am too tride to look it up to-nite.

They came to Georgia with there old Mistress. She was running from the Yankees—I mene the Federals. When the Army cot up with her in Atlanta the old Mistress said I will go no further-- so she stayed in Atlanta. Her girls left her there.

Nora is from Rome Georgia. She is very quite. She reminds me of Caroline. She told me she was the only slave on there farm, no other children black or wite. She said, 'I thot everything was like that place. I didnt no there was happiness for nobody—me nor nobody. When I got whiped I thot that was just a part of being alive.'

This makes me wonder, papa, what kind of peeple Caroline was sold to. Do they trete her well or do they bete her.

The girls do the washing for the officers. I help Manuel serve the meals. Cousin Aleck is Major Hitchcocks servant and a little boy named John takes care of the horses. More people come into camp every day. We are like a family now getting bigger every day!

Just think, Papa, all of us colored folks working for the Army in the daytime and singing and praying every nite and no one to tell us we cant!

Your loving daughter

Friday, November 18

A.C. MCCLURG, Lieutenant-Colonel and Chief Of Staff, Hdqrs. Fourteenth Army Corps, Eatonton Factory By order of BVT. MAJ. GEN. J. C. DAVIS

General Orders No. 22.

Useless negroes are being accumulated to an extent which would be suicide to a column which must be constantly stripped for battle and prepared for the utmost celerity of movement. We cannot expect that the present unobstructed march will continue much longer. Our wagons are too much overladen to allow of their being filled with negro women and children or their baggage, and every additional mouth consumes food, which it requires risk to obtain. No negroes, therefore, or their baggage, will be allowed in wagons and none but the servants of mounted officers on horses or mules....

JENNIE LEWIS, On the Freedom Road

Dear Papa,

Some of the colored people came rideing into camp today on horses they took from there old masters. Captain Pepper says it is not right to steal the horses, and he asked Rev. Quarles to preach about it at the meeting to-nite. But Rev. Quarles told him, 'You talks a heap about the niggers stealing. Well, you know what was the first stealing done? It was in africa when de white folks stole de negroes just like youd go get a drove of horses and sell em.' The people said

Amen Reverend but Captain Pepper turned red and left. He said I should meet him soon for our lesson but I stayed out in the brush to hear Rev. Steven Harris. Everyone who knew him from this place said he was not to be missed.

He preached a powerful lesson and I am glad I did not miss it: 'I joned the Church forty three years ago when I was a slave of Master Gaud. Till to-nite I was supposed to preach what they told me to. Master made me preach to the other slaves that the Good Book say that if niggers obey there master, they would go to Heaven. I knew there was something better for them but I darsent tell them so I done it on the sly. I told the black folks but not so Master could here it that if they keep praying the Lord would set them free. And He did so sure as Im standing here before you now!'

We all jumped up and shouted 'Amen Reverend. We are free! We are free!'

Rev. Harris never learned how to read and write but he knows how to read out of his hand. He knows the bible and he held his hand out like he was reading and preached for a long time about Daniel in the Lions Den. The meeting lasted till very late. The girls went rite to sleep. I stayed up to write you Papa but there is so much to tell that even if I stayed up every nite I could not write it all! Papa I miss you and think only that each day brings us closer together. I am,

Your loveing daughter

MAJ. HENRY HITCHCOCK, Assistant Adjutant General, Camp at Judge Harris' "Quarters" and Farm at X Rds, 1 ½ Miles from "Ulcofau" River

Marched only about eight miles today, having two rivers to cross. Weather cloudy and threatening rain all day, but no rain fell and now no matter. "This is the perfection of campaigning," said the General today, "such weather and such roads as this." It suits H.H.— all fatigue is gone, and I could easily go twenty-five miles per day to judge from my good spirits, good appetite and sound sleep.

Stopped for the day at the farm of Judge Harris. He and family reside in Covington: has only his "quarters" on the farm: is a "heavy man" (as our intelligent contraband last night called it), has quite a farm, and said to have sixty or more slaves. Nichols had a long talk with his negro driver and came back full of indignation. The women say that their master, though an elderly man, and with a family, obliges them to submit to him, and straps them if they refuse. One fine looking old darky has but one leg: his story, confirmed by the others, is that the white women shot him—years ago— deliberately, first picking a quarrel about the way he planted some potatoes, and so he lost his leg.

Went in and took possession—train up after a while, tents pitched in yard and lot across road. Plenty of forage, poultry, hogs, etc. and "foraged liberally." Camps all round us and frequent shots round through the woods, each the death knell of some luckless secesh pig or rebel fowl.

We had hardly got into the yard when four or five stout negro men appeared, who had skedaddled this morning early from their "kind masters" four or five miles off to join and go with us. Quizzed them a little about how we treat negroes. Asked them if they knew how the negroes fared at Atlanta. "Oh, yes, white folks tole us you burned the men in the houses and drowned the women and children." "Well, did you believe it?" "No, Sir!! We didn't believe it—we has faith in you!" One very black, but very quick and manly fellow, a model, physically, and "driver" for his "ky-ind master," though the youngest (say twenty-five to thirty), was the leading spirit. I asked him why he came to us—how he knew he would not be worse off. "I was bound to come, Sah,--good trade or bad trade, I'se bound to risk it."

"But did you not hear all the terrible things we did at Atlanta, to the negroes there?"

"Yes, Sir, but I didn't believe it"—and then added "Dey don't think nothing 'bout here of tying up a feller and givin' him 200 or 300 with the strap."

Another of them explained his presence by his having heard "the white folks" last night talking about the Yankee's approach, and their own intention to run off all their negroes this morning down to Macon and thence to Florida (!). He was ordered to have the horses, etc., all harnessed up early this morning; but instead rose very early and came over to the Yanks himself. It is most striking and touching, the faith in us these people show.

[66]

But the best case yet is old "Uncle Stephen," one of the Harris negroes, with whom the General had a long talk this P.M. I sat by and was equally amused at the shrewd, frank, easy way the questions were put, and his views, etc., explained by the General, and the really dignified but simply and manly way the old darkey answered. After diverse inquiries about roads, distances, etc., answered without hesitation, through sometimes "don't know." General said—"Well now old man, what do you think about the war?"

"Well, Sir, I've thought a great deal about it,--till I hardly does know what to think.

(S) "Well, but you do think something about it—come, now, tell me just what you think—don't be afraid, we are friends."

"Well, Sir, what I think about it, is this—it's mighty distressin' this war, but it 'pears to me like the right thing couldn't be done without it."

The old fellow hit it, exactly.

The General has a capital way of talking to these people-- frank, pleasant and unaffected, without being familiar, and they respond with a mingled respect and confidence which shows how well he understands them. He talks in the same simple, clear, way to all: tells them the war is because their masters refused to obey the laws, and must be made to: that we are their friends, that they are free if they choose, and that the able-bodied men among them who choose to may go with us, or those who choose may stay with their masters. ("I don't choose dat den!" said one steady-looking old fellow today, who came with old Stephen). He always explains that freedom means not being free to work or not as they please, but freedom to work for themselves——freedom from being bought and sold,--freedom to acquire and own property, bring up their children respectably and be secure in enjoyment of personal and family rights. As to their families he tells them we cannot now take care of these, nor take them with us, and advises those who have families to stay with them yet awhile and do the best they can: and repeatedly has—in a quiet way but emphatically—discountenanced any violence to their masters.

Indeed I have seen no evidence of any vindictive feeling among them—but Universal Hope and longing for freedom. As to their being made soldiers, he always explains that this must be wholly voluntary on their part, and that in this army we have no negro soldiers, though elsewhere we have: that among our people, some are in favor of and others opposed to it, but that the Government will receive as soldiers all who wish to enlist:--and the nearest he has come to persuading them to this was his saying today to Stephen and others around, "those of you who deserve to be free and wish to be, will certainly be free, and will no longer be sold like cattle, nor see their families separated and sold: but we think that any man, black or white, who wants his freedom, and is able to fight for it, ought to be willing to do so." They assented very heartily to this.

It is amusing to see how desperately the rebs have been lying to their slaves about us, and what a failure it is. The darkies receive it all very gravely, and then run away and join us and tell us about it, and beg to go along with the Yanks. In fact, they threaten already to become a serious impediment to the column.

PRIVATE THEODORE F. UPSON, 100th Indiana Infantry,
In Camp, near Covington

The Darkies come to us from evry direction. They are all looking for freedom but really dont seem to know just what freedom means. They all have a great desire to see General, or Massa Sherman. There were a lot of them, old and young, waiting at a cross roads as the troops were passing. An orderly who had come up from the rear of the column told them that General Sherman would soon be along, that when they saw a soldier with a red cut away uniform with a three cornered cocked hat with a feather in it come along driving a carriage with a span of mules, that was Massa Sherman.

The poor Darkies took it all in, and when a little after one of our bummers came along dressed in a captured uniform that no doubt had been some cherished family keepsake—our boys find many such—they marched along by the side of the road singing their songs till some one told them the truth. However, despite all discouragements we have a large following though General Sherman has tried in evry way to explain to them that we do not want them, that they had better stay on the plantations till the war is ended.

JENNIE LEWIS, On the Road to Freedom, late nite

Dear Papa!

Solders rushed into our tent to-nite and took Sevanda Ilene and Nora away. They woke us all up and said 'Gather your clothes girls. Your moveing out.'

Sevanda kept asking why but they only said 'No more sleeping in tents or riding in wagons. By order of General Davis.'

They loded us on a wagon and were about to drive away when Captain Pepper ran out and spoke to the soldiers. Then he took me off the wagon and back to the tent. 'Where are they takeing them?' I asked.

'Don't worry Jennie' he said. 'You are the General's personal servant. General Davis can not order you anywhere.'

'But those girls,' I cride. 'They are my...'

I cold not say the word to him. He wold not no what it means. It is like losing my dear Caroline all over again!

'Jennie' Captain Pepper said 'I can not help them. Those girls have to follow General Davis orders. But I promised your mother I wold look out for you. Those girls will be with the other Negroes--behind the wagons. They will have to look out for themselves.'

I fell back on the bed, sick, hideing my face from him.

I must speak to General Sherman tomorrow. He will not let this happen. He could bring them back here and damn! General

[70]

Davis could not stop him. He will do it if I ask. People ask him for things all the time. They don't have to ask. He stands right alongside the servants and hands clothes and food to the families. He says to them 'You deserve to be free and we think that any man, black or white, who wants freedom ought to be willing to fight for it.' Papa, that is just what Rev. Quarles has been saying. It is what we all beleve. I have never met a white man who speaks and thinks like General Sherman.

I must go to him. I am too tried to write more. I trust General Sherman will make things rite.

DOLLY S. L. BURGE, Burge Plantation, Near Covington

Slept very little last night. Went out doors several times and could see large fires like burning buildings. Am I not in the hands of a merciful God who has promised to take care of the widow and orphan?

Sent off two of my mules in the night. Mr. Ward and Frank took them away and hid them. In the morning took a barrel of salt, which had cost me two hundred dollars, into one of the black women's gardens, put a paper over it, and then on the top of that leached ashes. Fixed it on a board as a leach tub, daubing it with ashes. Had some few pieces of meat taken from my smoke-house carried to the Old Place and hidden under some fodder. Bid them hide the wagon and gear and then go on plowing. Went to packing up mine and Sadai's clothes.

I fear that we shall be homeless.

Oh, how I trust I am safe!

W. T. SHERMAN, In the Field, near Covington, Georgia,
midnight

We passed through the handsome town of Covington today,
the soldiers closing up their ranks, the color-bearers unfurling their
flags, and the bands striking up patriotic airs.

The white people came out of their homes to behold the
sight, spite of their deep hatred of the invaders, and the Negroes
were simply frantic with joy. Whenever they heard my name, they
clustered about my horse, shouted and prayed in their peculiar style,
which had a natural eloquence that would have moved a stone.

I rode on to a place designated for camp, at the crossing of
the Ulcofauhachee River, about four miles to the east of the town.
Here we made our bivouac, and I walked up to a plantation-house
close by, where were assembled many negroes, among them an old,
gray-haired man, of as fine a head as I ever saw.

I asked him if he understood about the war and its progress.
He said he did; that he had been looking for the "angel of the Lord"
ever since he was knee-high, and, though we professed to be fighting
for the Union, he supposed that slavery was the cause, and that our
success was to be his freedom. I asked him if all the negro slaves
comprehended this fact, and he said they surely did. I then explained
to him that we wanted the slaves to remain where they were, and not

to load us down with useless mouths, which would eat up the food needed for our fighting-men; that our success was their assured freedom; that we could receive a few of their young, hearty men as pioneers; but that, if they followed us in swarms of old and young, feeble and helpless, it would simply load us down and cripple us in our great task.

Major Henry Hitchcock was with me and made a note of the conversation… I believe that old man spread this message to the slaves.

Saturday, November 19

JOSEPH E. BROWN, Governor, State Of Georgia,

Executive Department, Milledgeville

The whole people understand how imminent is the danger that threatens the state. Our cities are being burned, our fields laid waste, and our wives and children mercilessly driven from their homes by a powerful enemy. We must strike like men for freedom, or we must submit to subjugation.

Death is to be preferred to loss of liberty. All must rally to the field for the present emergency, or the state is overrun.

I, therefore, by virtue of the authority vested in me by the statute of this state, hereby order a levy en masse of the whole free white male population residing or domiciled in this state between sixteen (16) and fifty-five (55) years of age, except such as are physically unable to bear arms, which physical defect must be plain and indisputable, or they must be sent to camp for examination, and except those engaged in the legislative or judicial departments of the government, which are by the recent act of the legislature declared exempt from compulsory service.

All others are absolutely required, and members of the legislature, and judges are invited to report immediately to Major General G. W. Smith, at Macon, or wherever else in Georgia his camp may be, for forty (40) days' service, under arms, unless the emergency is sooner passed.

[74]

The enemy has penetrated almost to the center of your state. If every Georgian able to bear arms would rally around him, he could never escape.

DOLLY S. L. BURGE, Burge Plantation, Near Covington

Like demons they rush in! My yards are full. To my smoke-house, my dairy, pantry, kitchen, and cellar, like famished wolves they come, breaking locks and whatever is in their way. The thousand pounds of meat in my smoke-house is gone in a twinkling, my flour, my meat, my lard, butter, eggs, pickles of various kinds—both in vinegar and brine—wine, jars, and jugs are all gone. My eighteen fat turkeys, my hens, chickens, and fowls, my young pigs, are shot down in my yard and hunted as if they were rebels themselves. Utterly powerless I ran out and appealed to the guard.

"I cannot help you, Madam; it is orders."

As I stood there, from my lot I saw driven, first, old Dutch, my dear old buggy horse, who has carried my beloved husband so many miles, and who would so quietly wait at the block for him to mount and dismount, and who at last drew him to his grave; then came old Mary, my brood mare, who for years had been too old and stiff for work, with her three-year-old colt, my two-year-old mule, and her last little baby colt. There they go! There go my mules, my sheep, and worse than all, my boys!

Alas! little did I think while trying to save my house form plunder and fire that they were forcing my boys from home at the point of the bayonet. One, Newton, jumped into bed in his cabin, and declared himself sick. Another crawled under the floor, --a lame boy he was,--but they pulled him out, placed him on a horse, and drive him off. Mid, poor Mid! The last I saw of him, a man had him going around the garden, looking, as I thought, for my sheep, as he was my shepherd. Jack came crying to me, the big tears coursing down his cheeks, saying they were making him go. I said:"Stay in my room."

But a man followed in, cursing him and threatening to shoot him if he did not go; so poor Jack had to yield. James Arnold, in trying to escape from a back window, was captured and marched off. Henry, too, was taken; I know not how or when, but probably when he and Bob went after the mules. I had not believed they would force from their homes the poor, doomed negroes, but such has been the fact here, cursing them and saying that "Jeff Davis wanted to put them in his army, but that they should not fight for him, but for the Union."

No! Indeed no! They are not friends to the slave. We have never made the poor, cowardly negro fight, and it is strange, passing strange, that the all-powerful Yankee nation with the whole world to back them, their ports open, their armies filled with soldiers from all nations, should at last take the poor negro to help them out against this little Confederacy which was to have been brought back into the Union in sixty days' time!

My poor boys! My poor boys! What unknown trials are before you! How you have clung to your mistress and assisted her in every way you knew.

Never have I corrected them; a word was sufficient. Never have they known want of any kind. Their parents are with me, and how sadly they lament the loss of their boys. Their cabins are rifled of every valuable, the soldiers swearing that their Sunday clothes were the white people's, and that they never had money to get such things as they had. Poor Frank's chest was broken open, his money and tobacco taken. He has always been a money-making and saving boy; not infrequently has his crop brought him five hundred dollars and more. All of his clothes and Rachel's clothes, which dear Lou gave before her death and which she had packed away, were stolen from her. Ovens, skillets, coffee-mills, of which we had three, coffee-pots - not one have I left. Sifters all gone!

Seeing that the soldiers could not be restrained, the guard offered me to have their remaining possessions brought into my house, which I did, and they all, poor things, huddled together in my room, fearing every movement that the house would be burned.

Such a day, if I live to the age of Methuselah, may God spare me from ever seeing again!

[77]

REV. G. S. BRADLEY, Chaplain, 22nd Wisconsin, In the Field, Madison

As I passed a house today, a lady, sitting on a piazza, inquired: "When do you think this thing will be over?"

"I do not know, but I hope soon."

"Well, I think our people are very foolish to continue the war any longer. We are not subdued in spirit, but we are whipped, and we might as well own up. We hate you, but you now have the power in your own hands, and sooner or later we must come under."

"Supposing you could gain your independence," I inquired, "what advantage would it be to you? Would you not be just as well off under the old government?"

"No, I don't think so."

"Why not?"

"Well I don't suppose it would make much difference with us as individuals, but then you know our government has just as much pride as you have."

"Don't you think Southern people have had wrong ideas about Northern people and Northern sentiment?"

"Yes, I suppose they have to quite an extent. So far as I have seen your army, I am quite well pleased with the soldiers. They seem to be under excellent discipline—much better than our soldiers."

Something was then said on the slavery question, when she remarked that she had no doubt that slavery was a curse to the country—that the South would be much better off without slaves.

"What do the people about here think of so many of them joining our army?"

"O, we are all glad of it, for your army has taken about all we have to live upon, and the less niggers we have to take care of the better for us."

Sunday, November 20

<u>DOLLY S. L. BURGE</u>, Burge Plantation, Near Covington

This is the blessed Sabbath.... But how unlike this day to any that has preceded it to me in my once quiet home. I had watched all night and the dawn found me watching for the moving of the Soldiers that were encamped about us. Oh, how I dreaded those that were to pass as I suppose they would straggle and complete the ruin that the others had commenced.

Some of my women had gathered up a chicken that they had shot yesterday, and they cooked it with some yams for our breakfast, the guard complaining that we gave them no supper. They gave us some coffee which I had to make in a tea kettle as every coffee pot is taken off. The rear-guard was commanded by Colonel Carlow, who changed our guard, leaving us one while they passed. They marched directly on scarcely breaking ranks. A bucket of water was called for and they drank without coming in.

About ten o'clock they had all passed save one who came in and wanted coffee made which was done and he too went on. A few minutes elapsed and two couriers riding rapidly passed, back again they came and this ended the passing of Sherman's army by my place leaving me poorer by thirty thousand dollars than I was yesterday morning. And a much stronger rebel.

MRS. ELLA GERTRUDE CLANTON THOMAS, Thomas House, Milledgeville

Oh God will this war never cease? Will we ever settle quietly in our old peaceful domestic relations? How strange it all seems. Even now I can scarcely realize the state of suspense in which we have all been placed during the past few days. I don't believe I have felt so gloomy at anytime tho as I did Saturday afternoon. The whole heavens overcast with clouds—All nature appearing to mourn over the wretched degeneracy of her children and weeping to see brothers arrayed in hatred against each other.

"Man, the noblest work of God." Verily, when I witness and read of the track of desolation which Sherman's army leaves behind them, I am constrained to think that the work reflects little credit upon the creator. I know that sounds irreverent but I sigh for the memory of those days when man's noblest, better nature was displayed, when the brute "the cloven foot," was concealed and I could dream and believe that ours was the very best land—ruled by the very best men under the sun!!

Mr. Scales spent Friday night with us. He was taking a gloomy view of our prospects, but he talked just this way I remember one year ago. Then I confess I felt more determined "to do and dare and die" than I do now.

THE WHIG, Macon, Georgia

The military authorities are active and vigilant, and every man is under arms. Confidence is being restored. The enemy is believed to be on our right, distant about thirty miles. The city will be defended to the last.

JOSEPH E. BROWN, Governor, The State House, Milledgeville, Georgia

President Davis: A heavy force of the enemy is advancing on Macon, laying waste the country and burning the towns. We have not sufficient force. I hope you will send us troops as re-enforcements till the exigency is passed.

HOUSE OF REPRESENTATIVES, Confederate States of America

To the People of Georgia:

We have had a special conference with President Davis and the Secretary of War, and are able to assure you that they have done, and are still doing, all that can be done to meet the emergency that presses upon you. Let every man fly to arms. Remove your negroes, horses, cattle, and provisions from Sherman's army, and burn what you cannot carry.

Burn all bridges, and block up the roads in his route. Assail the invader in front, flank, and rear, by night and by day. Let him have no rest.

J. A. SEDDON, Secretary Of War, Confederate States of America, Richmond, Va.

Governor Joseph E. Brown,

Your telegram to the President has been referred to the Department for answer. The movements of the enemy in Georgia are viewed with interest and concern. Whatever re-enforcements of men and means the Department can command from its limited resources, in consistency with general safety, will be afforded.

Monday, November 21

MAJOR JAMES A. CONNOLLY, 123rd Illinois Infantry, In
the Field

Tonight within 18 miles of Milledgeville. Rain falling
heavily all day. Roads in a horrible condition. Things have not
looked promising today. What would become of us if this weather
should continue two weeks? We couldn't march; would be
compelled to halt here in the midst of a hostile country, and thus let
the enemy have time to recover from his surprise and concentrate
against us. Well, let the worst come, we'll get to the capital of
Georgia anyhow, and my long desire to see it will at length be
gratified.

We are all wet through and covered with mud, and our horses
jaded, but our supper of coffee, fried chickens, sweet potatoes, &c,
and a good sleep will bring us out all right in the morning, and if our
horses give out, the stable of some wealthy Georgian must furnish us
a remount. Citizens everywhere look paralyzed and as if stricken
dumb as we pass them. Columns of smoke by day, and "pillars of
fire" by night, for miles and miles on our right and left indicate to us
daily and nightly the route and location of the other columns of our
army. Every "Gin House" we pass is burned; every stack of fodder
we can't carry along is burned; every barn filled with grain is
destroyed; in fact everything that can be of any use to the rebels is
either carried off by our foragers or set on fire and burned.

MAJOR HENRY HITCHCOCK, Assistant Adjutant General, At Mr. Vann's House—

Horrible weather and bad roads—very bad. Our luck for the last forty-eight hours in these respects has changed. Roads yesterday rather bad: but last night's rain made them infinitely worse today. We were delayed this morning till 11 a.m. before starting from last night's Headquarters, though tents were struck, etc., by 8 o'clock. Dismal sky and steady rain, and the wagons of advance brigade standing still in front of house where General waited for Davis to come up—in rear of which we had camped. At last we get off, floundered through heavy clay mud, and under rain sometimes heavy, sometimes drizzling, threading our way through and by wagons laboring along, up hill and down, or stuck fast. No wonder the weather is such an element in warfare.

Tonight we stop at home of Mr. Vann. Saw Aleck and his cousin Jennie with a very smart negro woman who had a child, almost white, by her master. Didn't hear her talk much, but Beckwith, Nichols, et al. talked with her—smart as a steel trap. She hid and fed three of our men, escaped prisoners: knew about Burnside, McClellan, and Sherman, also the fall of Atlanta, and even the recent unsuccessful rebel attack there. They pointed out Gen. S. to her in the door of the house—they were in an outbuilding. "Dar's de man dat rules de world!" she exclaimed.

She was about twenty-five, a common hand, negro brogue strong, but very quick and smart. Spoke most bitterly of her mistress, who she says has treated her most cruelly. Mistress never had a child: Sarah and Hagar case only worse. Mistress about forty-five or fifty, heavy sort of woman, sullen and slow, but civil to us: was in great troubling about "perishing." Soldiers "foraged liberally"—took all her peanuts drying on roof shed: and as we left the house, after riding some distance, saw her barn, old and rickety, on fire.

I am bound to say, while I deplore this necessity daily and cannot bear to see the soldiers swarm as they do through fields and yards,--I do believe it is a necessity. Nothing can end this war but some demonstration of their helplessness, and the miserable inability of J.D. to protect them,--with the understanding also that with the submission of their "leaders" and people to the laws, peace will come. If they do still hold out,--then the only alternative is to destroy or remove them. It is evident General believes the latter—indeed he says so.

Tuesday, November 22

W. T. SHERMAN, Ten miles short of Milledgeville

This afternoon was unusually raw and cold. My orderly was at hand with his invariable saddle-bags, which contain a change of under-clothing, my maps, a flask of whiskey, and bunch of cigars. Taking a drink and lighting a cigar, I walked to a row of negro-huts, entered one and found a soldier or two warming themselves by a wood-fire. I took their place by the fire, intending to wait there till our wagons had got up. I was talking to the old negro woman, when some one came and explained to me that, if I would come farther down the road, I could find a better place. So I started on foot, and found on the main road a good double-hewed-log house, in one room of which Colonel Poe, Dr. Moore, and others, had started a fire.

In looking around the room, I saw a small box, like a candle-box, marked "Howell Cobb," and, on inquiring of a negro, found that we were at the plantation of General Howell Cobb, of Georgia, one of the leading rebels. Of course, we confiscated his property, and find it rich in corn, beans, pea-nuts, and sorghum-molasses. Extensive fields are all round the house; I sent word to General Davis to explain whose plantation it was, and instructed him to spare nothing. To-night huge bonfires consume the fence-rails, keep our soldiers warm, and the teamsters and men, as well as the slaves, are carrying off an immense quantity of corn and provisions of all sorts.

[87]

In due season the headquarters wagons came up, and we got supper. After supper I sat on a chair astride, with my back to a good fire, talking with the girl Jennie and became conscious that an old negro, with a tallow-candle in his hand, was scanning my face closely. I inquired, "What do you want, old man?"

He answered, "Dey say you is Massa Sherman."

I answered that such was the case, and inquired what he wanted. He only wanted to look at me, and kept muttering. I asked him why he trembled so, and he said that he wanted to be sure that we were in fact "Yankees," for on a former occasion some rebel cavalry had put on light-blue overcoats, personating Yankee troops, and many of the Negroes were deceived thereby, himself among the number—had shown them sympathy, and had in consequence been unmercifully beaten therefore.

This time he wanted to be certain before committing himself; so I told him to look at the whole horizon lit up with camp-fires, and he could then judge whether he had ever seen any thing like it before. The old man became convinced that the "Yankees" had come at last, about whom he had been dreaming all his life. He said, "Dis nigger can't sleep dis night." Some of the staff-officers gave him a strong drink of whiskey, which set his tongue going.

MAJOR HENRY HITCHCOCK, Assistant Adjutant General, Howell Cobb's Plantation, 10 Miles W. of Milledgeville, Ga.

General Davis selected queer place for camp—exposed to wind, in ploughed field, etc.: general grumbling by Staff. Davis is odd to be sure. A Copperhead. Presently came orders from General Sherman for horses to go forward to house further on. Rode there—found it Howell Cobb's plantation, deserted by owner and able-bodied hands three days ago, and all moveable supplies taken. Plenty left—fodder, corn, oats, bin full of peanuts,--twenty sacks fine salt—500 gallons or more of sorghum molasses. Took possession and lodged there.

Old darky came to see "Mr. Sherman"—scared to death—"thought he was to be killed"—"Dis Mr. Sherman!" "Master, please give me dat light"—takes candle and surveys General trembling all over. "Well—well—and dis is Mr. Sherman! I shan't git done bein' skeered all day tomorrow! Dis nigger can't sleep this night."

General talked kindly—reassured him, etc. It seems that after Stoneman's raid a party of rebs went round among the negroes, disguised as Feds, coaxed them to leave, etc., and when they got as many as they could committed, revealed themselves and flogged the poor deluded negroes almost to death. This one was in deadly terror when he came in—thought he would be killed anyhow—and if it was Mr. Sherman, that he and his men were savages. Same stories of our cruelty, burning negroes alive, etc., at Atlanta, have been told these negroes. What fools the rebs are!

General told all the darkies to help themselves as well as the soldiers, to the supplies found here, and ordered the balanced burned. I don't feel much troubled about the destruction of H.C.'s property—one of the head devils.

JENNIE LEWIS, On the Freedom Road

Dear Papa,

General Sherman came by the mess wagon to talk to me to-nite. It is the first time I had a chance to speke to him since they took my girls away. I wanted to speke on there behalf but before I could he asked 'Well, Jennie what do you think of your freedom so far?'

What could I tell him Papa but this. 'It is the gratest thing, General.'

'Tell me what do the people think about me? Do they think I am the devil? Oh, dont worry. Ive been called worse.'

'But they love you, General Sherman. We all do. They think you rule the world. You and Mr. Lincoln.'

He sat down next to the fire took out one of his cigars and smoked and talked. 'How old are you, Jennie?'

'I'm 18, sir.'

'Do you have any family other than your Mother in Atlanta?'

I told him about Papa and Caroline and Papas letter. I took it from my pocket and he read it. 'He sounds like a strong man, your

Father. If I could have 500 like him. Oh, well—we'll lick these rebels with the Army we have, won't we Jennie?'

I asked him about his family. He told me about his wife and children and the little son who died. He said his last letter from home said the new baby was sick as well. He looked very sad. Then he asked me about my studies. I showed him my book of words from Captain Pepper. 'Captain Pepper says I am a quick study' I told him. 'He said my spelling was atrocious! But he teaches me how to spell words like that every night and I can look up other words in my book.'

'Jennie, your people will need many things once this war is over. You must continue to study with Captain Pepper and prepare to be of service to them and to your new country. There is a college in my home state—Oberlin College. They have been admitting Negro students for some time. Would you like to study there?'

'Yes, General' I whispered for I was in awe of him, but I do not know what a college is but if General Sherman thinks I should go there it must be wonderful. I must ask Captain Pepper what a college is.

Just then some of the elder men from this place walked up to the fire. They stood back at first because some white folks told them the General would sell them to Cuba. An old man held a shaky candle up to General Sherman. He stood still and let him look. 'Well—well—and this is Mr. Sherman!' the old man said. He had been afraid, but he came to see if it was really Mr. Sherman. He said

'I had to look you in the eye and thank you. He just kept saying 'This Nigger won't sleep this night!'

More people came to see him. General Sherman told all of the people to help themselves to everything found here. I love General Sherman with all my heart. He is truly an angel sent by God. He cares about the black people.

General Davis is not like General Sherman at all. He hates the Negroes. We all think so. He thinks we do not have a conscience. He asked a man who came into camp on an old horse 'Don't you think you did very wrong, Dick, to take your mistresses horse?'

'Well, I don't know, sir; I didn't take the best one. She had three; two of them first rate hosses, but the one I took is old, and not very fast, and I offered to buy him for eight dollars, sir.'

'But Dick, you took at least a thousand dollars from your mistress, besides the horse.'

'How, sir?'

'Why, you were worth a thousand dollars, and you should have been satisfied with that much, without taking the poor womans horse.'

'I don't look at it just that way, massa. I worked hard for missus more than thirty years, and I reckon in that time I about pay for myself. And this year missus gave me leave to raise a patch of cotton for my own. Well, I worked nights, and sabbaths, and spare times, and raised a big patch the way prices is, worth two hundred dollars, I reckon, and when I got it taken care of this fall, ole missus took it way from me; give some to the naybors, keep some for her own use, and sell some, and keep the money, and I reckon that pay for the ole horse!'

General Davis walked away. 'I find no conscience in these darkeys!' At my lesson to-night I asked Captain Pepper to spell that word for me and I asked him what it means.

'It is that part of you that knows what is right and what is wrong' he said. I wanted to know how General Davis knew that Negroes had no part of us like that. So I asked Rev. Quarles. He told me 'Fools come from all ranks, Virginia. General Davis cannot speak about your conscience. That is between you and God. You remember what your Mama told you. Keep her eyes set in front of you for you are guided by Providence. The Lord is on our side, Jennie. Not the side of those who hate us. He will carry us through.'

I know the Lord is on our side but which side is General Davis fighting for?

I never got around to asking General Sherman about the girls. Now I am still alone.

Wednesday, November 23

<u>MAJOR HENRY HITCHCOCK</u>, Headquarters, Governor's Mansion, Milledgeville, The Capital of Georgia

"First act of drama well played, General!" "Yes, sir, the first act is played."

General and staff started by 8 A.M.—rode slowly with column five miles,--met courier from Kilpatrick at Milledgeville asking to see him, rode in thence at gallop. K. met us this morning outside of town and rode in: at bridge, troops drawn up, grand reception, colors dipped, cheers, music,--all the horses scared and Button disgraced himself jumping and rearing like mad, but soon subdued. General and staff entered Milledgeville at head of troops with band, etc., without show of resistance. Best way for them, sure!

<u>BREVET MAJOR GEORGE WARD NICHOLS</u>, *In Camp, Milledgeville*

We are in full possession of the capital of the State of Georgia, and without firing a gun in its conquest. A few days ago, the Legislature, which had been in session, hearing of our approach, hastily decamped without any adjournment. The legislative panic spread among the citizens to such an extent as to depopulate the place, except a few old gentlemen and ladies and the negroes, the latter welcoming our approach with ecstatic exclamations of joy: "Bress de Lord! tanks be to Almighty God, the Yanks is come! de

[94]

day ob jubilee hab arribed!" –accompanying their words with rather embarrassing hugs, which those nearest the sidewalks received quite liberally

General Sherman is at the executive mansion, its former occupant having, with extremely bad grace, fled from his distinguished visitor, taking with him the entire furniture of the building. As General Sherman travels with a menage (a roll of blankets and a haversack full of "hardtack"), which is as complete for a life in the open air as in a palace, this discourtesy of Governor Brown was not a serious inconvenience.

Just before his entrance into Milledgeville, General Sherman camped on one of the plantations of Howell Cobb. It was a coincidence that a Macon paper, containing Cobb's address to the Georgians as General Commanding, was received the same day. This plantation was the property of Cobb's wife, who was a Lamar. I do not know that Cobb ever claimed any great reputation as a man of piety or singular virtues, but I could not help contrasting the call upon his fellow-citizens to "rise and defend their liberties, homes, etc., from the step of the invader, to burn and destroy every thing in his front, and assail him on all sides," and all that, with his own conduct here, and the wretched condition of his negroes and their quarters.

We found his granaries well filled with corn and wheat, part of which was distributed and eaten by our animals and men. A large supply of sirup made from sorghum (which we have found at nearly every plantation on our march) was stored in an out-house. This was also disposed of to the soldiers and the poor decrepit negroes which this humane, liberty-loving major general left to die in this place a few days ago. Becoming alarmed, Cobb sent for and removed all the able-bodied mules, horses, cows, and slaves. He left here some fifty old men—cripples—and women and children, with nothing scarcely covering their nakedness, with little or no food, and without means of procuring it. We found them cowering over the fireplaces of their miserable huts, where the wind whirled through the crevices between the logs, frightened at the approach of the Yankees, who, they had been told, would kill them. A more forlorn neglected set of human beings I never saw.

General Sherman distributed to the negroes with his own hands the provisions left here, and assured them that we were their friends, and they need not be afraid that we were foes. One old man answered him: "I spose dat you'se true; but, massa, you'se go way to-morrow, and anudder white man'll come." He had never known any thing but persecutions and injury from the white man, and had been kept in such ignorance of us that he did not dare to put faith in any white man.

We are continually meeting with comical incidents illustrative of the ignorance of the people, and more especially of the funny side of negro character

One old woman stood at her gate watching, with wondering eyes, a drove of cattle as they passed. "Lor' massy," said she, "whare did all them beef come from? Never seed so many in all my life."

"Those cattle were driven all the way from Chicago more than one thousand miles."

"Goodness, Lor'; what a population you Yanks is!"

General Sherman invites all able-bodied negroes (others could not make the march) to join the column, and he takes especial pleasure on some occasions, when they join the procession, in telling them they are free; that Massa Lincoln has given them their liberty, and that they can go where they please; that if they earn their freedom they should have it, but that Massa Lincoln had given it to them any how. They seem to understand that the proclamation of freedom had made them free; and I have met but few instances where they did not say they expected the Yankees were coming down some time or other, and very generally they are possessed with the idea that we are fighting for them, and that their freedom is the object of the war. They got this notion hearing the talk of their masters.

"Stick in dar," was the angry exclamation of one of a party of negroes to another, who was asking too many questions of the officer who had given them permission to join the column. "Stick in dar, it's all right; we'se gwine along; we'se free."

At a house a few miles from Milledgeville, we halted for an hour. In an old hut I found a negro and his wife, both of them more

[97]

than sixty years old. In the talk which ensued nothing was said which led me to suppose that they were anxious to leave their mistress, who, by the way, was a sullen, cruel-looking woman when all at once the old negress straightened herself up, and her face, which a moment before was almost stupid in its expression, assumed a fierce, almost devilish aspect.

Pointing her skinny black finger at the old man crouched in the corner of the fireplace, she hissed out, "What for you sit dar? you s'pose I wait sixty years for nutten? Don't yer see de door open? I'se follow my child; I not stay. Yes, I goes 'long wid dese people; yes, sar, I walks till I drop in my tracks."

A more terrible sight I never beheld. I can think of nothing to compare with it, except Charlotte Chushman's Meg Merrilies. Rembrandt only could have painted the scene, with its dramatic surroundings.

It was near this place that several factories were burned. It was odd to see the delight of the negroes at the destruction of places known only to them as task-houses, where they had groaned under the lash.

MAJOR JAMES A. CONNOLLY, *In Camp, Milledgeville*

Here I am, finally, at Milledgeville. My boyish desire is gratified, and I find that my boyish fancy in regard to the appearance of the city was quite correct. The dwellings are scattered and surrounded by large and tastefully decorated grounds. As one rides along its sandy streets, even at this season of the year, the faint perfume from every variety of tree and shrub, bud, blossom and flower fills the air with delicious fragrance. The exterior of the residences bespeak refinement within, and everything about the city serves to impress one with the idea that he is in an old, aristocratic city, where the worth of a man is computed in dollars and cents.

Our soldiers and even some officers have been plundering the State library today and carrying off law and miscellaneous works in armfuls. It is a downright shame. Public libraries should be sacredly respected by all belligerents, and I am sure General Sherman will, some day, regret that he permitted this library to be destroyed and plundered. I could get a thousand dollars worth of valuable law books there if I would just go and take the, but I wouldn't touch them. I should feel ashamed of myself every time I saw one of them in my bookcase at home. I don't object to stealing horses, mules, niggers and all such little things, but I will not engage in plundering and destroying public libraries.

MAJOR FREDRICK C. WINKLER, *In Camp, Milledgeville*
The white people of Milledgeville are cold and for the most part intensely Secesh, and remain true to the most terrible resolutions that they will never give up, but the negroes, black and white--for it is difficult to distinguish them from white men--are the most devoted friends of the Yankee soldiers. Their demonstrations are literally

frantic. They dance and shout and clap their hands when they see our column approach.

Whatever a soldier may ask for, they hasten to do for him. Whatever their masters have, he will get. It is claimed the negroes are so well contented with their slavery; if it ever was so, that day has ceased to be. Hundreds of men go with us, and thousands would if they could take their families along. Most of them have more or less white blood in their veins, and though they are not taught even to count, they are by no means unintelligent.

Up to this time I have thought the South could organize a formidable military force out of their negroes, but I am satisfied now that they dare not attempt it. Every negro in the land will defend a Yankee soldier to the utmost of his power; many of our prisoners have escaped by their aid, and not one I believe has ever been betrayed by them. At Madison they burned the calaboose or whipping post, and the wild transports of men, women and children, dancing about, was really a spectacle worth seeing.

JENNIE LEWIS, in camp, Milledgeville

Oh, if every day cold be like this one. I just returned from a frolic given by the colored folks of Milligeville. It was the best time ever. I must never forget it from beginning to end so I must rite it all down before I dreme it all over again in my sleep.

After morning chores, the yung girls from the camp got baths out of large tubs set up in the kitchen houses. The older women added in petals and oils and we filled the tubs with heated water. When it was my turn to get undressed and into the bath Sevanda wissled. 'You been fooling us Jennie. Hiding a womans body under those clothes you wear one on top of the other. Look at you. You got bigger ones than me.' They laffed but I did not find it funny. I looked at my brest as they bobbed in the water. I cupped my hands to cover them. They felt like the ripe peaches we used to pick from the trees in Miss Mary's yard. A feeling came over me like I was a grown woman. I slipped deeper into the tub and let the warm sweet water cover me whole.

When we got back to the rooms Captain Pepper brout us four dresses strate from the white womens closets. He gave me first pick. I new what I wanted. It had white lace all up to the neck and a full skirt that flared out and swung when Captain Pepper gave it to me like it was alredy alive and just looking for a body to get going. A silver clasp held a soft blue ribbon around the middle that formed a bow in back. It was soft inside and a little cool, like a dress out of a misty dreme. It was a better dress than any Miss Mary had. I ran behind the screen and pulled it on. It hung loos in places but held me tite around my waist. I put it on and wear it still. I wish I had never to take it off.

Before the dance Sevanda piled my hair up to the top of my head and pinned a blue flower to match the ribbon. She fixed all of our hair and together when walked out into the night.

You cold here the music from across the field before the stone bilding where the dance was to be. Inside a man with a short arm played the banjo and two more men played the bones. On the crowded floor colored folks cut the pigeon wings, went to the East and went to the West. Old Uncle Ned who got here on an old mule all the way from Atlanta called out the figures just as he had done for us at home: 'Ladies sache' and 'Gents to the Left' and 'Now all swing!' We watched and clapped on the side, then accepted a yung mans hand and joned the dance. When it was time to Set the Floor Ilene and her partner did the best and won two slices of peach pie.

Then the music stopped and the hole place took in a breth. In walked General Sherman, Major Hitchcock, and some other officers. All the laffing died away. 'Hello!' the General shouted, and then a roar of cheers followed. We cheered for a long time and General Sherman moved along before us. He cut a handsome figure shakeing hands with the men and bowing to the ladies. He took off his hat and the firey hair shone under the candle lite. He wore a fresh uniform and shined boots. I watched him and the hole way and yet still cold not believe it when he stood in front of me and lifted his hand.

'Miss Jennie Lewis. Wold you honor me with a dance.'

Thankfully my skirt covered up my shaking nees. The band play a song at the Generals request. The Blue something or other. I did not care what tune they played. Once I took the Generals hand and we swung onto the dance floor I did not here or see anyone or anything else but him. I brethed in the smell of his shaving powder mixed with the smell of cigar. I felt warm in my hands held in his and where he placed his other hand on my back. I felt him move me around on the floor and felt as lite as the air itself. I watched him the hole time and he never took his eyes off of mine. Then the song ended and we stood before each other and did not move while all around us the people clapped and shouted. Then he bowed and I curtseyed and he said to me, 'Miss Jennie that is the most pleasant feeling Ive had since the cruell war began. Thank you.' Then he took my arm and led me back where the others stood. Then with a wave to every one he was gone. And everyone looked at me with new eyes.

After the dance, Sevanda said 'We see now why you still sleeping in that ten by yourself—and we's sleeping on the ground. I seen the General whispering in your ear. We all did. You planning on a ron day vu to-nite?'

I wanted to slap her face but I held my anger inside. How cold she think that way about General Sherman.

'Well, Jennie' said Ilene. 'You know what they say about a Yankee officer and a Colored woman...'

'They the two free-est things in the world,' Sevanda said.

'General Sherman is a gentleman.' But the words had no effect on them. Part of me felt mad but another part wished it were so. For I had in the space of two weeks fallen in love with General William Tecumseh Sherman. But I cold never tell them—or anyone. Never ever let General Sherman himself no this was so.

[103]

'Its nothing to be ashamed of,' Sevanda said as if she had seen my thots running threw my head. 'Colored women and white mens have been lying together since Day One.'

'Hush!' I said 'before someone heres you.'

Sevanda said 'It aint nothing to be shamed for, Jennie. My former master didn't even have no children by white womens. He had all his sweethearts amongst his slaves. The slave girls went to the mistress and told her 'bout the master forcing them to let him have something to do with them and the mistress told them, 'Well go on. You belongs to him.'

'Slavery is over' I said. 'We don't belong to people now.'

'Still and all,' Sevanda said.

We walked together to my tent and sat down at a nereby campfire. Ilene began to talk about once when her Old Mistress had gone away to spend the day. 'I always worked in the house and I was alone. Some white boys from town came in and threw me down on the floor and tied me down so I couldn't struggle and one after another used me as long as they wanted, for the whole afternoon. My Old Mistress had them whipped when she came home, but it was too late. When the baby was born, she sold him away and I aint never even got a good look at him and wouldn't know him now if I did.'

We were quite for a long time. Then they walked back to there pallets in camp behind the Army. I am alone in my tent once more with such thots and feelings I can not describe. And now someone is wissling outsite my tent. Its that song. The Blue something.

DANIEL P. CONYGHAM, War Correspondent,
Milledgeville

To-night the camps roared with laughter and the songs of revivals and music halls. Negroes danced and sang, juggled, played banjos and fiddles and homemade drums, rattled bones and entertained the troops. Soldiers and black girls are making love all about the camps.

L. M. DAYTON, Aide-de-Camp By order of MAJ. GEN. W. T. SHERMAN, Hdqrs. Mil. Div. of the Mississippi, Milledgeville, Ga.

Special Field Orders, No. 127:

The first movement of this army having proved perfectly successful and the weather now being fine, the second stage of the campaign and the movement will commence to-morrow, November 24.

Thursday, November 24

ANNA MARIE COOK, *Cook House, Milledgeville*

We are despondent our heads bowed and our hearts crushed--
The Yankees in possession of Milledgeville. The yankee flag waving
from the Capitol-- Our degradation is bitter, but we know it can not
be long, our trust is still strong. No, we go through the house
singing, "We live and die with Davis."

How can they hope to subjugate the South. The people are
firmer than ever before. This morning we walked into town, and we
heard the cry "Our cavalry is coming" how our hearts leaped for joy,
and as a few ragged men came riding up and bowed and brandished
their pistols the tears streamed from our eyes-- strong men wept--
God bless our soldiers our poor suffering soldiers—

Many negroes left with the yankees. Ours were true.
Anderson is gone I fear to suffer—Oh! how dreadful is war, we now
know something of its terrors. God grant to this a speedy and
glorious issue-- May not only peace but honor perch upon banners in
triumph. May He grant that never again may their hostile tread
darken our city and may He comfort the afflicted and distressed and
suffering and poor.

[106]

MRS. ELLA GERTRUDE CLANTON THOMAS,

Thomas House, Milledgeville

Mrs. Gen. Sherman:

A few days hence I read your husband's farewell telegram to you dated Atlanta. Will you believe it? For a moment I felt sorry for you, forgetting who you were and for what purpose he was coming among us, so my heart went out in womanly sympathy for you. This week your husband's army found me in possession of wealth, tonight our plantations are a scene of ruin and desolation.

You bade him Godspeed on his fiendish errand, did you not? You thought it a gallant deed to come amongst us where by his own confession he expected to find "only the shadow of any army," a brave act to frighten women and children! desolate homes, violate the sanctity of firesides and cause the "widow and orphan to curse the name Sherman for the cause" and this you did for what? To elevate the Negro race!

Be satisfied Madame your wish had been accomplished. Enquire of Gen. Sherman when next you see him Who had been elevated to fill your place?.... Did he tell you of the girl for whom he was so much concerned that she rides in a specially designed wagon as he continues his vandal march? This girl he dances with in his arms in public. She is spoken of by the Negroes as "Sherman's wife."

[107]

Rest satisfied Mrs. Sherman and the apprehension of your northern sisters with regard to the elevation of the Negroes. Your husbands are, most of them, provided with "a companion du voyage"

I will only add that intensely Southern woman as I am *I pity you.*

PART THREE: NOVEMBER-DECEMBER 1864

Friday, November 25, 1864

CAPT. DAVID P. CONYNGHAM, War Correspondent,
Observations In the Field, Central Georgia

"How were you treated in slavery, Robert?"

"Pretty well, sar."

"Did your master give you enough to eat and clothe you comfortably?"

"Pretty well, till dis year. Massa have no money to spend this year. Don't get many clothes this year."

"If you had a good master, I suppose you were contented?"

"No, sar."

"Why not, if you had enough to eat and clothes to wear?"

"Cause I want to be free. Sar."

CAPT. GEORGE W. PEPPER, In Camp, 9 mi. from the
Oconee River

Who are these slaves?

I have in the course of this journal mentioned some circumstances to illustrate the character and habits of the Negro population of the South; and a little closer view of it may not be unpleasant.

[109]

The Negroes are remarkable for their ingenuity, docility, religious enthusiasm and quick conception. That they are not naturally lazy is evident from the quantity of laborious work which they will perform, and perform well. In the beautiful city of Huntsville, a lady informed me, that the lordly mansion in which she dwelt, with all the inside furniture, was conceived and executed by the genius and handicraft of three slaves. Their hospitality, when their circumstances are not too wretched to display, is remarkably great. The brother Negro's white visitor finds every man's hut open, and to walk in without ceremony and to partake of his humble fare is sure to give pleasure to every one of the Negroes.

The attachment of the slave mothers to their children is very great. To play with the child is her highest delight; and for this indulgence, she will, by an injudicious, but natural miscalculation of maternal duty, omit the care of herself and husband. Of the docility of the Negroes, when kindly treated there are many instances on record. In battle, on shore, and at sea, the Negro soldier and sailor have been remarkable for their valor, steadiness and subordination; it is said on good authority that over two hundred thousand of them have joined the Union army.

The instruction of this class of persons is in the lowest state of degradation. In many States it was made a crime to teach them to read and write. Gifted with more than ordinary intellect, more exercised than cultivated, the negroes have been kept in a frightful state of degradation, which is too well known, and which ought to

[110]

call forth the immediate attention of the General Government. The aptness to learn and acquire knowledge is attested by my own pupil, Jennie Lewis, the young slave girl who left with us from Atlanta. It's true she had rudimentary reading and writing skills before I came along, taught to her, she said, by her father. Under my nightly instruction, she shows remarkable improvement in vocabulary and spelling and a strong desire to learn. This is the true War we are fighting, against ignorance imposed upon the innocent. And Jennie and I are winning that war every night. In all my endeavors as a minister or a soldier, I have never felt such a sense of worthy accomplishment as I do witnessing the flowering of her intellect.

This night I had a good long talk with a negro who has not yet attained even to the dignity of a "contraband," but is under the yoke. When I spoke to him of liberty, he kindled and said, "That's just all I ask for. Every man has a right to his own sweat, and not to be squandered like cattle, working all his life just for other people to live by. I've seen men and women chained together, driven in squads up this valley, just like cattle. All I ask is to have my own sweat; and if I could get that, I'd work for my wife and children, and never trouble nobody."

I advised him to be discreet and watchful, and bide his time; and gave him written directions how to apply to me in the future--for though he cannot read, he knows Jennie can "spell mighty smart," and she has promised to assist him when the time comes. I found him a true Christian, full of faith and hope, yet having withal a

[111]

touching resignation. For when I spoke of the prospects of his people, he said, "What's for us, we'll get; and what isn't for us, we can't have." Surely, it is my duty to rescue such men from the hands of the spoiler.

Such is the character of the Southern Negro. I appeal not to the affections or humanity, but to the justice of every one to whom chance may direct these pages, whether men so constituted present no character which a wise government can mould to the great purpose of augmenting the prosperity of the country, and the happiness of society.

CAPT. DAVID P. CONYNGHAM, War Correspondent,
Observations in the field, Central Georgia

As we pass through Georgia, colonies, squads, whole families, from the feeble old folks, supported on their canes, and tottering under heavy bundles, down to the muling infant in the mother's arms, while her back was burdened with a heavy bundle, fell in. The young and the old leave home, at a moment's notice, to go, they know not where, nor ask where, in search of freedom. Such was their simple faith that they trudged along, "bressing de Lord, de day of jubilou is come." They were invariable dressed in their best and had packed into bundles their most valuable dresses and a small stock of provisions and then, feeling happy and jubilant, fall in with the sable column that flanks the roads and bring up the rear on all sides.

Black children of all ages and sizes, I might add, of all shades, toddle along in rags and filth, urged on by the application of the maternal rod. Babies squeal in their mothers' laps. Old buggies and wagons, that they took from massa, block up the way, and literally line it with their debris. Galled and jaded mules and horses carry hampers and bags, stuffed with children and wearables, balanced on each side. It is no unusual sight to see a black head, with large, staring eyes, peeping out of a sack at one side, and a ham of bacon or a turkey balancing it at the other.

Even here beauty conquers, for the good-looking lead luxurious lives, stowed away in wagons during the day, and feasting at the servants' mess at night.

Saturday, November 26

<u>JENNIE LEWIS</u>, On the Road to Freedom

Dear Papa,

I attended a camp meeting in the woods. Everywhere you looked colored people stood and sang and shouted, too many people to count. I found Sevanda, Ilene and Nora and was so happy to see them. They say it is better to be in the rear than in the officers camp. 'Much better material to make a husband with,' Sevanda said. 'So many men we have our pick!'

A lot of black folks joined us in Milledgeville, some of them riding into camp on good wagons waring there best. But most of them rode there feet and toted all there belongs on there backs. We hold meetings every night. Mothers and fathers sit on blankets and children run around until the mothers quite them down. The young men line along one side and the young women on the other. The elders sit on chairs up front. Then, the singing starts and the whole congregation (look, Papa! what words I can tell you now that I can spell) rises. If no white soldiers are present, the ring shout begins. That can go on for a long time until we are all spent and spread out in the grass, waiting to hear the word.

The main speaker to-night was a man named Fortune Bell. He started off saying 'In the name of God the mercyful may the prayer of God be on our Lord—' and here he said some word Ive never heard and can not find in my word book—'Mo ha met'— He said 'I stand before you now and I say to you that there aint nothing like Freedom.' People started to shout.

'There aint nothing like working hard and keeping the money you make for yourself.'

'Amen Brother Bell!'

Owning your own self, not belonging to someone else.'

People jumped up from the blankets and the benches and started stomping the ground.

'Nothing like reuniting with your family, finding loved ones who have been sold away.'

I shouted 'Amen Brother Bell'. Mama would not have liked the way I behaved in meeting to-night. I have heard some good preaching all along this road, and it has moved me to sing and holler, but no one put such a spirit into me as Brother Fortune Bell.

He came from Milledgeville but before that he came from some place he called an eyeland. I must ask Captain Pepper to help me find the word eyeland in my speller. When the War started his master took all the strong men and women from the eye-land and walked them to Milledgeville. Now they are going to walk all the way back with the Union Army and clame there homes on the eye-land. 'We got as much right to own and work that land as the white folks had.' He told us his father was a 'mus lamb' and he is too and he has 11 brothers and 7 sisters and they are all also 'mus lambs'. They read and write in erabek. Papa, I do not know what any of that means and I could not find hide nor hare of these words in my book.

[115]

He said the eyeland is a place between the land and the sea. He said it is rich. Oh, Papa, you must know about these things since you are on a ship. How I wish we were together and we could go to an eyeland. There is so much to see and do that we never ~~new~~ knew about in slavery.

Fortune Bell told us we are the Chosen People and that this War is our deliverance from evil slavery for sure. We all believe it.

I did not want to come back to this tent alone. I wanted to stay with the Chosen People. General Sherman has left our camp to ride with another general. He left General Davis in charge. I stay away from General Davis if I can. To-morrow I will move out of my tent and sleep in the rear with the Chosen People.

Your loving daughter,

MRS. L.J.F., Jones Plantation, Sandersville, Georgia

Solemn and sad rose this November sun. Breakfast passed, untasted. Confederate soldiers were stationed in battle-line, even up to our front doors. Sitting in the parlor windows, I could put out my hand and touch the files of soldiers. Soon the skirmish fighting began; volley after volley was poured forth and returned by the advancing army. Wildly beat my heart, and regardless of danger, I sprang into the window, when a Confederate soldier rushed into the room, saying, "For God's sake, ladies, go into your cellar! Don't you know these bullets will kill you?"

For the first time I thought of danger, and told him we had no cellar.

"Go into the back rooms, then, and stand in front of your middle chimney."

Soon mother, myself, and the little Negroes were all huddled up at the fireplaces, while the bullets rattled like hail-stones against the house.

The "fighting" had continued but a short time, when a second soldier rushed into the room where we were and exclaimed: "My God, ladies, we are fighting the whole of Sherman's army; we thought we were fighting a skirmishing party, but it's the whole army. Take care of yourselves, ladies, we'll have to run.... Lock your doors; keep inside. If the Yankees come to the doors, unlock them and stand in them. Be sure to ask for a guard. Be polite, and you will not be mistreated I hope. Good-bye; God bless you ladies...."

I now looked out. Over the fences and fields our Confederates were flying. The last horse I saw leap the fences was that ridden by the kind soldier, who had come in to speak to us. One wave of his cap, and he was gone, like a flash.

The fighting was now over, so I ventured to a front window. These windows faced the two roads leading to the Capital of Georgia. Looking out, I screamed in horror. It seemed to me the whole world was coming.

All day long, the men and wagons poured into town. "Rip! rip," went the yard and garden fences, as they tore them down and pitched their white-winged tents at our very doorsteps—no yards, no gardens, were spared in our ill-fated village. Now the soldiers, with hateful leers from their red eyes, would walk up to the steps of the back veranda, on which we stood, and throwing down the hams and shoulders of our meat, which they had found, would cut them up with savage delight, in our very faces. Next they found the sugar, flour, lard, salt, syrup, which mother had stored away in a cellar, dug beneath one of the Negro houses, by a trusty servant.

Tonight we went to bed supperless; all day long we had fasted, for our breakfast was untasted because of excitement, and dinner we had none....

One of the housemaids ran in, crying and wringing her hands.

"Oh, Missy, de bu'ful courthouse is all burnin' up; and dem soldiers say dey is gwine to burn dis town, dis berry night. Please Missy, you and ole Miss go out to de plantation—dey will shorely burn you all up!"

Poor Betsy wrung her hands and wept bitterly. Now I shut my mouth firm and hard, packed some of Baby's clothes in a small carpet-sack, and placed it behind the door, where I could easily put my hands upon it, if I must go.

I had told the Masonic officers...that I was a Mason's daughter, had asked them for a guard, and they had placed one at either door. I now went to one of these guards, and asked him if the town would be burned.

"Not to-night," he answered; "the courthouse is a signal fire."

Lonely and sad, mother and I sat around the little handful of coals in the fireplace.... Outside countless white tents gleamed in the chill night air.

Old black Tom told us, at dark, that he would keep watch round the house, and come to a certain window and tap every few hours. "I'll tell you what's gwine on outside," he said, "and if anything berry serious am a gwine to happen, den I'll git you off to de plantation somehow."

One of our servants accepted her freedom and went into the army camp—this one was old Tom's daughter. He pursued her, found her, gave her a sound thrashing and brought her home. As he led her into mother's room he said: "Dar she is, mistis! I'se tried mighty hard to make gemmen and ladies outer my chillun, but it 'pears dis one won't do right no how."

Such is the loyalty of our Negroes.

ELLA MITCHELL, Mitchell Home, Sandersville, Georgia

Mr. Ben R. Smith gave a sumptuous dinner this evening to a dozen of the Washington Rifles home on furlough. About the time the guests were seated, one of the house servants named Isham came in hurriedly, he was ashen with fright. He exclaimed, "Lord, Marse Ben, the woods on the hill are full of blue coats."

Mr. Smith answreed, "Isham, you rascal, if you are fooling me, I'll skin you."

"Isham said, "Marse Ben, come and see."

All hurried to the front piazza. Sure enough, the blue coated enemy were on the hill. No one stood on the order of his going. Fortunately their horses stood bridled and saddled. For once, forgetting the ladies and Southern chivalry, they dashed away.

R. D. ARNOLD, Savannah Mayor, Mayor's Office,
Savannah, Georgia
Fellow Citizens,

The time has come when every male who can shoulder a musket can make himself useful in defending our hearths and homes. Our city is well fortified, and the old can fight in the trenches as well as the young; and a determined and brave force can, behind entrenchments, successfully repel the assaults of treble their number.

The general commanding this division has issued a call for all men of every age, not absolutely incapacitated from disease, to report at once to Captn. C. W. Howard, at the Oglethorpe barracks, for the purpose of organizing into companies for home defense. I call upon every man not already enrolled in a local corps to come forward at once and report to Captain Howard. Organization is everything. Let us emulate the noble examples of our sister cities of Macon and Augusta where the whole male population is in arms. By manning the fortifications we will leave free the younger men to act in the field. By prompt action a large local force can be organized from our citizens above the military age, and from those who have been exempted from field service.

No time is to be lost. The man who will not comprehend and respond to the emergency of the times, is forsworn to his duty and to his country.

Sunday, November 27

MAJOR JAMES A. CONNOLLY, 123rd Illinois Infantry,

On the march, near Sandersville, Georgia

Where can all the rebels be? Here we are riding rough shod over Georgia and nobody dares to fire a shot at us. We burn their houses, barns, fences, cotton and everything else, yet none of the Southern braves show themselves to punish us for our vandalism. Perhaps they are preparing a trap to catch us all, but I don't think we will go into their trap, if we can find any way to go around it. We don't care where we come out; would a little rather come out at Savannah, but if we can't do that we'll go somewhere else.

Georgia is an excellent state for foraging. Our foragers came into camp tonight pretty well loaded, and I can't imagine where they found so much stuff through this country. I suppose the negroes assisted them.

We are living finely, and the whole army would have no objection to marching around through the State for the next six months. Indeed, the whole trip thus far has been a holiday excursion, but a very expensive one to the rebels.

The rebel papers we get hold of from Augusta also call on all the citizens to turn out and fall timber across the roads—destroy their forage and provisions, and do everything possible to harass us and retard our march. Let them do it if they dare. We'll burn every house, barn, church, and everything else we come to; we'll leave their families houseless and without food; their towns will all be destroyed, and nothing but the most complete desolation will be found in our track. The army will not be trifled with by citizens.

CAPT. DAVID P. CONYNGHAM, War Correspondent,
Observations, In Camp, near Sandersville

Near this RR station we found several locomotive houses inhabited by a very peculiar people. Some western squatters live on rafts; the Chinese have their floating populations, and the poor Irish their mud cabins; but here we found new tenants who inhabit the box-cars that have been thrown off the track, or switched on sidelings. In some of these were families of blacks, whose masters had been burned out, and they were now shifting for themselves. All the able-bodied men had been carried off by massa, leaving the women and children to enjoy the combined luxury of freedom and starvation.

Greasy negro wenches stuck out their heads through the windows to survey us, while young picaninnies rolled and tumbled about like porpoises on the land. Some had octoroon lightness of color and clearness of features; others approached the brown olive of the Indian; while others displayed the thick lips, woolly heads, and dusky skins of the pure Ethiopian. Such a medley would send your miscegenation disciples into ecstasies; but it would take a whole herald college to trace their relationships to one another.

I learned that the octoroon boy, whom, if you met with, you would set down as the child of white parents, was the offspring of brother and sister. His mother was the child of a planter, and his slave; while the boy was the child of the planter's son.

"Did you know," said I to the boy's mother, who was certainly good-looking, "that he was your brother?"

"Spects I did."

"And why did you live with him?"

"Me gwine to oppose massa? Catch a slave do it."

Two box-cars near the black colony were inhabited by white families. They did not appear to be a bit better off than the blacks. Their clothing was scant, and their sense of shame or moral rectitude, if they ever had any, was perfectly blunted. In one car I found two young and rather good-looking women. They had three children between them.

"Where are your husbands?" I asked.

"We never had none," was the reply

"How do you manage to live?"

"Well, I reckon as well as we can. Can't get no coffee nor snuff, now. Have you a chew of 'backer, stranger?" These wretched families appeared content in their filth, and rags, and wretchedness.

I then dropped into a clean negro shanty to rest and await the column. Its occupants were an old patriarch who had no hair on the top of his head, the place where the wool ought to grow, two young picaninnies, and a good-looking negress in a fair way of soon increasing the slave population.

The old man was quite communicative, and enlightened me very much on the blessings of slavery. Soon a strapping negro rode up to the door, and, hitching his horse, ran in in the best possible spirits.

"Whar you gwine, Jake?" said the young woman.

"I'm gwine wid de rest, to be sure. De Lord has sent 'em to burst our bondage."

"Am I gwine wid you?" asked the wife.

"No, so, Cal; a lady in you'ns state ain't fit to travel. I will come back to get you when we lick them rebs. Jist do pack up, and I'll gwine along."

"What will become of your family?" I asked.

He scratched his head, and replied,--"Well, I guess de Lord will take care of dem."

So he packed up a few things, and with scarcely a parting good bye, jumped on the miserable animal which he had helped himself to from massa, and joined the moving throng.

JENNIE LEWIS, On the Road to Freedom, near
Sandersville, Georgia
Dear Papa,
To-day Captain C. said he met a man and his wife named Cal. I asked him to tell me what she looked like but he could not. He

[125]

says they live in a cabin near the railroad track. Papa, I am going to look for this Cal. It may be Caroline. You know how she used to like us to call her Cal.

I must hurry before Captain Pepper misses me.

Monday, November 28

REV. G. S. BRADLEY, Chaplain, 22nd Wisconsin , In Camp, near Davisboro:

May blacks have joined us to-day. Women came with large bundles on their heads, children also carried quite large packages on their heads, and some of the larger ones carried the little ones. All seemed bent on having their freedom, poor, ignorant, miserable people! They little know the hardships before them. Many of them come into our ranks with expectations that will fall far below realization. Our soldiers urge them to go along with us, without stopping to think how they will manage to make their way to a land of freedom.

CAPTAIN GEORGE PEPPER, In Camp, Davisboro

I went to the Negro meeting to-night to find Jennie. Spoke with the Rev. Quarles. He had not seen Jennie all day but he allowed she was in camp behind the supply wagons, staying the night with the growing throng of negroes now marching with us.

Jennie has missed two nights of lessons, and now I learn she has abandoned our headquarters camp. Perhaps I have held the reigns too loosely. I did promise her mother I would keep watch over her. I must speak with her sharply tomorrow.

I caught some of the good Rev.'s sermon. "Family we knew this day was coming. We knew about Emancipation before that man up in Washington knew about it. Only we didn't let on to Ole Massa. We pretended not to know. I said to my ole massa, 'What's this Massa Lincoln is going to do to the poor nigger? I hear he is going to cut 'em up awful bad. How is it, massa?" I just pretended foolish. We knew from the start the Yankees are going to win cause they always marching to the South, but none of the South soldiers marches to the North. And with their victory comes the end of slavery. I didn't say that to the white folks before, but I sure say it to you now. Walk together children. Don't you get weary."

It seemed rather a radical message to give to the untutored masses—that they know more about freedom than President Lincoln or any white man. I spoke with him afterwards about it and he nodded but would not comment on the subject further.

BREVET MAJOR GEORGE WARD NICHOLS, Near Johnston, south side of the Georgia Railroad

The most pathetic scenes occur upon our line of march daily and hourly. Thousands of negro women join the column, some carrying household goods, and many of them carrying children in their arms, while older boys and girls plod by their side. All these women and children are ordered back, heartrending though it may be to refuse them liberty. One begs that she may go to see her husband and children at Savannah. Long years ago she was forced from them and sold. Another has heard that her boy was in Macon, and she is "done gone with grief goin' on four years."

But the majority accept the advent of the Yankees as the fulfillment of the millennial prophecies. The "day of jubilee," the hope and prayer of a lifetime, has come. They can not be made to understand that they must remain behind, and they are so satisfied only when General Sherman tells them, as he does every day, that we shall come back for them some time, and that they must be patient until the proper hour of deliverance arrives.

The other day a woman with a child in her arms was working her way along among the teams and crowds of cattle and horsemen. An officer called to her kindly: "Where are you going, aunty?"

She looked up into his face with a hopeful, beseeching look, and replied, "I'se gwine whar you'se gwine, massa."

PVT. THEODORE F. UPSON, 100th Indiana Infantry In the Field, Georgia

We have been crossing a large River on our pontoon boats. I think it is called the Oconee. Here we turned back a large number of Negroes who have been following us. We cannot feed them and must look out for ourselves.

It aint right to have them thinking we're here just to free the slaves. We're fighting secession. This slavery business has just been hung on us.

Tuesday, November 29

REV. G. C. QUARLES, Camp Meeting, Middle Georgia

We hear grumbling from the soldiers. They say that the growing number of freed people coming into our camps swell the Army's lines and are an encumbrance—threatening to put the Army in harm's way. They say old men and young women with children should stay with Massa until the war ends and the North is victorious. They say we consume too much food and threaten to starve the Army that must be well fed to survive and win this war. This is what the soldiers say--and some of their officers.

We must remind these gentlemen what it is they are fighting for.

"Yes, Lord!"

They are fighting for our freedom, for the very right of those old men and young women to bid adieu to old Massa and take up with Uncle Sam. Or stay and make a claim for the land inhabited and worked by generations of their families. Their right to choose.

They say they are fighting to preserve the Union, but are we not the Union's best friend? We are working for the Union, for this army. We are the pioneers--repairing the roads that the rebels have torn apart. We are the scouts and spies giving valuable information to the generals. We are the teamster, the laundresses, the errand boys, the cooks—and we—people—

"Say it!"

"We go out into the countryside and get our own food. I suppose the rich georgia families who have lived off of the sweat of our brow have enough food in their fields to feed a few thousand Negroes! And the whole of Sherman's army!

"Amen, Lord!"

They say we don't know what freedom means. We think it means freedom from work. We know free men have to work—can't live without work. There's the great difference between free and slave. When you free, you work and the money belongs to yourself.

"Thank the Lord!"

They say—with freedom, the Negroes will take retribution upon their masters. But have we taken advantage of this War to commit acts of lawlessness and violence?

"No, never!"

It is their own soldiers who are taking advantage—commiting atrocities against citizens—black and white. They leave them with no food and no stock. Yet they want our people to stay put and continue to suffer oppression and want. And they call us primitive. Hah!

"That's a joke!"

I say to you. Do not listen to what the white men say. Watch what they do. Those complaining the loudest are still fighting to defeat our enemy. The Yankees will defeat the Rebels. And we shall all be free.

*We will march thro' the valley in peace, We will march thro'
the valley in peace;*

*If Jesus himself be our leader, We will march thro' the valley
in peace.*

Amen.

<u>MAJOR JAMES A. CONNOLLY</u>, 123rd Illinois Infantry ,
In camp, near Davisboro

A lot of refugee negroes who are encamped near our
headquarters got up a regular "Plantation Dance" tonight, and some
of us went over and watched the performance which was highly
amusing. The dress, general appearance, action, laughter, music and
dancing of the genuine plantation negro is far more grotesque and
mirth-provoking than the broadest caricatures of "Christy's
Minstrels."

They require neither fiddle nor banjo to make music for their
ordinary plantation dances, and the dancers need no prompter, but
kick, and caper and shuffle in the most complicated and grotesque
manner their respective fancies can invent, while all who are not
actually engaged as dancers stand in a ring around the dancers,
clapping their hands, stamping their feet, swinging their bodies, and
singing as loud and as fast and furious as they can, a sort of barbaric
chant, unlike anything I ever heard from the lips of white mortals; I
observed, however, that there is a tone of melancholy (I know of no
other mode of describing it) pervading all their rude music, which

was plainly discernible even when the mirth of the dancers and singers had apparently reached its highest pitch.

There is more fact than fiction in the saying that a "Soldier's life is always gay," for here we are in the midst of a hostile country, engaged in a campaign which probably the whole world, at this moment, is predicting will end in our complete destruction, and yet I have spent the evening laughing at the oddities of these negroes until my head and sides are aching.

Wednesday, November 30

JENNIE LEWIS, On the Freedom Road

Papa!

I have found Caroline!

My dear sister sleeps next to me in my tent and her son lies curled beside her.

I found her and right where Captain C. described. She was dressed in rags Papa but now she has good dresses and stockings and shoes, all given to her by the women in camp. Magdelena has been feeding her and taking care of the little boy during the day. At night she brings the baby to my tent and we talk until near morning.

And--oh, Papa—soon Caroline will be a mother again!

We rode a wagon from sandersville to catch the army lines. How we got away I do not know but that God was protecting us. Rebels soldiers rode all around in the words. But they left us alone so we rode all day and finely are now safe with the Union.

Caroline is married to a man named Jake Smothers. She was forced to marry him by her new master. That is why he bought her to his farm. 'Caroline' he said 'You are a big fine looking woman and Jake is a big fine looking man. I want you to bring forth big fine looking children.'

'All he wanted me for was to make more children he could sell. Well, I could not go for that. The first night Jake tried to come

[134]

to my bed I picked up the poker and said 'Get away from me before I bust your brains out and stomp on them.'

For an hour he glared at her and she glared right back. Then he stomped out the door and she barred it. 'The next day I went to tell Master what Jake had done and he told me 'I paid good money for you Caroline, and I did that because I want you to raise me children. You are to live with Jake for that purpose. Now if you don't want whipping at the stake, you do as I want.'

'What could I do Jennie, but submit. And there is little Jake.'

Oh but you have never seen such an angel, Papa. He is just one but walks and runs about as if he owns the place. He never meets a stranger but has a smile for everyone. To hear him laff is to beleve there is no war, Papa.

Caroline is with the Army now. No one can sell her baby away.

I will stop now, Papa, for there are things between sisters that even you should not ~~no~~ know. Just know that we are, always,

Your too loving daughters who long to be united with you,

Thursday, December 1

SUE SAMPLE, Sample House, Summertown

They shot all the hogs in the pen. Two Yanks came first, a
Dutch and Negro, telling Rachel it would be best to turn the hogs
out, but she had no time before they were there. The yard, Negro
houses, and kitchen, were crowded with the yankees. We could hear
nothing but guns all day and the squeals of hogs. We begged them to
leave something, but no answer.

They camp here tonight, and until 11 o'clock, the camp was
ringing with music, which made our hearts bleed. We had but little
to eat and do not sleep at all tonight.

NORA M. CANNING, Canning Home, Jefferson County,
near Louisville

For several days, squads of Wheeler's cavalry have passed
and tell us where Sherman's army is, and of the depredations they
are committing, and warn us to prepare for the worst, as they were
showing no mercy; and on Sunday, we heard that the destroyers
were encamped just above our upper plantation. That night, the
heavens looked as if they were on fire, from the glare of hundreds of
burning houses, and yesterday morning, a Negro man came from the
upper plantation and told us they were crossing the river and that
some of them were in Louisville, about two miles off; also that they

were searching the houses, breaking open the stores and setting fire to them, and killing all the stock they could find.

About noon today, just as we were ready to sit down to dinner, a little Negro boy came running in half breathless from fright.

"Marster," he cried, "dey's coming down the lane."

"Who is coming?" asked the master.

"Two white men's wid blue coats on," the little Negro answered.

We left the dining-room and looked out. Instead of "two white men with blue coats," we saw about a dozen at the Negro houses, talking to the Negroes. My husband went out, and two of them came up and spoke very politely to him, asking if he could let them have something to eat. They said they wanted some flour, and were willing to pay for what they got. They looked around the pantry and smoke-house, and one of them said, "You had better have those provisions carried into your house; some of our men are not very particular to ask for what they want," while another offered to take down some pieces of meat that were hanging in the smoke-house and bring them into the house for me.

I began to think they were not so bad after all, but I soon had reason to change my mind. We had hardly got the meat inside of the house before hundreds of the "Blue Coats" could be seen everywhere. One man came up to me and asked if I could tell him how long it was since the last "Rebs" passed the place. I made no reply to him, whereupon he cursed me and demanded to know why I did not answer his question.

"Don't you know the Southern women know no such persons as 'Rebs,'" another soldier observed.

"Then," said the first, "will you please tell me, madam, how long since the last Confederate soldier passed here?"

I told him General Wheeler's men had been passing for several days, and that some of them had passed that morning. "I suppose," I added, "that they are waiting for you down in the swamp," and I hoped in my heart they would give them a warm reception.

BRAXTON BRAGG, Commanding General of North Carolina, CSA, Military Secretary, Richmond:

Following just received from Major-General Wheeler:

Jos. Wheeler,, Major General, CSA, Four Miles West Buck Head Church, November 29—9 p. m.

We fought General Kilpatrick all night and all day, charging him at every opportunity. Enemy fought stubbornly, and a considerable number of them killed. We stampeded and came near capturing Kilpatrick twice, but having a fleet horse he escaped bare headed, leaving his hat in our hands. Our own loss about 70, including the gallant General Robertson, severely wounded. Our troops all acted handsomely.

W. J. HARDEE, Lieutenant-General, CSA, Savannah, Georgia

Major General L. McLaws:

General Wheeler says that prisoners report that Sherman is going to Savannah by way of Augusta. The force at the Oconee bridge cannot be spared yet. Be prepared to press negroes if you need them.

Friday, December 2

W. T. SHERMAN, Major-General, Headquarters, near
Millen, Georgia

The southern newspapers predict our "utter annihilation." But
our advance through this country has been steady and mostly
unopposed. After the skirmish in Sandersville, General Wheeler's
cavalry has all but disappeared from our midst, and I expect no
serious opposition from here on.

On entering Sandersville, I told certain citizens (who would
be sure to spread the report) that, if the enemy attempted to carry out
their threat to burn their food, corn, and fodder, in our route, I would
most undoubtedly execute to the letter the general orders of
devastation made at the outset of the campaign.

I accompanied the Twentieth Corps from Milledgeville to
Sandersville. I now shift to the Right Wing, and am accompanying
the Seventeenth Corps (General Blair) on the south of the railroad,
till abreast of Station 91/2 (Barton), General Howard, in person, with
the Fifteenth Corps, keeping farther to the right, and about one day's
march ahead, ready to turn against the flank of any enemy who
should oppose our progress.

At Barton I learned that Kilpatrick's cavalry had reached the
Augusta railroad about Waynesborough, where he ascertained that
our prisoners have been removed from Millen, and therefore the
purpose of rescuing them, upon which we had set our hearts, was an

[140]

impossibility. But as Wheeler's cavalry had hung around him, I ordered him to leave his wagons and all incumbrances with the Left Wing, and move in the direction of Augusta; if Wheeler gave him the opportunity, to indulge him with all the fighting he wanted.

The Seventeenth Corps has taken up the destruction of the railroad at the Ogeechee, near Station 10, and will continue it to Millen, the enemy offering little or no opposition.

Pierce the shell of the Confederacy and it's hollow, all hollow inside.

Tomorrow I enter Millen with the Seventeenth Corps and there will pause one day, to communicate with all parts of the army. Will send word to Capt. Pepper for Jennie to return with the courier to Millen. Manuel is complaining about her absence and one must keep the cook happy.

Restless to-night.

JENNIE LEWIS, On the Freedom Road

Captain Pepper scolded me for leaving camp. 'I thought you were serious about your studies, Jennie. But it appears you have abandoned your hopes for elevation above ignorance and want.'

He gave me no chance to speak.

'You left camp without my knowledge. Had something happened to you what could I tell your mother? Nothing, for I had no clue where you went off to. You could have been just another dead black body along this road. It is utterly irresponsible.'

[141]

I dare not ask him how to spell these words, so I have spent all night with my books trying to write what he said. I could not answer back except to show him Caroline and the baby in my tent. He humped his back and went away. Then little Jake stood up and did the same thing and Caroline and I laughed behind our hands.

When Jake fell asleep Caroline had me put on the ball gown I got in Milledgeville. 'Oh, it is fine' she said. Then she went about camp and found some thread and a needle. She began to sew the dress to fit me better, talking softly as she did.

I have only one regret, Jennie, she said. 'I wish Jake could have been free from birth. If I knew freedom was coming so soon, I would have wanted to wait until then to have a baby. But then, I was nothing but a slave, so how could I know. And if I did know how could I wait. I had no choice to wait. Master took that away.' She looked at me. 'But you do. We free now, Jennie. You can choose.'

'There now' she said, looking at me. 'You are the prettiest girl in camp.'

If the General was here he would understand. He would not mind me going to get Caroline and Jake. I told him I will meet papa wherever the Army ends up and Papa will bring all our family together again. He would not mind Jake in camp at all. He loves children. He told me so. He told me how much he misses his children especially the son who died. General Sherman understands. He loves me. He told me so.

Saturday, December 3

U.S. GRANT, Lieutenant- General City Point, Va.,
December 3, 1864

Maj. Gen. W. T. Sherman, Commanding Armies, near
Savannah, Ga.:

The little information gleaned from the Southern press indicating no great obstacle to your progress, I have directed your mails, which had been previously collected in Baltimore by Colonel Markland, special agent of the Post-Office Department, to be sent as far as the blockading squadron off Savannah, to be forwarded to you as soon as heard from on the coast.

Not liking to rejoice before the victory is assured I abstain from congratulating you and those under your command until bottom has been struck. I have never had a fear of the result. After all becomes quiet, and roads up here so bad that there is likely to be a week or two that nothing can be done, I will run down the coast and see you. If you desire it, I will ask Mrs. Sherman to go with me.

W. T. SHERMAN, Major-General, Headquarters, In camp,
Millen Georgia

Notes for Report: I entered Millen with the Seventeenth Corps (General Frank P. Blair), and here paused to communicate with all parts of the army. General Howard is south of the Ogeechee River, with the Fifteenth Corps, opposite Scarboro. General Slocum is at Buckhead Church, four miles north of Millen, with the Twentieth Corps. The Fourteenth (General Davis) is at Lumpkin's Station, on the Augusta road, about ten miles north of Millen, and the cavalry division is within easy support of this wing. Thus the whole army is in good position and in good condition. We have largely subsisted on the country; our wagons are full of forage and provisions; but, as we approach the sea-coast, the country will become more sandy and barren, and food will no doubt became more scarce; still, with little or no loss, we have traveled two-thirds of our distance, and we will push on for Savannah.

General Hardee is ahead, between us and Savannah. We will resume the march directly on Savannah, by the four main roads. The weather is fine, the roads good, and every thing seems to favor us.

CAPTAIN JAMES M. RANDALL, 21st Wisconsin, In the Field, near Lumpkin's Station, Georgia

We crossed Buckhead Creek, a deep stream, on a pontoon bridge. The 21st Wis. was in the rear of the 14th Corps. Following us were probably three hundred black refugees, men, women and children. Some had followed our army fifty miles or more. All were joyous as they marched toward freedom. But for some reason Gen. Jeff. C. Davis, our Corps commander, desired to get rid of these followers, and he chose to do it at the crossing of Buckhead Creek. He ordered that as soon as the last soldier, and those blacks who were employed by officers, had crossed, the pontoon bridge should be immediately removed. Thus the poor creatures were left in the swamp to their doom. I saw the bridge removed and heard the piteous pleadings of these people to be allowed to cross. As they came to realize their helpless condition, they presented a sad sight. I regard this as an inhuman act ordered by Gen. Jeff. C. Davis, and without an excuse.

MAJOR JAMES A. CONNOLLY, 123rd Illinois Infantry, In the field, near Lumpkin's Station, Georgia

We heard from the rest of our corps tonight and from the extreme right of the army. General Sherman with the right wing is probably within 20 miles of Savannah tonight. Our withdrawal from Waynesboro and march to this place this afternoon closes all demonstrations against Augusta. We have kept up the delusion of an attack on that place as long as we can, and with the sunlight of tomorrow the true design of our campaign will break upon the bewildered minds of the rebels. It is over a hundred miles tonight between the two extremes of our army, and tomorrow morning we commence closing up as rapidly as possible. The road we are encamped on tonight leads straight to Savannah. I heard tonight that General Davis turned back a lot of contrabands at Buckhead Creek, and I don't doubt it, for he is a copperhead.

CAPTAIN GEORGE W. PEPPER, Aide-de-Camp In camp, near Lumpkin's station

General S. sent note requesting Jennie go to Millen and meet up with his Headquarters wagon there. Not sure whether this request was in the form of a direct order. But I sent word to the General that, as I am remaining here with the 14th Corps on General Davis' orders, perhaps Jennie had better remain as well.

If this was a direct order, I suppose I face reprimand. Well, so be it. I cannot consider sending her away from here after lecturing her about staying afoot.

I heard there was some trouble at Buckhead Creek and that some of the Negroes there were left behind, on Davis' orders. All the more reason to keep a tighter watch on Jennie's whereabouts.

Sunday, December 4

CAPTAIN JAMES M. RANDALL, 21st Wisconsin, In the
Field, Georgia

Our Division moved at noon, and after a march of 6 miles
went into camp at dark. We passed through a poor country. A few of
those black refugees whom we left at Buckhead Creek overtook us.
We learned that several were drowned in an attempt to cross this
stream.

JENNIE LEWIS, On the Road to Freedom

The colored people are in an uproar. Last night the solders
pulled up the boat bridge and left people behind the wagons on the
other side of a creek. Some turned back and said they were going
home. Some people almost drowned trying to get across. The men
had to tie logs together with there own clothes. It took till this
morning to get everyone across. I was in the mess tent when a solder
came to General Davis and said 'Sir the niggers are back.'

'Con found it!' General Davis said. 'I ordered that bridge to
be taken up. Which ones of my lincoln-loving john brown
abolishioniss solders refused a direct order? They will be tried and
shot! I will not have my lines clogged up with niggers, if I have to
remove every bridge from here to Sa-van-da' (that's what it sounds
like to me). 'Let them stop up the creeks instead.'

[147]

He did not see me in the room or he saw me and did not care that I heard. I ran strate to Rev. Quarles as soon as I could get away. I repeted as best I could word for word what the general said. Rev Quarles called some of the men and women in camp together and they talked for a long time. While words flew around to the colored folks in camp. 'We should all go back to our homes and let the army fend for itself' some people said. Caroline and I did not like that talk at all. Our Papa is ahead of us, not behind.

Folks sat around camp fires shivering and grumbling and crying and praying until finely the men and women came out of there meeting and spred through the camp to talk to the rest of us. Rev. Quarles, Fortune Bell, and some of the other men from Milledgeville came to my tent.

'Jennie we are sending a delegation to General Sherman. We want him to know what happened last night. We want him to order General Davis to keep the bridges up and we need you to come along.' This was Fortune Bell talking. My heart skipped a beat. Caroline and I looked at each other. 'What do you want me for?'

'You are an eye witness to what General Davis said. And'— he stopped and looked at Rev. Quarles. Then he looked at me. 'General Sherman trusts you. He knows you and likes you. He will listen to what you say.'

I could not say a word but just stood there looking at everyone. Finely I said 'Im just the cooks assistant.' As I said the words I no know my eyes spoke another truth. I know General

Sherman will listen to me because he has done just that before. I also want to go. But how can I leave Caroline and little Jake when I have just found them!

Fortune Bell then said 'They call you Shermans wife.'

'Says who?' I shouted. Caroline took my hand. She said 'Jennie is not going. It is not safe for my sister to be on the roads in this country. It is crawling with rebels.'

'We will ride with the carriers going to the generals headquarters. No one will dare molest us and if they try, we will protect Jennie' Fortune Bell said.

I heard him talking but I could not get the other words out of my ears Shermans wife! Is that what Fortune ~~thot~~ thought of me? Did ever one think the same? I looked at Rev. Quarles but his face gave no answer. I asked him if he thought I should go.

'It is a big responsibility, Jennie. You are the only one who should decide whether you will take it. I will only say that if you decide to go I will answer for you to your mother and father.'

'It is not the way people think Reverend' I said. 'General Sherman is a good, kind man.'

'I know Jennie. I know you are a good, smart girl. I know you will do what is right.'

They left and I looked at Caroline. She looked back at me. 'Shermans wife?' she said. We laughed and fell upon the bed.

Now Caroline and Jake are asleep and I am still awake writing all of this in my book. Now I must think about what to do. I do not want to leave Caroline. Captain Pepper has told me never to leave camp without him. And yet, there is a part of me that itches to see General Sherman again.

I must sleep.

Monday, December 5

BRAXTON BRAGG, Headquarters Armies Of The
Confederate States, Augusta
Col. John B. Sale, Military Secretary:

The following just received from General Wheeler: Near
Walker's Bridge, December 5, 1864—4.30 a. m.

*Enemy's infantry and cavalry left Waynesborough going
toward Millen; they were in very large force, both infantry and
cavalry. Everything now appears to be moving toward Savannah.*

H. W. HALLECK, Major-General and Chief of Staff,
Surgeon-General U. S. Army, Washington:

The Secretary of War directs that all supplies, stores, and
material for General Sherman's army be immediately sent to
Savannah., to be landed at such place, or places, as may be there
ordered. Competent officers of each department should be at that
place to forward and issue stores without delay.

Very respectfully, your obedient servant,

(Copies to the Chief of Commissary Department, Chief
Engineer, Chief of Ordnance, and the Quartermaster-General,
Washington.)

C.W. THOMAS, Major and Chief Quartermaster, Hilton Head, S. C.

Maj. Gen. J. G. Foster, Commanding Department of the South:

General:

The telegraph operator here has just received a dispatch from Port Royal Ferry, stating that a rebel officer who has deserted brings information that General Sherman is within sight of Savannah.

I am, very respectfully, your obedient servant,

Tuesday, December 6

<u>A. LINCOLN</u>, U.S. President, Washington, D.C., 1864 State
of the Union Address

Fellow-Citizens of the Senate and House of Representatives:

The war continues. Since the last annual message all the important lines and positions then occupied by our forces have been maintained and our arms have steadily advanced, thus liberating the regions left in rear, so that Missouri, Kentucky, Tennessee, and parts of other States have again produced reasonably fair crops.

The most remarkable feature in the military operations of the year is General Sherman's attempted march of 300 miles directly through the insurgent region. It tends to show a great increase of our relative strength that our General in Chief should feel able to confront and hold in check every active force of the enemy, and yet to detach a well-appointed large army to move on such an expedition. The result not yet being known, conjecture in regard to it is not here indulged.

Important movements have also occurred during the year to the effect of molding society for durability in the Union. Although short of complete success, it is much in the right direction that 12,000 citizens in each of the States of Arkansas and Louisiana have organized loyal State governments, with free constitutions, and are earnestly struggling to maintain and administer them. The movements in the same direction, more extensive though less

[153]

definite, in Missouri, Kentucky, and Tennessee should not be overlooked. But Maryland presents the example of complete success. Maryland is secure to liberty and union for all the future. The genius of rebellion will no more claim Maryland. Like another foul spirit being driven out, it may seek to tear her, but it will woo her no-more.

At the last session of Congress a proposed amendment of the Constitution abolishing slavery throughout the United States passed the Senate, but failed for lack of the requisite two-thirds vote in the House of Representatives. Although the present is the same Congress and nearly the same members, and without questioning the wisdom or patriotism of those who stood in opposition, I venture to recommend the reconsideration and passage of the measure at the present session. Of course the abstract question is not changed; but an intervening election shows almost certainly that the next Congress will pass the measure if this does not. Hence there is only a question of time as to when the proposed amendment will go to the States for their action. And as it is to so go at all events, may we not agree that the sooner the better?

It is not claimed that the election has imposed a duty on members to change their views or their votes any further than, as an additional element to be considered, their judgment may be affected by it. It is the voice of the people now for the first time heard upon the question. In a great national crisis like ours unanimity of action among those seeking a common end is very desirable--almost indispensable. And yet no approach to such unanimity is attainable unless some deference shall be paid to the will of the majority simply because it is the will of the majority. In this case the common end is the maintenance of the Union, and among the means to secure that end will, through the election, most dearly declare in favor of such constitutional amendment.

The most reliable indication of public purpose in this country is derived through our popular elections. Judging by the recent canvass and its result, the purpose of the people within the loyal States to maintain the integrity of the Union was never more firm nor more nearly unanimous than now. The extraordinary calmness and good order with which the millions of voters met and mingled at the polls give strong assurance of this. Not only all those who supported the Union ticket, so called, but a great majority of the opposing party also may be fairly claimed to entertain and to be actuated by the same purpose. In affording the people the fair opportunity of showing one to another and to the world this firmness and unanimity of purpose, the election has been of vast value to the national cause.

The election has exhibited another tact not less valuable to be known--the fact that we do not approach exhaustion in the most important branch of national resources, that of living men. While it is melancholy to reflect that the war has filled so many graves and carried mourning to so many hearts, it is some relief to know that, compared with the surviving, the fallen have been so few. While corps and divisions and brigades and regiments have formed and fought and dwindled and gone out of existence, a great majority of the men who composed them are still living. The same is true of the naval service. The election returns prove this. So many voters could not else be found. Thousands, white and black, join us as the national arms press back the insurgent lines. We have more men now than we had when the war began; that we are not exhausted nor in process of exhaustion; that we are gaining strength and may if need be maintain the contest indefinitely.

The public purpose to reestablish and maintain the national authority is unchanged, and, as we believe, unchangeable. The manner of continuing the effort remains to choose. On careful consideration of all the evidence accessible it seems to me that no attempt at negotiation with the insurgent leader could result in any good. He would accept nothing short of severance of the Union, precisely what we will not and can not give. His declarations to this effect are explicit and oft repeated. He does not attempt to deceive us. He affords us no excuse to deceive ourselves. He can not voluntarily reaccept the Union; we can not voluntarily yield it. Between him and us the issue is distinct, simple, and inflexible. It is an issue which can only be tried by war and decided by victory. If we yield, we are beaten; if the Southern people fail him, he is beaten. Either way it would be the victory and defeat following war. What is true, however, of him who heads the insurgent cause is not necessarily true of those who follow. Although he can not reaccept the Union, they can. They can at any moment have peace simply by laying down their arms and submitting to the national authority under the Constitution.

In presenting the abandonment of armed resistance to the national authority on the part of the insurgents as the only indispensable condition to ending the war on the part of the Government, I retract nothing heretofore said as to slavery. I repeat the declaration made a year ago, that "while I remain in my present position I shall not attempt to retract or modify the emancipation proclamation, nor shall I return to slavery any person who is free by the terms of that proclamation or by any of the acts of Congress." If the people should, by whatever mode or means, make it an Executive duty to re-enslave such persons, another, and not I, must be their instrument to perform it.

Wednesday, December 7

W. T. SHERMAN, Major-General, Commanding, HDQRS.

Military Division Of The Mississippi,

In the Field, Two Miles and a Half from No. 3

Major-General Slocum, Commanding Left Wing:

GENERAL: Owing to the rain, General Blair did not reach Guyton to-day, but is at this point, about two miles and a half northwest of Guyton. Early in the morning, his column will move right forward on the road which passes about two miles west of Guyton and about the same distance east of Eden, where your road and ours come together. It will be well if you can find a road passing from Springfield to Monteith and Pooler, and General Davis should be instructed to reach Saint Augustine and the vicinity of Cherokee Hill. He must first secure the road indicated from Cherokee Hill to Silk Hope and Litchfield. Press upon him that he must arrive when expected. We hear that the enemy is fortifying in a semi-circle around and about four miles from Savannah.

I am, general, respectfully, yours

H. C. ROGERS, Assistant Adjutant- General, Headquarters Left Wing, Army Of Georgia, Four Miles from Springfield, December 7 1861—11 a. m.

Maj. Gen. J. C. Davis, Commanding Fourteenth Corps:

The major-general commanding is of the opinion that the enemy will not give up the Charleston and Savannah road without a fight, and thinks you may be attacked at any time before you reach that road. He desires me to suggest that you strengthen your advance guard, keep your column well closed up, and let Kilpatrick take care of your rear. He expects your corps to be at St. Augustine as agreed. He also sends word that you should keep your bridge down until everyone is across.

Please indicate where you will probably encamp to-night, and, if possible, communicate with us to-morrow. We shall not move beyond Springfield until further orders and until we know where your column has caught up.

Very respectfully, your obedient servant

JEF. C. DAVIS, Brevet Major-General, Commanding, Headquarters Fourteenth Army Corps, Five Miles North of Sister's Ferry,—3.10 p. m.

Col. H. C. Rodgers, Chief of Staff, Left Wing:

COLONEL: Your dispatch by Corporal Cureton and party is just received. My advance division took dinner at Sister's Ferry; my rear will reach there to-night. My headquarters will be about five miles from that place.

The enemy shows himself at all the ferries on the opposite bank of the river. A little skirmishing has been reported in my rear this morning. We find fallen timber across all the creeks and swamps. I sent a messenger to you at daylight this morning. Our roads are bad, but I will make nearly twenty miles to-day by dint of hard work and rapid marching. I had already made arrangements to place more troops in my front.

I have and will keep my bridge down as long as necessary for the safe crossing of the army.

Yours, respectfully

CAPTAIN GEORGE W. PEPPER, In camp

The roads are bad, execrable; swamps, creeks, and pathless marshes have to be bridged and crossed. We cross the streams one after another on pontoons until we are now within 30 miles from Savannah. We anxiously await the issue of the day, which may materially affect the immediate capture of the city. We will not be defeated. The absolute necessity of a complete victory over the rebels has been so intensely infused into our army that they must conquer. How anxiously we wait the blast that orders our brave veterans forward.

I have had an interesting conversation with Lieutenant William L. Reteley, an escaped prisoner from Columbia, South

Carolina. The Lieutenant is a dashing officer of the Fifty-first Ohio, and was captured at the battle of Chickamauga. For fifteen months he has endured unparalleled hardships and privations, reducing him to a mere skeleton. He had been in Richmond, Danville, Macon, Savannah, Millen, Andersonville, Charleston and Columbia. He confirms the usual tales of the inhumanity and brutal treatment of the rebel officers to our brave men, incarcerated in Southern dungeons. He left his prison, traveled by night, and lay concealed during the day in the swamps and woods. He found the much abused and despised negro to be a Samaritan, a friend indeed.

The slaves gave him directions where to hide, what ferry to cross, when to travel, and replenished his scanty haversack with sweet potatoes, cereals, molasses and chickens. He came within nine miles of Augusta, supposing the army to be there; here again the trusty negro came to his aid, and piloted him through to our lines. The Lieutenant, though formerly prejudiced against the African, is now enthusiastic in his praises of the down-trodden, but soon to be emancipated slave. I only echo the feelings of thousands escaped Federals, when I say: God Almighty bless the African race.

Larger caravans of negroes than before are now following in our path, frequently being cut off by the enemy's cavalry, but by circuitous routes and much hard marching, making their appearance again. Some of these are mere babes in arms. Jennie has found her sister Caroline and frequently chooses to spend her time with them rather than on her studies. I have warned her that she has lost her

[161]

focus, and today, I ordered her to return her sister to the columns of negroes behind us as she is not employed or sponsored by an officer and therefore is prohibited by General Davis's orders from riding in the wagons, sleeping in a tent in our camp, and so forth. I told Jennie I thought the General (meaning General Sherman) might come into camp unexpectedly. I could not promise to her what his reaction would be to this lack of respect for camp rules.

The truth is, General Sherman is with the advance of the 15th Corps and miles away from here. But Jennie must learn the discipline one needs to truly benefit from any instruction. And she must follow the army way. You obey orders.

Once we cross the next creek, I think it is called Ebenezer, I'll work it out with Davis to let the sister and the child ride again. He's in too black a mood right now, what with all the delays.

JENNIE LEWIS, On the Road to Freedom

Dear Papa,

I must write this qwickly because Captain Pepper is sending Caroline and Jake to the rear. He says it is against General Davis orders having them in the tent with me. 'But she is my sister' I said to him. 'Only servants to officers can stay in the headquarters camp' he said back. 'Then I will go with them' I said. 'So be it,' he said.

I don't mind for myself. But it ranes much of the time now. How will we keep little Jake warm and dry. He is always on the move. He runs laughing around camp and into and out of the solders tents. No one minds him. They love him. They call 'Come here Jake. You fat little rascal you.' And then they give him some trinket or sing and clap. Jake has more friends than anyone. No one minds him in our camp except Captain Pepper and General Davis.

Must go, Papa. The solders are at the tent.

Thursday, December 8

<u>H. W. SLOCUM</u>, M. G., Army of Georgia, Head Qrs., Left
Wing, Springfield, Dec. 8, 7 A. M.

Genl. Davis,

Genl. Sherman has information that the line of defense
around Savannah is about four miles from the city. He desires to take
the road extending from Cherokee hill through Silk Hope to
Litchfield, as our first position.

Your corps should be at or near Cherokee hill to night.

Yours very respectfully

<u>MAJ. JAMES A. CONNOLLY</u>, 123rd Illinois Infantry, in
the field, near Ebenezer Creek, Georgia

This night's work was harder than that of last night, and I
never was so utterly exhausted and worn out as I am after crossing
Ebenezer Creek. The enemy was just in our rear, undoubtedly
listening for every sound that would indicate a movement on our
part, and to cross the creek we had to pass through at least a mile of
the most gloomy, dismal cypress swamp I ever saw, on a narrow
causeway, just wide enough for a wagon to drive along. If the enemy
had discovered our movement and had planted a piece of artillery in
the road to rake that causeway while we were on it, they could have
killed or wounded three-fourths of the men in the division, and we

[164]

should have been utterly helpless to defend against it. If there were no other road to approach Savannah except by this one over Ebenezer Creek, five thousand rebels could defend the city against the world. I don't believe they thought we would be foolish enough to try to cross here.

When the head of the column reached the "Ebenezer Causeway" I went ahead with one of Genl. Davis' aids who had come back to point out our ground for camping, and as I reached the bridge, I found there Major Lee, Provost Marshal of the Corps, engaged, by Genl. Davis' order, in turning off the road, into the swamp all the fugitive negroes that came along. When we should cross I knew it was the intention that the bridge should be burned, and I inquired if the negroes were not to be permitted to cross. I was told that Genl. Davis had ordered that they should not.

This I knew, and Genl. Davis knew, must result in all these negroes being recaptured or perhaps brutally shot down by the rebel cavalry to-morrow morning. The idea of five or six hundred black women, children and old men being thus returned to slavery by such an internal copperhead as Jeff. C. Davis is entirely too much for my Democracy; I suppose loss of sleep, and fatigue makes me somewhat out of humor too, and I told his staff officers what I thought of such an inhuman, barbarous proceeding in language which may possibly result in a reprimand from his serene Highness, for I know his toadies will repeat it to him, but I don't care a fig; I am determined to expose this act of his publicly, and if he undertakes to vent his spleen on me for it, I have the same rights that he himself exercised in his affair with Nelson. I expect this will cost me my Brevet as Lieut. Colonel, but let it go, I wouldn't barter my convictions of right, nor seal my mouth for any promotion.

Everybody is tired, sleepy and worn out. I don't think I could stand this kind of soldiering more than a month or two without some rest.

Friday, December 9

JOHN HIGHT, Chaplain, 14th Corps, in Camp near
Ebenezer Creek, 5 a.m.

Where can you find in all the annals of plantation cruelty anything more completely inhuman and fiendish than what I witnessed this last night. On the pretense that there was likely to be fighting in front, the negroes following our wagons were told not to go upon the pontoon bridge until all the troops and wagons were over. A guard was detailed to enforce the order. But, patient and docile as the negroes always are, the guard was really unnecessary. After the army wagons were across, General Davis ordered the pontoon bridge to be taken up, and to not let a negro cross on pain of court marshall. He left those people on the other side of that swollen, racing creek without any means of crossing. Some of them plunged into the water and swam across. Others ran wildly up and down the bank, shaking with terror. Someone shouted "Rebels!" and Wheeler's cavalry charged on them, driving them pellmell, into the waters, and mothers and children, old and young, perished alike! Many were drowned—how many is not known. There went up from that multitude a cry of agony.

Davis is a military tyrant, without one spark of humanity in his makeup. He was an ardent pro-slavery man before he entered the army, and he has not changed his views since.

COLONEL CHARLES D. KERR, 126th Illinois Cavalry,

Head Quarters Cavalry Corps, near Savannah

To-night I witnessed a scene the like of which I pray my eyes may never see again. Hundreds of old men, women and infants abandoned by "General Reb" on the north side of Ebenezer Creek. With Wheeler's cavalry closely pressing from the rear, the negroes raised their hands and implored from the corps commander the protection they had been promised; the prayer was in vain and, with cries of anguish and despair, men, women and children rushed by hundreds into the turbid stream and many were drowned before our eyes.

Some of our soldiers returned and cut down trees to float across. And the negro men themselves built rafts to ferry the terrified refugees across. Some of these makeshift rafts overturned and women and their babies were swept downstream. So many bodies piled up they formed a human dam across the 100 foot creek. The others huddled as close to the edge of the water as they could, crying, praying, and fearful that the rebels would come before they could get over.

From what we learned afterwards, the rebels did return and of those who remained upon the land, their fate at the hands of Wheeler's troops was scarcely to be preferred.

[168]

J. WHEELER, Maj. Genl., CSA, Near Ebenezer Creek

Lt. Coln. T. B. Roy, A. A. Genl. Hd. Qs. Dept., etc.

Colonel: On the night of Dec. 8th, we shelled the camp of the 14th Corps with good effect, throwing the corps into confusion and causing it to leave camp at midnight, abandoning clothing, arms, etc. By breaking up the camp during the extreme darkness, a great many negroes were left in our hands whom we sent back to their owners. We also captured three wagons and teams, and caused the enemy to burn several more wagons.

The whole number of negroes captured from the enemy during the movement was nearly 2,000.

Respy. Col., Your Obt. Servt.

FORTUNE BELL, Camp Meeting, south of Ebenezer Creek

My master used to throw me in a buck and whip me. He would put my hands together and tie them. Then he would strip me naked. Then would make me squat down. Then he would run a stick through behind my knees and in front of my elbows. My knee was up against my chest. My hands was tied together just in front of my shins. The stick between my arms and my knees held me in a squat. That's what they call a buck. You couldn't stand up and you couldn't get your feet out. You couldn't do nothing but just squat there and take what he put on. You couldn't move no way at all. Just try to. You just fall over on one side and have to stay there till you were turned over by him. He would whip me on one side till that was

[169]

sore and full of blood and then he would whip me on the other side till that was all tore up. The blood flew. It ran all down my back and dripped off my heels.

But that don't compare to our betrayal at the hands of this Union Army. You thought the Yankees was going help the nigger. What kind of help you call this? We should have known it. What can you expect from a hog but a grunt.

Family we must rely on God and ourselves. We are between two poisonous snakes. Their names are slavery and freedom. The snake called slavery lay with his head pointed south and the snake called freedom lay with his head pointed north. Both are riled up against the nigger. General Davis just made it obvious, that's all. Dont get too close to either one of them, people, or they will bite.

JEF. C. DAVIS, Brevet Major-General, Commanding, Headquarters Fourteenth Army Corps, Two Miles South of Ebenezer Creek—9 a. m.

General Slocum, Commander, Left Wing:

My troops skirmished all day. Fewer attacks in rear. I have destroyed the bridge behind me, and do not think I shall be troubled from the rear to-day.

I am, very respectfully yours

PART FOUR: DECEMBER 1864

Saturday, December 10, 1864

BRIG. GENERAL G. T. BEAUREGARD, CSA, Charleston,
S. C.

Lieut. Genl. Hardee, Savannah, Ga.:

Having no army of relief to look to, and your forces being
essential to the defense of Georgia and South Carolina, whenever
you shall have to select between their safety and that of Savannah,
sacrifice the latter.

REV. G. S. BRADLEY, Chaplain, 22nd Wisconsin, In the
field, near Savannah, Georgia

Came to a halt about noon. We lay in the woods till nearly
night, when our brigade was ordered into camp near the railroad.
And here we are at last before Savannah.

MAJOR JAMES A. CONNOLLY, 123rd Illinois Infantry, in
the field, near Savannah

Mine eyes have beheld the spires of the city!

This forenoon Capt. Biddle and myself rode down to the
river, visited the rice plantations, and rice mills, saw a rebel
steamboat, captured by our foragers yesterday, saw the spires of

Savannah, saw the sacred soil of South Carolina, saw and talked with the real genuine plantation nigger, and indeed were surfeited with sights to us entirely new. There is as much difference between niggers on rice plantations and "up-country" ones, as there is between negroes and baboons.

Many of those I saw to-day were scarcely a single remove from brutes, and they speak a broken sort of English that I can scarcely understand.

On one plantation I saw about 150 niggers principally women and children, and nearly every one of them sick, not a mouthful for them to eat on the whole plantation, except the rice which was stacked up, in the straw, in huge ricks that look like large wheat ricks.

Negroes employed on rice plantations live but a few years, and I suppose from this fact, the idea has become prevalent that white men could not stand it to labor on southern plantations. If they would take any decent care of their negroes on rice plantations, they would live as long as on any other plantations, but the proprietors of rice plantations live in cities or in Europe. Everything is done by overseers, and the negroes are treated with just the same brutality as our army mules; profits are large, and if a nigger dies it makes but little difference, another can easily be bought.

After returning from my visit to the rice plantations, I gave the General a description of what I saw, and he went down himself this afternoon.

BREVET MAJOR GEORGE WARD NICHOLS, Aide-de-Camp, in the field, less than 10 miles from Savannah

This evening a movement of the greatest importance has begun. Hazen's division of the 15th Corps is marching to the other side of the river. Fort McAllister must be taken. To-morrow's sun will see the veterans whom Sherman led upon the heights of Missionary Ridge within striking distance of its walls. Warm words have been uttered by the Generals of the 15th and 17th Corps because the second division has been assigned the honor of this expedition. The possibility of repulse, the fear of wounds and death, do not seem to be considered in the rivalry. These brave men of ours have seen too many wounds, and death has passed too near them to suggest any terrors now. The glory of the flag and victory is the noble thought which animates and stimulates officers and men alike.

We have now connected our lines, so that the four corps are within supporting distance of each other. The soldiers are meanwhile in most cheerful spirits, displaying the unconcern which is the most characteristic feature of our troops.

Sunday, December 11

<u>JENNIE LEWIS</u>, in camp, Hospital Tent

I herd the singing while I was still asleep. at first I thot they were angels singing but they were too sad so I ~~new~~ knew I was not in heven. then I opened my eyes and saw they were nurses praying and singing and standing over me holding my hands.

They say I have slep for 3 days. I asked for Caroline and Jake, someone finely said 'They did not make it Jennie you nearly drownd yourself. Now rest.'

God—plese. Let them be rong. Plese don't take Caroline, not now. we 've only just united again. Let them be alive or make me dead to be with them.

Monday, December 12

<u>G.T. BEAUREGARD</u>, General, CSA, Charleston, S.C.,—
11.30 p. m.

General S. Cooper, Adjutant and Inspector General:

Lieutenant-General Hardee reports enemy developed in strong force along his entire front yesterday, and that he has been compelled to extend his lines. He asks for immediate re-enforcements.

<u>G.T. BEAUREGARD</u>, General, CSA, Charleston, S. C.

Lieutenant-General Hardee, Savannah, Ga.

About 450 men will be sent you to-day with instructions to General Jones to divert them, if necessary. These re-enforcements are the last you and Jones can hope for.

Keep yourself well advised, through staff officers and otherwise, of his ability to hold your communication, for Savannah must be held only so long as is consistent with the safety of its garrison.

<u>W. T. SHERMAN</u>, Major-General, King's Bridge

I rode over and spent the night at Mr. King's house, where I found General Howard, with General Hazen's division of the Fifteenth Corps. I gave General Hazen, in person, his orders to march rapidly down the right bank of the Ogeechee, and without hesitation to assault and carry Fort McAllister by storm. I explained to General Hazen, fully, that on his action depended the safety of the whole army, and the success of the campaign.

Tuesday, December 13

REV. G. S. BRADLEY, Chaplain, 22nd Wisconsin,

Cheeve's Rice Mill,

Outside Savannah

At 1 O'clock joined Generals Sherman and Howard, at Dr. Cheeve's rice mill, on the Ogeechee, opposite Fort McAlister. I found Sherman on the roof of the mill, surrounded by his staff and signal officers and Bekley and Cole, waiting to communicate with Hazen on the island. While patiently waiting for Hazen's signals, Sherman's keen eye detected smoke in the horizon seaward. Up to this time he had received no intelligence from the fleet. In a moment the countenance of the chieftain lightened up, and he exclaimed:

"Look! Howard; there is a gunboat!"

Time passed on, and the vessel now became visible, yet no signal from the fleet or Hazen. Half an hour passed and the guns of the fort opened simultaneously with puffs of smoke that rose a few hundred yards from the fort, showing that Hazen's skirmishers had opened. A moment after, Hazen signaled.

"I have invested the fort and will assault immediately."

At this moment Sickley announced. "A signal from the gunboat." All eyes are turned from the fort to the gunboat that is coming to our assistance with news from home. A few messages pass that inform us that Foster and Dahlgreen are within speaking distance. The gunboat now halts and asks:

[177]

"Can we run up? Is Fort McAlister ours?"

"No," is the reply. "Hazen is just ready to storm it. Can you assist?"

"Yes," is the reply. "What will you have us to do?"

But before Sherman can reply to Dahlgreen, the thunders of the fort are heard, and the low sound of small arms inborne across the three miles of marsh and river. Field glasses are opened, and, sitting flat upon the roof, the hero of Atlanta gazed away off to the fort. "There they go grandly; not a waiver," he remarks.

Twenty seconds pass, and again he exclaims: "See that flag in the advance, Howard; how steadily it moves; not a man falters. There they go still; see the roll of musketry. Grand, grand."

Still he strains his eyes, and a moment after speaks without raising his eyes—"That flag still goes forward; there is no flinching there."

A pause for a minute.

"Look!" he exclaims, "it has halted. They waver, no! it's the parapet! There they go again; now they scale it; some are over. Look, there is a flag on the works! Another, another. It's ours. The fort's ours!"

The glass dropped by his side, and in an instant the joy, the great leader at the possession of the river and the opening of the road to his new base, burst forth in the words the old darkie had used, "dis chile don't sleep tonight." And turning to one at his side, Captain Andereid, he remarked: "Have a boat for me at once, I must go

[178]

there," pointing to the fort, from which half a dozen battle flags floated grandly in the sunset.

BREVET MAJOR GEORGE WARD NICHOLS, Fort McAllister

Fort McAllister is ours. It has been gallantly and bravely won. I saw the heroic assault from the point of observation selected by General Sherman at the adjacent rice-mill.

During the greater part of to-day the General gazed anxiously toward the sea, watching for the appearance of the fleet. About the middle of the afternoon he decried a light column of smoke creeping lazily along over the flat marshes, and soon the spars of a steamer were visible, and then the flag of our Union floated out. What a thrilling, joyful sight! How the blood bounded, when, answering the signal waved above us, we saw that they had recognized us, and knew that our General was here with his army!

The sun was now fast going down behind a grove of water-oaks, and as his last rays gilded the earth, all eyes once more turned toward the Rebel fort. Suddenly white puffs of smoke shot out from the thick woods surrounding the line of works. Hazen was closing in, ready for the final rush of his column directly upon the fort. A warning answer came from the enemy in the roar of heavy artillery—and so the battle opened.

General Sherman walked nervously to and fro, turning quickly now and then from viewing the scene of conflict to observe the sun sinking slowly behind the tree-tops. No longer willing to bear the suspense, he said: "Signal General Hazen that he must carry the fort by assault, to-night if possible. Say to him that on his action depends the safety of the whole army, and the success of the campaign." The little flag waved and fluttered in the evening air, and the answer came:

"I am ready, and will assault at once!"

The words had hardly passed when from out the encircling woods there came a long line of blue coats and bright bayonets, and the dear old flag was there, waving proudly in the breeze. Then the fort seemed alive with flame; quick, thick jets of fire shooting out form all its sides, while the white smoke first covered the place and then rolled away over the glacis. The line of blue moved steadily on; too slowly, as it seemed to us, for we exclaimed, "Why don't they dash forward?" but their measured step was unfaltering. Now the flag goes down, but the line does not halt. A moment longer, and the banner gleams again in the front. We, the lookers-on, clutched one another's arms convulsively, and scarcely breathed in the eager intensity of our gaze. Sherman stood watching with anxious air, awaiting the decisive moment. Then the enemy's fire redoubled in rapidity and violence. The darting streams of fire alone told the position of the fort. The line of blue entered the enshrouding folds of smoke. The flag was at last dimly seen, and then it went out of sight altogether.

"They have been repulsed!" said one of the group of officers who watched the fight.

"No, by Heaven!" said another; "there is not a man in retreat—not a straggler in all the glorious line!"

The firing ceased. The wind lifted the smoke. Crowds of men were visible on the parapets, fiercely fighting—but our flag was planted there. There were a few scattering musket-shots, and then the sounds of battle ceased. Then the bomb-proofs and parapets were alive with crowding swarms of our gallant men, who fired their pieces in the air as a *feu de joie*. Victory! the fort was won.

Then all of us who had witnessed the strife and exulted in the triumph, grasped each the other's hand, embraced, and were glad, and some of us found the water in our eyes.

In half an hour we were congratulating General Hazen, and in an hour more Generals Sherman and Howard were pulling down the stream, regardless of torpedoes, in search of the signaled vessel of the navy.

The victory of Fort McAllister, and the way it was done, is a grand ending to this most adventurous campaign. It is in reality the end, for here terminates our march. We set out for a new base, and we have found it. The capture of Savannah is another matter, and with its siege will begin a new campaign. Our soldiers are electrified by the brilliant episode just enacted, and are eager to go wherever the General directs.

L. M. DAYTON, A. A. G., By Order of MAJ. GEN. W. T.
SHERMAN, Headquarters,
Military Division of the Mississippi, In the Field, Near
Savannah General Field Order No. 13.

The General-in-Chief announces, with pleasure, that, to-day at four and a half o'clock, P. M., the Second Division, of the Fifteenth Army Corps, assaulted Fort McAllister, and carried the place, capturing the entire garrison and armament, giving full communication with the fleet and army of General Foster.

W. T. SHERMAN, Cheeve's Rice Mill
This nigger will have no sleep this night!

Wednesday, December 14

W. T. SHERMAN, Major General, On Board Dandelion, Ossabaw Sound

General H. W. Halleck, Washington:

Yesterday, at 5 p.m., General Hazen's division of the Fifteenth Corps carried Fort McAllister by assault, capturing its entire garrison and stores. This opened to us the Ossabaw Sound, and I pulled down to this gun boat to communicate with the fleet. Before opening communication, we had completely destroyed all the railroads leading into Savannah and invested the city. The left is on the Savannah River, three miles above the city, and right on the Ogeechee, at King's Bridge. Were it not for the swamps, we could march into the city, but as it is, I would have to assault at one or two places over narrow causeways, leading to much loss; whereas in a day or two, with my communications restored and the batteries in position within short range of the city, I will demand surrender.

The army is in splendid order, and equal to anything. Weather has been fine, and supplies abundant. Our march was most agreeable, and we were not at all molested by guerrillas. We reached Savannah three days ago, but owing to Ft. McAllister we could not communicate, but now we have McAllister we can go ahead. We have on hand plenty of meat, salt, and potatoes; all we need is bread, and I have sent to Port Royal for that.

[183]

We have not lost a wagon on the trip, but have gathered in a large supply of negroes, mules, horses, & c. and our teams are in far better condition than when we started. My first duty will be to clear the army of surplus negroes, mules, and horses, and suppose General Saxton can relieve me of these.

Yours, truly

PVT. THEODORE UPSON, 100th Indiana, in the field
before Savannah

We learn that General Hazens 2nd Division of the A. C. has captured Fort McAllister. This gives us communication with our Fleet and now Savannah is doomed without a doubt. We feel proud to think that a Division from our Corps was selected to make the desperate assault upon fort McAllister. The boys did the work in grand style though it cost them dear—24 killed and 110 wounded. The Johnnys fought to the last, and even after our men got into the Fort they got into their "bomb proofs" and had to be overpowered in detail.

We are getting ready to assault the works. It will be hard work in our front for the water is nearly 5 ft deep and there are a great many ditches and bad places to get over and through. But if we make a start we are going through and I think the Johnnys know it for they do not talk as saucy as they did at Vicksburg.

[184]

MAJOR FREDERICK C. WINKLER, in the Field, siege of

Savannah

We have good news today. We heard heavy firing, both musketry and artillery, a considerable distance to our right yesterday, and this morning we received an order from General Sherman, in which he announces with pleasure that yesterday, at 4:30 P. M., the second division, 15th Army Corps, assaulted and carried Fort Mc Allister, capturing its entire garrison and armaments, thereby opening communication with the Fleet and the army of Major General Foster. It is good news indeed--it is the crowning victory of the most successful campaign known in military history. Now we have a base by which we can receive an abundance of supplies and, if need be, reinforcements for further operations.

Savannah must fall; there is no hope for that city. We have batteries on the river shore and infantry on an island above the city, completely commanding the river, so that the rebels have nothing left but the few miles of river below that; that they are still using and can cross straight over into South Carolina. I went over to the river today; there are immense rice plantations there and a large number of mills, both on the main land and on the islands, for threshing and grinding rice. Each plantation has a village of negroes, and they are all hard at work threshing and pounding their rice for the Yankees. They all do it cheerfully and are evidently sincere in their protestations that they are glad the Yankees have come.

Thursday, December 15

WATT MCKINNEY, Ex Slave, Camp Meeting near Savannah

My mammy, she said I was born two hours before day on the fourth of July. Independence Day. I knowed I would be free one day. I has been in good health all my days. I ain't never been sick in my life. I just keep on living and trusting in de Lord 'cause de Good Book say, "Wherefore de evil days come and de darkness of de night draw nigh, your strength, it shall not perish. I will lift you up amongs dem what abides with me." Dat is de Gospel, Boss.

Before dis War broke out, I can remember dere was some few of de white folks what said dat niggers ought to be set free, but dere was just one now and den dat took dat stand. One of dem dat I remember was de Reverend Dickey what was de parson for a big crowd of de white folks in that part of the county. Rev. Dickey, he preached freedom for de niggers and say dat dey all should be set free and given a home and a mule. Dat preaching de Rev. Dickey done sure did rile up de folks—the white folks. Dey fired him from the church, and abused him, and some of dem say dey going to hang him to a limb. No sir, Boss, they say they ain't going divide up no land with the niggers or give them no home or mule or there freedom or nothing. They say they will wade knee-deep in blood and die first. Well, here is the War they longed for. And now they spilling buckets of blood. But the blood is being spilt from all of us.

[186]

These Yankees, they is some of 'em bad and aint got no care about the niggers. But they is dying all the same and the reason is because niggers must be free just like everybody else. That's the Gospel, Boss. Dis here is a bad War, here in Georgia. We have lost precious souls to this War and we will lose some more. But we niggers will be free. I know I will. I was born on Independence Day. So, I just keep on living and trusting in de Lord 'cause de Good Book say, "Wherefore de evil days come and de darkness of de night draw nigh, your strength, it shall not perish. I will lift you up amongst dem what abides with me." Dat is de Gospel, Boss.

SARAH GUDGER, Ex-Slave, Camp Meeting

I 'members when my ole mammy die. She sick a long time. One day white man come to see me. He say: "Sarah, did you know you mammy was dead?" "No," I say, "but I wants to see my mother afore dey puts her away." I went to the house and say to Ole Missie: "My mother she die today. I wants to see my mother afore they puts her away," but she look at me mean and say: "Get on out of here, and get back to work afore I wallop you good." So I went back to my work, with the teres streaming down my face, just a-wringing my hands, I wanted to see my mammy so. In slavery, we couldn't even mourn our loved ones the right way. But we free now. We goin mourn these lost souls right.

[187]

GEORGE M. HORTON, Ex Slave, Poet, Camp Meeting

O death, thy power I own, whose mission was to rush

And snatch the rose, so quickly blown, down from its native bush;

The flower of beauty doom'd to pine, ascends from this to worlds divine.

Death is a joyful doom, let tears of sorrow dry,

The rose on earth but fades to bloom and blossom in the sky.

Why should the soul resist the hand that bears her to celestial land.

Then, bonny bird, farewell, till hence we meet again;

Perhaps I have not long to dwell within this cumb'rous chain,

Till on elysian shores we meet, till grief is lost and joy complete.

REV. G. C. QUARLES, Ex Slave, Camp Meeting

Let the people say Amen.

For many days now, we have come together to tell our stories. We have recorded the names of the thousands lost to the waters of Ebenezer Creek or returned to bondage. With the help of Brother George Horton and Sister Jennie Lewis, we have committed your stories to paper. We cannot bury our loved ones who died in those raging waters. But we can make sure they are never forgotten. What happened at Ebenezer Creek is recorded in these pages for all time, and the names of our loved ones are written down. They may

[188]

be unburied, but they will not die un-noted, un-named, un-known, like the thousands who died before them--enslaved.

Friday, December 16

<u>JENNIE LEWIS</u>, The Rice Mill House of Mr. Cheeves

Yesterday soldiers brought me to the Generals headquarters. It is a large house—a manson. This room where I sleep, has tall windows where the sun lite streams in. There are flowers in little vases along the mantal. An empty bird cage hangs in a corner. This bed is large and covered in ruffled spreads. A fire roars against the chill.

When I came here I was given a towel and a bath of warm water and told to soak myself clean. Then I was given a new dress to wear, and stockings and shoes. And a night gown and undergarments. I was told to rest and get better, Generals orders. He was standing at the door but he said nothing. He nodded and walked away. All the love I have for him came rushing over me. His kindness to me filled me up. But a second later I thot again of Caroline and Jake and all the others swept to the sea never to be herd from again and I cried myself back to sleep into the soft white pillows.

To-night the General returned to my room. I told him about Caroline and Jake and he held me as I ~~eride~~ cried. He told that I must find a way to be strong for my mother and father for this will beat them down. He told me he is sorry about Caroline and Jake but glad that I am safe. He said the war would end soon, for it was already as much as over and that I must think about my future. 'We will take

Savannah in a few days. They cannot resist us. Then, I will turn North and when I go through South Carolina it will be one of the most horrible things in the history of the world. The devil himself wont be able to restrane my men in that state. Im going to march this Army to Richmond. Will you come along, Jennie?'

I told him I wold and we fell into each others arms. In this we gave ourselves to each other.

This was not the first time. In Milledgeville, the general came to my tent and said, 'Jennie, you are so lovely. I have become fond of you. You are a free woman. This is not the plantation. You can tell me no.'

I did not say no then nor did I to-night. I needed the strength of his comforting words and his strong embrace. I needed him to make me want to live.

Now I am staying here with General Sherman. No one will send me to the rear. I am safe from General Davis. He cannot hurt me anymore. No one can hurt me. I am the Generals wife.

W. T. SHERMAN, Headquarters, Military Division of the Mississippi, Cheeve's Mill Plantation, near Savannah

Dearest Ellen,

I have no doubt you have heard of my safe arrival on the Coast. The fact is I never doubted the fact, but these southern Blatherscytes have been bragging of all manner of things but have done nothing. We came right along living on turkeys, chickens pigs

&c. I suppose Jeff Davis will now have to feed the People of Georgia, instead of collecting provisions of them to feed his armies.

We have destroyed nearly 200 miles of Railroad and are not yet done. As I approached Savannah, I found every river & outlet fortified. The Ogeechee River emptying into Ossabaw Sound was best adapted to our use, but it was guarded by Fort McAlister, which has defied the Navy for 2 years. I ordered Howard to carry it with our Division. The detail fell on the 2nd Division of the 15th Corps and it was the handsomest thing I have seen in this war.

As soon as we got the Fort I pulled down the Bay & opened Communication. General Foster & Admiral Dahlgren received me, manned the yards & cheered, the highest honor at sea. They had become really nervous as to our safety and were delighted at all I told them of our early success. I can now starve out Savannah. I never saw a more confident army. The soldiers think I know everything and that they can do anything.

I have some heavy guns coming from Port Royal, and as soon as they come I shall demand the surrender of Savannah, but will not assault, as a few days will starve out its Garrison about 15,000, and its People 25,000. I do not apprehend any army to attempt to relieve Savannah, except Lee's, and if he gives up Richmond it will be the best piece of strategy ever made, to make him let go there.

We have lived Sumptuously, turkeys, chickens and sweet potatoes all the way, but the poor women & children will starve. All

[192]

I could tell them was, if Jeff Davis expects to found an empire on the ruins of the South, he ought to afford to feed the People.

The newspapers & mischief mongers will give you gorgeous details of our march across Georgia. It was just 30 days from Atlanta till I was sitting with the Admiral in a Steamer at sea. Grant's letter of the 3rd proposed to bring you down to see me, but his of the 6th looked to my coming to James River. Await Events and trust to Fortune. I'll turn up when & where you least expect me. I Should like to hear how you all are, but suppose of course you are at South Bend. Write me, care of Adjt. Genl. Washington D.C.

Love to all. Yrs. Ever

W.T. SHERMAN, Major-General, Headquarters Military
Division of the Mississippi, In the Field, near Savannah
General William J. Hardee, Commanding Confederate Forces
in Savannah:

GENERAL: You have doubtless observed from your station
at Rosedew that sea-going vessels now come through Ossabaw
Sound and up Ogeechee to the rear of my army, giving me abundant
supplies of all kinds, and more especially heavy ordnance necessary
to the reduction of Savannah. I have already received guns that can
cast heavy and destructive shot as far as the heart of your city; also, I
have for some days held and controlled every avenue by which the
people and garrison of Savannah can be supplied; and I am therefore
justified in demanding the surrender of the city of Savannah and its
dependent forts, and shall await a reasonable time your answer
before opening with heavy ordnance.

Should you entertain the proposition I am prepared to grant
liberal terms to the inhabitants and garrison; but should I be forced to
resort to assault, or the slower and surer process of starvation, I shall
then feel justified in resorting to the harshest measures, and shall
make little effort to restrain my army -- burning to avenge a great
national wrong they attach to Savannah and other large cities which
have been so prominent in dragging our country into civil war. I

inclose you a copy of General Hood's demand for the surrender of the town of Resaca, to be used by you for what it is worth.

I have the honor to be your obedient servant

W. J. HARDEE, Lieutenant General, CSA, Head Quarters Department S. C., Ga. & Florida, Savannah, Ga.

Major General W. T. Sherman, Commanding Federal Forces, near Savannah, Ga.

General:

I have to acknowledge receipt of a communication from you, of this date, in which you demand "the surrender of Savannah and its dependent forts," on the ground that you "have received guns that can cast heavy and destructive shot into the heart of the city;" and for the further reason that you "have for some days held and controlled every avenue by which the people and garrison can be supplied." You add, that should you "be forced to resort to assault or to the slower and surer process of starvation, you will then feel justified in resorting to the harshest measures, and will make little effort to restrain your army, etc., etc."

The position of your forces half a mile beyond the outer line for the land defense of Savannah, is, at the nearest point, at least four miles from the heart of the city. That and the interior line are both intact.

Your statement that you have, for some days, held and controlled every avenue by which the people and garrison can be supplied, is incorrect. I am in free and constant communication with my department.

Your demand for the surrender of Savannah and its dependent forts is refused.

With respect to the threats conveyed in the closing paragraph of your letter of what may be expected in case your demand is not complied with, I have to say that I have hitherto conducted the military operations entrusted to my direction in strict accordance with the rules of civilized warfare, and I should deeply regret the adoption of any course by you that may force me to deviate from them in future.

I have the honor to be, very respectfully, your obedient servant

PRESIDENT JEFFERSON DAVIS, CSA, Richmond, Va.
General W. J. Hardee, Savannah, Georgia:

Beyond the force sent sometime since to Augusta, General Lee has not thus far found himself able to detach troops from his command. Should a change of circumstances permit further aid to be sent no time will be lost. Whether General Beauregard can secure the communication between Charleston and Savannah in the contingency referred to by you he can best inform you. Close observation will, I hope, enable you to know when the enemy shall send from your front any considerable force, that you may then provide for the safety of your communications and make the dispositions needful for the preservation of your army.

Sunday, December 18

<u>H. W. HALLECK</u>, Major-General and Chief of Staff, Headquarters of the Army, Washington (Via Hilton Head.)

Confidential: HDQRS, Armies of the United States, Washington, D.C.

Maj. Gen. W. T. Sherman, Savannah:

My Dear General: Yours of the 13th, by Major Anderson, is just received. I congratulate you on your splendid success, and shall very soon expect to hear of the crowning work of your new campaign in the capture of Savannah. Your march will stand out prominently as the great one of this great war. When Savannah falls, then for another raid south through the center of the Confederacy. But I will not anticipate. General Grant is expected here this morning, and will probably write you his own views.

Should you capture Charleston, I hope that by some accident the place may be destroyed, and if a little salt should be sown upon its site, it may prevent the growth of future crops of nullification and secession.

Yours, truly

U.S. GRANT, Lieutenant-General, City Point, Va.

Maj. Gen. William T. Sherman, Commanding Military Division of the Mississippi:

My Dear General: I have just received and read, I need not tell you with how much gratification, your letter to General Halleck. I congratulate you and the brave officers and men under your command on the successful termination of your most brilliant campaign. I never had a doubt of the result. When apprehensions for your safety were expressed by the President, I assured him, with the army you had, and you in command of it, there was no danger but you would strike bottom on salt water some place; that I would not feel the same security—in fact, would not have entrusted the expedition to any other living commander.

If you capture the garrison of Savannah it certainly will compel Lee to detach from Richmond, or give us nearly the whole South. My own opinion is that Lee is adverse to going out of Virginia, and if the cause of the South is lost, he wants Richmond to be the last place surrendered. If he has such views, it may be well to indulge him until everything else is in our hands.

Congratulating you and the army again upon the splendid result of your campaign, the like of which is not read of in past history. I subscribe myself, more than ever, if possible,

Your friend,

W. T. SHERMAN, Major-General, Commanding, Headquarters Military Division of The Mississippi, In the Field, near Savannah, Ga--8 p. m.

Lient. Gen. U. S. Grant, City Point, Va.:

General: I wrote you at length by Colonel Babcock on the 16th instant. As I therein explained my purpose, yesterday I made a demand on General Hardee for the surrender of the city of Savannah and received his answer, refusing. Copies of both letters are herewith inclosed. You will notice that I claim that my lines are within easy cannon range of the heart of Savannah, but General Hardee claims we are four miles and a half distant. But I, myself, have been to the intersection of the Charleston and Georgia Central railroads, and the three-mile post is but a few yards beyond, within the line of our pickets.

By to-morrow morning I will have six 30-pounder Parrotts in position, and General Hardee will learn whether I am right or not.

We have a good strong bridge across Ogeechee at King's Bridge, by which our wagons can go to Fort McAllister, to which point I am sending the wagons not absolutely necessary for daily use, the negroes, prisoners of war, sick, &c., en route for Port Royal.

In anticipation of leaving this country, I am continuing the destruction of their railroads, and at this moment have two divisions and the cavalry at work breaking up the Gulf railroad from the Ogeechee to the Altahama; so that even if I do not take Savannah, I will leave it in a bad way. But I still hope that events will give me time to take Savannah, even if I have to assault with some loss.

With Savannah in our possession at some future time, if not now, we can punish South Carolina as she deserves, and as thousands of people in Georgia hoped we would do. I do sincerely believe that the whole United States, North and South, would rejoice to have this army turned loose on South Carolina to devastate that State, in the manner we have done in Georgia, and it would have a direct and immediate bearing on your campaign in Virginia.

I have the honor to be, your obedient servant

MAJOR JAMES A. CONNOLLY, 123rd Illinois Infantry, in the field, near Savannah

Orders received this evening for the army to hold itself in readiness to make an assault on the enemy's entire line; this means business.

I wrote a rough draft of a letter to-day relative to Genl. Davis' treatment of the negroes at Ebenezer Creek. I want the matter to get before the military committee of the Senate; it may give them some light in regard to the propriety of confirming him as a Brevet Major General. I am not certain yet who I had better send it to.

PRESIDENT JEFF'N DAVIS, CSA, Richmond, Va.

General R. E. Lee, Petersburg, Va.:

The following dispatch just received from General Beauregard:

Savannah, December 18, 1864.(Via Hardeeville.)

General Sherman demanded the surrender of Savannah yesterday of General Hardee, which was refused. The loss of Savannah will be followed by that of the railroad from Augusta to Charleston, and soon after of Charleston itself. Cannot Hoke's and Johnson's divisions be spared for the defense of South Carolina and Georgia until part or whole of Hood's army could reach Georgia?

G. T. Beauregard

I cannot realize the consequences as portrayed. But General Bragg has just returned; if you can have a conference with him you can better judge. Let me have your advice, and, if you choose, communicate with General Beauregard.

ROBERT E. LEE, CSA, Headquarters Army Of Northern Virginia

His Excellency Jefferson Davis:

Dispatch of to-day received. Beauregard and Hardee must judge of necessity of evacuating Savannah. If done troops can be saved, and by uniting all in direction of Branchville any column marching on Charleston would be threatened and communication preserved. I cannot find that any troops have left Grant. He has united to him the Sixth and Nineteenth Corps. If Hoke and Johnson are sent south, it will necessitate the abandonment of Richmond with the present opposing force.

Monday, December 19

M. C. MEIGS, Quartermaster-General, Brevet Major-General, Quartermaster-General's Office, Washington City

Major-General Sherman, Commanding, at Savannah

General:

I wrote you fully a day or two since in regard to supplies. I have ordered six of the most suitable light steamers to be sent to Kings Bridge via Hilton Head. The Planter, a very fine iron steamer, goes this morning, and I write by her unless my other dispatch may miscarry.

I see you are aware of the importance of stripping your army of all useless mouths. I hope that you will get rid of every mule and horse and negro not absolutely needed about Savannah. Wishing you continued success, I am, very truly, your friend

L.M. DAYTON, Aide-de-Camp By order of MAJ. GEN. SHERMAN, Headquarters, Department Of The Army Of Tennessee

SPECIAL FIELD ORDER No.199. Near Savannah, Ga., December 19, 1864

The major-generals commanding the Four Corps will each cause to be immediately sent from their columns one regiment, of an average strength of 350 men, and a working party of fifty negroes, to report to Colonel Beckwith, chief Commissary, at the landing at King's Bridge for quartermaster and fatigue duties.

JEF. C. DAVIS, Brevet-Major-General, Commanding, Headquarters, Fourteenth Army Corps, Before Savannah, Ga.

Lient. Col. H. C. Rodgers, A. A. G. and Chief of Staff, Left Wing, Army of Georgia:

I have the honor to state for the information of the general commanding that the regiment required was ordered to report to Colonel Beckwith, at King's Bridge, for fatigue duty this morning. Efforts have been made to find fifty negroes in the corps who could be sent with the regiment, but without effect as all the unemployed negroes had already been sent away, 544 in number, and a large proportion of them able-bodied men.

I have the honor to be, colonel, very respectfully yours servant

MAJOR JAMES A. CONNOLLY, 123rd Illinois Infantry, in the field, near Savannah

The fugitive negroes were collected to-day throughout this wing of the army, and marched off to King's Bridge on the Ogeechee, from where they will be shipped to Hilton Head, S.C.

It was a strange spectacle to see those negroes of all ages, sizes, and both sexes, with their bundles on their heads and in their hands trudging along, they knew not whether, but willing to blindly follow the directions given to them by our officers. At least 5 thousand of them must have marched by our Head Quarters.

All our surplus mules and horses were sent off to-day too. The decks are being cleared for action, and if it must come, I care not how soon.

Tuesday, December 20

JENNIE LEWIS, The Rice Mill House of Mr. Cheeves

Dear Papa,

I hope this letter finds you well and on your way here. General Sherman said he would make sure this letter finds you on the Plantar, so I want you to no know that I am fine. I am doing well. I am with the General in a mill house belonging to Mr. Cheeves. It is near Savannah.

Papa, come as soon as you can to get me.

In haste, Your loving daughter

I had only a few moments to write Papa. General Sherman has gone to South Carolina. He promised me he would see my letter delivered to Papa on the Plantar. He said Papas ship is making its way to Savannah. I am so happy Papa will be here soon. But for now, I am just alone.

I am no longer an excellent cook's assistant. Manual no longer cooks for the general. Mr. Cheeves cook wont let him in her kitchen and theres servants enough that he does not need me. I have all day to read and write letters. But I do neither one. I just watch the sea waters for the Plantar with such a mix of desire and despare. As soon as I see Papa and fall into his happy arms, I must brake his heart with the awful news: we will never see Caroline again in this life. Her little boy Jake his only grandson drouned at Ebenezer Creek. And me, now his only child, no longer the girl I used to be.

When I am not down at the docks I am here in this bedroom watching myself in the looking glass. Who is this girl with Mamas hair and Papas eyes and a form and figure I no longer know? I wear the gowns of a millers daughter long gone from here. I sleep in her bed. The servants here bring me my food and draw my bath and treet me like I am a fine lady. The Generals wife. So this is freedom.

Today I rode back to General Davis camp. Nerely everyone was gone. I found Reverend Quarles and Fortune Bell in a servants tent. They said boats came and all the others were put onboard and saled away. Fortune Bell said they were sent by General Shermans orders. I did not beleve him.

'The great general dose not share everything with you then' Fortune said 'only his bed.' This brought on such a rush of feeling. I thought I wold fall right to the floor. Reverend Quarles rushed to my side. I cold not speke not even to say it wasn't true.

'Fortune, you are out of your place' said Rev. Quarles.

'Somebody got to tell her the truth. That Sherman sent for you to join him in camp. Ordered Captain Pepper to have you sent to headquarters. But Pepper sent you to the rear instead. Did you know that?'

'That's enough Brother Bell' Reverend Quarles said. But Fortune was shouting.

'You and Caroline and little Jake would have been in the General's camp, miles away from Ebenezer Creek. But your good minister captain teacher sent you to the rear instead. Do not trust the white man, Jennie. Remember what I said about the two poisonous snakes. It don't matter if your slave or free, you need to rely on your own people. You should be here with us. We can protect you.'

'No' I said. 'You cannot. Sevanda was here, Ilene and Nora. Who protected them.' I would be gone just like they are, to who knows where. Gone somewhere where Papa would never find me."

I ran from there and found the courier. I rode back to headquarters silent, thinking--I have the only protection I need. I have the General.

Wednesday, December 21

PVT. THEODORE UPSON, 100 Indiana, In the Field, near Savannah

The Johnnys are moving out. Our officers know they are going and do not try to stop them for we can hear them all night moving about and most of us think if we push the fighting on our right front a little harder we might cut them off and capture the whole of them. I am awfully glad we did not have to charge their works for we would have lost a good many lives, that's sure.

We got some Northern papers to day. It seems that the good people up there were terribly worried about us. They called us the Lost Army. And some thought we never would show up again. I dont think they know what kind of an Army this is that Uncle Billy has. Why, if Grant can keep Lee and his troops busy we can tramp all over this Confederacy; and by the time we were through with that, there would be nothing left but the ground and that would be in a state primeval as the Poet says.

BREVET MAJOR GEORGE WARD NICHOLS, Savannah

The fall of Fort McAllister has been quickly followed by the evacuation of this great commercial city, which we gain without a battle. I have already written of the nature of the obstacles which confronted us, and the life-blood which must of necessity have been shed had we been forced to capture it by assault. I most devoutly thank God that, through the prudent strategy of our General, the lives of our brave soldiers are spared to their wives and homes, and for future use to dear old fatherland.

It was fortunate that our troops followed so quickly after the evacuation of the city by the enemy, for a mob had gathered in the streets, and were breaking into the stores and houses. They were with difficulty dispersed by the bayonets of our soldiers, and then, once more, order and confidence prevailed through the conquered city.

We have won a magnificent prize—the city of Savannah, more than two hundred guns, magazines filled with ammunition, thirty-five thousand bales of cotton, three steamboats, several locomotives, one hundred and fifty cars, and stores of all kinds.

MAJOR JAMES A. CONNOLLY, 123rd Illinois Infantry, In the field, Savannah

Almost with electric speed the word ran around the entire lines of our army: "Savannah is evacuated," and in less time than it takes to tell it, the heaviest sleepers in the army, as well as the lightest, were out, some dressed, and some en deshabille, shouting and hurrahing from the bottom of their lungs. This was indeed a joyful morning. Savannah is ours. Our long campaign is ended. If the world predicted our failure, the world must acknowledge itself mistaken.

I am glad I was permitted to have a part in this campaign. Geary's Division of the 20th Corps marched in and took peaceable possession of the city this morning. Savannah is a beautiful city—the finest I have seen in the South. The rebels left all their heavy artillery, and considerable field artillery—they didn't dare to remove it, lest we should discover them, and make an attack. They left the city on a pontoon bridge, and took the only road left them, toward Charleston.

Here my Diary must end.

Thank God that I am yet alive, and permitted thus to end it.

SAVANNAH REPUBLICAN EDITORIAL
To the Citizens of Savannah:

By the fortunes of war, we pass today under the authority of the Federal military forces. The evacuation of Savannah by the Confederate army, which took place last night, left the gates to the city open, and General Sherman, with his army will, no doubt, to-day take possession.

The Mayor and Common Counsel leave under a flag of truce this morning, for the headquarters of Gen. Sherman, to offer the surrender of the city, and ask terms of capitulation by which private property and citizens may be respected.

We desire to counsel obedience and all proper respect on the part of our citizens, and to express the belief that their property and persons will be respected by our military ruler. The fear expressed by many that Gen. Sherman will repeat the order of expulsion from their homes which he enforced against the citizens of Atlanta, we think to be without foundation. He assigned his reason in that case as a military necessity; it was a question of food. He could not supply his army and the citizens with food, and he stated that he must have full and sole occupation. But in our case food can be abundantly supplied for by both army and civilians. We would not be understood as even intimating that we are to be fed at the cost of the Federal Government, but that food can be easily obtained in all probability, by all who can afford to pay in the Federal currency.

It behooves all to keep within their homes until Gen. Sherman shall have organized a provost system and such police as will insure safety in persons as well as property.

Let our conduct be such as to win the admiration of a magnanimous foe, and give no ground for complaint or harsh treatment on the part of him who will for an indefinite period hold possession of our city.

In our city there are, as in other communities, a large proportion of poor and needy families, who, in the present situation of affairs, brought about by the privations of war, will be thrown upon the bounty of their more fortunate neighbors. Deal with them kindly, exercise your philanthropy and benevolence, and let the heart of the unfortunate not be deserted by your friendly aid.

FRANCES HOWARD, Howard Home, Savannah

It has come at last. To-night, the town will be evacuated.

Confidential Circular. Head Qrs. Savannah,

The troops in and around Savannah will be transferred to-night to the left bank of the Savannah river, and will proceed thence to Hardeeville.

By command of Lt. Genl. Hardee

My poor father came in jaded and worn out. Nelly and I packed up everything for him He left us at three this morning. In his feeble condition I am glad to know that he has secured a mule and will not have to walk. Heaven protect us!

Thursday, December 22

W. T. SHERMAN, Major-General, Headquarters, Military
Department of Mississippi, Savannah
To His Excellency President Lincoln, Washington, D. C.:
I beg to present you as a Christmas-gift the city of Savannah
with one hundred and fifty heavy guns and plenty of ammunition,
and also about twenty-five thousand bales of cotton.

PART FIVE: DECEMBER 1864-JANUARY 1965

Friday, December 23, 1864

ROSE TAYLOR, Ex-slave, Taylor Residence, Savannah, Georgia

Us looked for the Yankees like us looked for the Savior and the host of angels at the second coming. I'd always thought about this time, and wanted this day to come, and prayed for it and knew God meant it should be here sometime, but I didn't believe I should ever see it, and it is so great and good a thing, I cannot believe it has come now; and I don't believe I ever shall realize it, but I know it is though, and I bless the Lord for it.

Ye's long been a-coming, Ye's long been a-coming, Ye's long been a-coming, For to take de land.

And now ye's a-coming, And now ye's a-coming, And now ye's a-coming, For to rule de land.

R. SAXTON, Brigadier General of Volunteers Headquarters U. S. Forces, District Of Beaufort, Beaufort, S. C.
Maj. Gen. W. T. Sherman, U. S. Army, Commanding Army of Occupation, Savannah, Ga.:

General: Rather than sending any more blacks to me at Beaufort, I would respectfully suggest that a large number of contrabands might be sent to Saint Simon's Island, Ga., and Edisto, S. C. There are a large number of vacant houses on each of these islands and a regiment of colored troops could hold them securely. These islands have both been occupied by our troops, but were vacated in 1863 by order of General Hunter, then commanding this department. I presume there are no rebels on either of them, and it would require but a small force to hold them securely. If one of the colored regiments now at our front in the vicinity of the railroad could be sent to OCCUPY these islands, they perhaps might aid your operations as much as they are now doing.

I very much regret, general, that my power to relieve you of the burden of these people is not equal to my inclination, but I have no means at all under my control. Even a small steamer sent to me by the War Department for special service, the control of which is absolutely essential to this service, has been taken from me by General Foster. I greatly fear that if these contrabands are sent to this post, there will be much suffering among them, as I have neither men nor means at my command to provide them with shelter.

With this statement of my situation and of facts as they exist at present, which I deem it my duty to make, I beg to assure you, general, that I am prepared to do all that you may desire me to do in this matter, and am ready to report to you at Savannah for the purpose, or anywhere else you may desire. Every cabin and house on these islands is filled to overflowing—I have some 15,000. It has occurred to me that I might render you more service by coming to

Savannah. I shall be governed entirely by your wishes or orders in the case.

I am, very respectfully

JENNIE LEWIS, Headquarters, The Green House, Savannah, Georgia

I am now in Savannah. I am living in the Generals headquarters. We arrived two days ago and I have scarcely left my room.

We are in the home of Mr. Green. The servants here say this is the grandest home in all of Savannah. It sits on something called a squire. Around the squire are big trees with heavy drooping branches. They cast wide shadows. But the paths of the squire, neat as cotton rows, are bright with sunlight and still blooming gardens. In the middle of the square a man of stone holds up a flag and looks to be marching right off into the air. From the windows of my rooms I watch the people of Savannah line the paths coming to Mr. Greens house, coming to see the general.

He meets people in downstairs all day. Then he comes up here to see me. 'How are you, Jennie. Are you enjoying your leisure? This is your room, Jennie,' he tells me. 'All the dresses and shoes yours to wear.'

So many dresses and shoes for one girl? And so many glasses to gaze into. Who was this room meant for? I do not think for me. Yet here I am.

My bed has four posts, one at each corner. On top of each post is a spike. The wood is so smooth it feels like cloth. The blankets and pillows have white ruffles sown all around. When I first saw it I did not want to sleep there. But now I lie here much of the day reading books I find on the shelves, writing whatever I want in my papers, and wondering, wondering what is to become of me now.

The fences around the house and the rails on the stairways are made of black iron, curved like branches. In the grand hallway the floors shine and a curved staircase rises up to the second floor. A great circle of candles opens up to the sky above the staircase, letting the smoke rise into the night and the heat and light fall upon the people below.

The general said Papa is sure to have my letter soon. But for now I am alone. I can come and go as I please he tells me. Where would I go? I dare not seek Rev. Quarles in the city. I may have to face Fortune Bells wrath again. I know no one here except the Army staff. I cannot face Captain Pepper with my question. I see only the General and the servants and take no notice of any one else.

Mr. Greens cook will not let Manual in her kitchen. So I have no chores to do. The servants bring me trays of food. I eat and try on dresses. And shoes and stockings and hats and gloves and stare at myself in the three looking glasses. I wonder who is this girl with my mothers heavy black hair piled up on her head and a sad look in her eyes. Wearing a lace flower in her hair and a lace collar as tight as the metal ones the slaves used to wear. Who is this now free woman? What does a free woman do?

Mr. Greens servants call me Miss Lewis. They call me Sherman's Wife. As my letter travels to find Papa and bring us together, I stare at myself and wonder how will I tell him why I am here, in this house, as Sherman's Wife. And why Caroline is not with me. How will I tell him I am no longer the daughter he left? Nor will he ever see his Caroline again in this life? I shudder when I think about it and my heart aches. I will watch his face fall from joy at our reunion to the sadness of knowing what all we have lost.

Saturday, December 24

CAPT. GEORGE W. PEPPER, Savannah

I attended a meeting of colored people tonight in the Baptist Church. The building was packed to its utmost capacity, and hundreds stood during the whole evening, while hundreds of others came and went away, being unable to find even a place to stand. The meeting was opened by one of "our own" the Rev. Quarles, in a prayer of great pathos and rare power. He paused in the midst of his supplications and offered up a thrilling supplication for the great army that had delivered them. In a strain of rude but hearty eloquence, he thanked God that the black people were free, and forever free. The whole congregation here gave vent to their joyous emotions, in bursts of: Glory to God! Hallelujah! Praise his name!

The following hymn was read and sang with wonderful power:

Blow ye the trumpet, blow, The gladly solemn sound,
Let all the nations know The year of jubilee has come.

The effect of this stirring poetry on the assembly was thrilling. The elder, who read the hymn, when he came to the words: The year of jubilee is come! was so overwhelmed with emotion, that it was impossible for him to proceed. The audience caught the magical influence, and then a scene ensued which baffles description. All classes, black and white, old slave owners, and the soldiers of the army were alike affected

That staunch patriot and eloquent minister, Mansfield French, well known in Ohio as the friend of the negro, was the principal speaker. He called the attention of the emancipated to the duties and responsibilities devolving upon them in their present position. He recommended them to cultivate habits of honesty, purity, thrift and enterprise; admonishing them of the necessity of industry on their part; advising them to love their old masters, and not cherish feelings of revenge.

At every mention of the Union, and Liberty, and the names of Lincoln and Sherman, the walls almost trembled beneath the thunder which followed. When the orator declared the re-election of Mr. Lincoln as the guarantee of their freedom for all time, the vast gathering rose to their feet, and with shouts and tears, returned thanks to Almighty God. Never did the painter find a nobler sight for his pencil than the spontaneous uprising of that liberated people.

What a lofty ambition for one man to be the emancipator of the oppressed! History, who keeps a record of events, will hand down the name of Abraham Lincoln to posterity on her brightest page. Our hearts yearn to thee, noble patriot. We are lifted up in wonder and admiration; when we see thy cheerful endurance, thy uncomplaining spirit; we respect and honor thee. Brother French electrified the multitude by earnest outbursts of glowing patriotism, which was received with cheer upon cheer. But it is useless to attempt to convey any adequate idea of the great meeting held in the Baptist Church. The colored population of Savannah send greeting, a solid, enthusiastic greeting to their brethren in other States and cities throughout the length and breadth of the land, and ere long, we trust and expect similar meetings will be held everywhere.

JENNIE LEWIS, Headquarters, The Green House, Savannah

I have just come from the meeting at Third African Baptist Church. We have been singing and praising the Lord since early night. I could fall asleep in the middle of a sentence but I must write what I learned today. Thousands of colored people are now living in Savannah, and the Federal Army means to send them away from here. Some men say they have been forced to join the army.

Fortune Bell spoke out at the meeting. "I will not be shipped to any place. I am going back to farm on St. Simons, and no Army will stop me. They say we need the Federals to protect us. That we will need to sign a contract to work the land for the white people. I will not sign such a contract. I will work my own land. I have as much right to sign a white man to a contract to work for me!"

The church leaders agreed with Fortune. Now they are going to see the General. They will tell him the people should be allowed to go where they choose. No one asked me to go with them this time.

Captain Pepper was at the meeting today. I stayed away from him. I did not talk to Rev. Quarles or Fortune. I have let them all down. The Planter is not yet here. I am alone. This is my saddest Christmas ever.

Christmas Day 1864

<u>FANNY COHEN TAYLOR</u>**,** Taylor Residence, Savannah

This was the saddest Christmas that I have ever spent and my only pleasure during the day was in looking forward to spending my next Christmas in the Confederacy.

This morning my uncle Mr. Myers and his daughter Mrs. Yates Levy came to see us and told us of a party given Christmas Eve by the negroes at Genl. Geary's Hd. Qtrs. The Gen. went into the kitchen and desired an introduction to the ladies and gentlemen there assembled. After the introduction he asked who were slaves and who were free. There was but one slave present, a servant girl of my Aunt's who acknowledged the fact.

This elegant gentleman inquired into her private history and finding that she was a married woman begged an introduction to her husband, Mr. Valentine. He then presented Mr. Valentine, *as a Christmas gift*, with a free wife. The girl was so much amused having always been a favorite servant and treated like one of the family that she told it to her mistress as a good joke.

<u>DOLLY S. L. BURGE</u>**,** Burge Plantation, Near Covington

Sadai jumped out of bed very early today to feel in her stocking. She could not believe but that there would be something in it. Finding nothing, she crept back into bed, pulled the cover over her face, and I soon heard her sobbing. The little negroes all came in: "Christmas gift, mist'ess! Christmas gift, mist'ess!"

'T is the last Christmas, probably, that we shall be together, freedmen! Now you will, I trust, have your own homes, and be joyful under your own vine and fig tree, with none to molest or make afraid.'

I pulled the cover over my face and was soon mingling my tears with Sadai's.

FRANCES HOWARD, Howard Residence, Savannah

Miss Moodie and Nelly went to the house of Mr. Green, a British resident, where German Sherman had quarters. Mrs. Randolph's cotton had been taken and she wished to ask Mr. Green if it were possible to take any steps toward recovering it. They were in the parlor when Mr. Green entered closely followed by General Sherman.

"There are some ladies in the parlor," said Mr. Green.

"Not to see me; not to see me, I hope," said Sherman roughly.

"Do you wish to be introduced to General Sherman?" asked Mr. Green in an undertone to Miss Moodie.

"Not for the world," she replied in a distinct voice. "I have no wish to make his acquaintance; my business is private and entirely with you, Mr. Green, entirely with you."

Sherman walked to the piano, looked at some music and then left the room.

When Miss Moodie had concluded her conversation with Mr. Green, he asked them upstairs to look at a fine picture, and they passed the open doors of some beautifully furnished rooms. In one of these fine rooms they saw a young Negro woman, admiring herself before a mirror!

"Those apartments are occupied by General Sherman and his--staff," said Mr. Green to Nelly, who must have looked her disgust, for he continued as they passed a door through which a handsome bed was visible, "don't you want him to rest comfortably?"

"No, indeed, I do not!" she exclaimed. "I wish a thousand papers of pins were stuck in that bed and that he was strapped down on them."

W. T. SHERMAN, Headquarters, Military Division of the
Mississippi, Savannah
Dearest Ellen,

I hope truly & really that you and the Little ones enjoyed Christmas Day, in the full Knowledge that I am all safe after our long march—I am at this moment in an elegant chamber of the house of a Gentleman named Green. The house is elegant & splendidly furnished with pictures & Statuary—my bed Room has a bath & dressing Room attached which look out of proportion to my poor baggage. My clothing is good yet and I can even afford a white Shirt.

It would amuse you to See the negros, they flock to me old & young they pray & shout—and mix up my name with that of Moses, & Simon, and other scriptural ones as well as Abram Linkum the Great Messiah of "Dis Jubilee."

I have no doubt you hear enough about "Sherman" and are sick of the name, and the interest the public takes in my whereabouts leaves me no subject to write about. Charley & Dayton promise to write details. All I can do is make hasty scrawls assuring you of my health and Eternal affection,

JENNIE LEWIS, Headquarters, Savannah

The general gave me a golden locket. Now I have two. It is finer than Mama's locket, tho I treasure both. What photograph will I place inside this one?

I were it every day but when I go out, I wear it under my garments. Where no one else will see it.

Monday, December 26

General Sherman:

When you were about leaving Atlanta for the Atlantic coast, I was anxious, if not fearful; but, feeling that you were the better judge, and remembering "nothing risked, nothing gained," I did not interfere. Now, the undertaking being a success, the honor is all yours; for I believe none of us went further than to acquiesce; and, taking the work of General Thomas into account, as it should be taken, it is indeed a great success.

Not only does it afford the obvious and immediate military advantages, but, in showing to the world that your army could be divided, putting the stronger part to an important new service, and yet leaving enough to vanquish the old opposing force of the whole, Hood's army, it brings those who sat in darkness to see a great light.

But what next? I suppose it will be safer if I leave General Grant and yourself to decide.

[227]

Tuesday, December 27

<u>MAJOR FREDRICK C. WINKLER</u>, In Camp, Savannah

We have such cheering news from all quarters, it seems the war must come to a speedy end. Movements in Tennessee, which were looked upon with apprehension, now present the most cheering aspect. The Battle of Frankton seems to have been well fought on both sides, yet General Hood was badly whipped and lost heavily, both in numbers and morale of his troops. Now, in front of Nashville, it would seem that he has met with a crushing defeat. His disaster promises to become complete before he can recross the Tennessee.

Here is this big army without an enemy before it. The rebels are crippled everywhere. Lee cannot stay in Richmond much longer; he would have left before this time if only he had some place to retreat to. North Carolina is his only chance, and there he will have Grant's forces in front and an army equal to his own under Sherman in his rear.

Wednesday, December 28

U. S. GRANT, Lieutenant-General, City Point, Virginia

Maj. Gen. William T. Sherman, Commanding Military

Division of the Mississippi:

General: Before writing you definite instructions for the next campaign, I wanted to receive your answer to my letter written from Washington. Your confidence in being able to march up and join this army pleases me, and I believe it can be done. The effect of such a campaign will be to disorganize the South, and prevent the organization of new armies from their broken fragments.

Hood is now retreating, with his army broken and demoralized. His loss in men has probably not been far from 20,000, besides deserters. If time is given the fragments may be collected together and many of the deserters reassembled; if we can, we should act to prevent this. Your spare army, as it were, moving as proposed, will do this.

Without waiting further directions, then, you may make preparations to start on your northern expedition without delay. Break up the railroads in South and North Carolina, and join the armies operating against Richmond as soon as you can. I will leave out all suggestions about the route you should take, knowing that your information, gained daily in the progress of events, will be better than any that can be obtained now.

I shall establish communication with you there by steam-boat and gun-boat. By these means your wants can be partially supplied. I shall hope to hear from you soon, and to hear your plan and about the time of starting. Please instruct Foster to hold on to all the property captured in Savannah, and especially the cotton. Do not turn it over to citizens or Treasury agents without orders of the War Department.

Very respectfully, your obedient servant,

P.S. Jeff. Davis is said to be very sick; in fact, deserters report his death. The people had a rumor that he took poison in a fit of despondency over the military situation. Of course, I credit no part of this, except that Davis is very sick, and do not suppose his reflections on military matters soothe him any.

J. WHEELER, Confederate States Army, Hardeeville, S. C.
General Braxton Bragg, Headquarters Armies of the Confederate States:

Dear General: The loss of Savannah I presume you anticipated. I felt convinced myself it could not be saved immediately upon my arrival and learning that no more enforcements could be expected. presume you have been mortified to hear the complaints and charges which have been made against my command. The first charge was that my command straggled. This is partially true, but the great cause was the issuing of an illegal order by General Taylor directing General Clanton to organize all absentees from the army into regiments. This order was, of course, abused, as all illegal orders generally are, and his officers enlisted men directly from my ranks and this nearly ruined one brigade and had a bad effect on my entire command. After such action on his part he was so unkind as to heap upon me abuse for the very thing which he has caused.

Of course there was other apparent straggling, always while watching or engaging an enemy.

You have no doubt heard that I burnt mills after the enemy had passed. This is false. In my anxiety to save property I placed guards at mills, directing them to remain until the enemy drove them off, and only to fire the mill when they saw it was impossible to remain any longer.

I make these explanations to you as I feel grateful for the kindness you have shown me on so many occasions, and I knew you would regret to see me neglectful. I have made two written applications for a board of officers of rank to investigate the entire matter and report the facts.

The world is getting worse and worse every day. It is astonishing what false representations are made by some parties. I beg, if any representations are made regarding my command, they will be referred to me and not allowed to rest until I am held accountable or am able to prove the charges incorrect.

We were all much shocked at hearing of the President's death, but were much relieved this morning to hear that the report was incorrect.

I hope Hood will meet with success in Tennessee, but reports indicate that we may be disappointed.

With high regard, your obedient servant and friend

Thursday, December 29

ELLEN E. SHERMAN, South Bend Indiana

Dearest Cump:

Considering your orders to me not to write until I heard from you I think you have been a long time in getting a letter to me. You must have known I was in South Bend yet you sent your letter to Lancaster and today is the first of my receiving anything in your hand writing. A dispatch came to me after all the telegraphic news was old and at long last I have got a letter. I had about made up my mind that I was not to get any more from you. I did not know how to send my letters and I have therefore written only one. That you will probably not receive as I did not know how to address it. Now I have but a short time to write as I am expecting a carriage to go to the Academy. I have been out there since the day before Christmas and only came in to spend the day and to get my letters.

I have been watching the office most anxiously for your letter & had just given it up and made up my mind to do without any when I got it. Long before this you have seen in the papers the notice of the dear baby's death. His long agony & my woe in witnessing & recalling it I will not dwell upon at present. The loss, aside from the present loneliness it involves, I do not deplore on my own account for it is so much better to have him safe with his heavenly Father than to feel that we ever might leave him here without our care. Part we must and it is better to send them on before to pray for and await our coming. God grant that his prayers and Willy's may ensure my perseverance and obtain for you the gift of faith.

The other children are well & have all enjoyed their Christmas very much. Elly & Rachel are still at the Academy with Emily. Tommy is to commence his school on Monday the 2nd day of Jan, when I intend to keep him closely to it as he is very backward for eight years. I will try and write you a long letter tomorrow.

I receive compliments innumerable on your account and am even stared at myself as a wonder. The children are very anxious to see you and so am I but I dread another journey and hope we may meet short of a southern city. They are projecting a handsome present to you either a farm or a residence in Ohio. Should they really offer it you must not decline as I shall despair of ever having a home if you do. I hope they will make it a house in Cin: & then I could have all the children with me and educate them well too and I would also be near enough to Father to see him at any time.

I am suffering today from cold and sore throat - Truly I have great cause to be thankful that you have been preserved through so many dangers. I think you ought to have telegraphed me earlier and more than once, for I have been too long alone here without hearing from you or the means of writing to you. I hope it will be different hereafter. I don't care about hearing from Dayton - after the letter he wrote to Henry Reese which Henry read for me. Dayton is ungrateful to me and I will not pretend that I don't know it.

In haste for the carriage,

[234]

JENNIE LEWIS, Headquarters, Green House, Savannah

Today Fortune Bell asked me to marry him! He is leaving for St. Simons Island tomorrow and he wants me to come with him. 'Jennie, you are a strong woman with a good mind. I am a strong man. We will own our own land and raise a strong family.' I sat with my mouth and ink dripping onto paper. We were in the church basement where I have come every day to help people write letters to their families. He came right up to me while I was in the middle of a letter and said 'Jennie, I want to marry you.'

I thought Fortune Bell hated me! It's a good thing Rev. Quarles came upon us or we might be there still waiting for me to answer.

Rev. Quarles took us into the pastors office and sat us both down before him. 'Now whats this all about Fortune?'

'I'm leaving tomorrow. I want Jennie to go with me, you know, marry me.' Rev. Quarles looked at me, but I must have still been in shock. He turned back to Fortune.

'Have you two discussed any of this before?' We both shook our heads. 'Then why, Brother Fortune, would you do this in this manner?'

Fortune looked at me. 'Jennie—I like you—a lot. I think about you all the time.'

'But, Fortune, you have always said the meanest things to me.' He could not deny it.

[235]

Then he said 'I loved you. And I didnt know how to tell it.'

I started to cry. I looked to Rev. Quarles for help but he could not help me say *I don't love you Fortune. Im in love with General Sherman. And he loves me.*

Rev. Quarles said 'Fortune, you cannot just spring this on a woman like that. And Jennie could not answer, in any case. She must discuss a thing as important as marriage with her mother and her father. He will be here in a few days and—'

I stopped him. 'What did you say about Papa?'

'He will be arriving on the Planter in a few days time.'

I jumped up, forgetting all about Fortune and his marriage. 'How do you know, Rev. Quarles?'

'I heard General Fosters report to General Sherman. Its coming from the Chesapeake with other supply ships.'

I wanted to scream and shout for joy. But instead I got up and said to Fortune 'I am honored Fortune Bell, but I can not think of marrying anyone right now. And I cant go to your Island if my Papa is on his way here. I wish you the best in your life, Brother Bell. I wish you the best.'

Then I ran out of the room. I heard the news from Rev. Quarles. Now I wanted to hear it from the general.

As usual many people had come to the Green house to see General Sherman. In and out all day long, white people, colored people, bringing there children to hug Mr. Sherman. It was long after supper before I could find him alone.

'Ah, Jennie' he said and waved me into his rooms. 'I have something for you.' He gave me a white envelope.'

'Another gift?' I asked, smiling.

'No. No gift. This is your army pay.' I opened the envelope and many papers fell out. General Sherman reached down and picked them up, and put them in my hand. 'Greenbacks. Good old U.S. dollars. Now what will you do with it?'

'Im sure I dont know, general. Ive never had any before. What should I do with it?'

'Why spend it! Or save it! Its yours to decide.'

I handed the papers back to him. 'Please keep it for me and I'll ask—' I stopped because I wanted to get to the reason I had come to see him. 'Is Papas ship on its way here at last?'

'Why, yes, Jennie, the Planter is making her way south. She should arrive in a couple of days.'

I hugged him and kissed him and danced around the room. It seemed I could float. I became so happy that I began talking about everything I could think of. I told the general about Fortune Bells offer. The general grew sober.

'Well, Jennie, what will you do? Will you stay in Savannah? Our army must leave here soon. We're heading North, to Richmond, where we will end this cruel war. Then we will all have to rebuild our country. Will you come to Ohio and go to college?'

This felt like my second proposal of marriage to-day. And for the second time *I could not answer*.

Friday, December 30

MAJOR HENRY HITCHCOCK, Assistant Adjutant
General, Headquarters, Green House, Savannah

The greatest in-door feature of our residence in Savannah has
been the General's new-found colored friends who have come by
hundreds to see "Mr. Sherman." The morning we entered the city he
rode down at once to the river-bank and went up to a signal station
on the roof of a warehouse; and by the time we got down to the
street again a crowd of them had gathered who pressed round him to
welcome him and shake hands and tell him how long they had
watched and prayed for his coming.

After we came to this house they soon began to find out that
he would see them, and for several days there was a constant stream
of them, old and young, men, women and children, black, yellow
and cream-colored, uncouth and well-bred, bashful and talkative—
but always respectful and well-behaved—all day long, anxious to
pay their respects and to see the man they heard so much of, and
whom—as more than one of them told him,--God had sent to answer
their prayers. Frequently they came in a dozen or twenty at a time, to
his room up-stairs where he usually sits, and where, as my writing is
done there, I have been in the way of seeing it all. He has always had
them shown in at once, stopping a dispatch or letter or a
conversation to greet them in his off-hand—though not undignified
way—"Well, boys,--come to see Mr. Sherman, have you? Well, I'm

[238]

Mr. Sherman—glad to see you" —and shaking hands with them all in a manner highly disgusting, I dare say, to a "refined Southern gentleman."

Almost all of them who have talked at all have spoken of our success and their deliverance with an apparently religious feeling,-- "Been prayin' for you all long time, Sir, prayin' day and night for you, and now, bless God, you is come"—etc. One old preacher likened himself to Simeon of old, kindly reminding the General of all the particulars as given in the Gospel. Indeed there have been some quite touching scenes. The General gives them all good advice—briefly and to the point, telling them they are free now, have no master nor mistress to support, and must be industrious and well-behaved, etc.

Meanwhile, the white citizens are "subjugated," and, what is more, they—or their leading men, lately "loyal" to Jeff. Davis,--say openly that the C.S.A. is "played out."

BREVET-MAJOR GEORGE WARD NICHOLS, Aide-de-Camp, Headquarters, Savannah

Along the whole line of our march, General Sherman has never lost an opportunity of talking with and advising the negroes who came into our camp, and his great heart has overflowed in kindly counsels to these poor people. Since his arrival in this city he has kept open house for all who choose to call upon him, white or black. His rooms in the splendid mansion of Mr. Green, a British resident, are constantly thronged with visitors, and the negroes are greeted by him with the same courtesy that is extended to the whites. In truth, I honestly believe the General entertains a more profound respect and love for these loyal blacks than for the rebellious white men who formerly called themselves masters.

The negroes all tell the General that the falsehoods of the Rebel papers never deceived them, and that they believed that his "retreats" were victories; that they would serve the Union cause in any and all ways that they could, as soldiers, as drivers, or pioneers. Indeed, the faith, earnestness, and heroism of the black men is one of the grandest developments of this war. When I think of the universal testimony of our escaped soldiers, who enter our lines every day, that in the hundreds of miles which they traverse on their way they never ask the poor slave in vain for help; that the poorest negro hides and shelters them, and shares the last crumb with them—all this impresses me with a weight of obligation and a love for them that stir the very depths of my soul.

H. W. HALLECK, Headquarters of the Army, Washington, D.C.

Major-General W. T. Sherman, Savannah

My Dear General: I take the liberty of calling your attention, in this private and friendly way, to a matter which may possibly hereafter be of more importance to you than either of us may now anticipate.

[240]

While almost every one is praising your great march through Georgia, and the capture of Savannah, there is a certain class having now great influence with the President, and very probably anticipating still more on a change of cabinet, who are decidedly disposed to make a point against you. I mean in regard to "inevitable Sambo." They say that you have manifested an almost criminal dislike to the negro, and that you are not willing to carry out the wishes of the Government in regard to him, but repulse him with contempt! They say you might have brought with you to Savannah more than fifty thousand, thus stripping Georgia of that number of laborers, and opening a road by which as many more could have escaped from their masters; but that, instead of this, you drove them from your ranks, prevented their following you by cutting the bridges in your rear, and thus caused the massacre of large numbers by Wheeler's cavalry.

To those who know you as I do, such accusation will pass as the idle winds, for we presume that you discouraged the negroes from following you because you had not the means of supporting them, and feared they might seriously embarrass your march. But there are others, and among them some in high authority, who think or pretend to think otherwise, and they are decidedly disposed to make a point against you.

I do not write this to induce you to conciliate this class of men by doing any thing which you do not deem right and proper, and for the interest of the Government and the country; but simply to call your attention to certain things which are viewed here somewhat differently than from your stand-point. I will explain as briefly as possible.

Some here think that, in view of the scarcity of labor in the South, and the probability that a part, at least, of the able- bodied slaves will be called into the military service of the rebels, it is of the greatest importance to open outlets by which these slaves can escape into our lines, and they say that the route you have passed over should be made the route of escape, and Savannah the great plane of refuge. These, I know, are the views of some of the leading men in the Administration, and they now express dissatisfaction that you did not carry them out in your great raid.

Now that you are in possession of Savannah, and there can be no further fears about supplies, would it not be possible for you to reopen these avenues of escape for the negroes, without interfering with your military operations? Could not such escaped slaves find at least a partial supply of food in the rice-fields about Savannah, and cotton plantations on the coast?

I merely throw out these suggestions. I know that such a course would be approved by the Government, and I believe that a manifestation on your part of a desire to bring the slaves within our lines will do much to silence your opponents. You will appreciate my motives in writing this private letter.

Yours truly

[242]

Saturday, December 31: Watch Night

REV. JAMES LYNCH, Third African Church, Savannah

A few short years ago I left Savannah a slave.

"Hallelujah, oh yes!"

I now return a man.

"Amen."

"I have the honor to be a regular minister of the Gospel."

"Glory to God, Amen!"

"...and also a regularly commissioned chaplain in the American Army."

"Amen!"

"One week ago you were all slaves; now you are all free."

"Thank God the armies of the Lord and of Gideon has triumphed and the Rebels have been driven back in confusion and scattered like chaff before the wind."

"Amen! Hallelujah"

"I listened to your prayers, but I did not hear a single prayer offered for the President of the United States or for the success of the American Army."

"Amen! O yes, I prayed all last night!"

"But I know what you meant. You were not quite sure that you were free, therefore a little afraid to say boldly what you felt. I know how it is. I remember how we used to have to employ our dark symbols and obscure figures to cover up our real meaning. The profoundest philosopher could not understand us."

"Amen! Hallelujah! That's so!"

Sunday, January 1, 1865

<u>FRANCES HOWARD</u>, Howard Residence, Savannah

To-day a little Negro amused herself by jumping up and down under my window, and singing at the top of her voice:

"All de rebel gone to hell, Now Par Sherman come."

The city authorities have seen fit to declare the city once more in the Union.

<u>ELLA GERTRUDE CLANTON THOMAS</u>, Thomas House, Milledgeville, Georgia

Another Christmas has come and gone and another year has passed. I could bow my head and weep, oh so bitterly, did I permit my mind to follow its impulse & think of the bright hopes which have been dashed to the earth, the sad condition of our loved country, but God disposes of all things and it is too late. I do not know what to think.

Sometimes I am inclined to look upon our defeat as a Providential thing and then I grow skeptical and almost doubt whether Providence had anything to do with the matter. Slavery had its evils and great ones and for some years I have doubted whether Slavery was right and now I sometimes feel glad that they have been freed and yet I think that it came too suddenly upon them. As it is, we live in troublous times. Lawless acts are being committed every

[245]

day and the papers are filled with the robberies which are constantly taking place.

It has been raining all day. Mr. Thomas left this morning to go to Burke to have a settlement with the Negroes. They have made nothing and he has little inducement to plant. Indeed he does not know what to do and were it not too serious a subject to jest upon I should say he was "waiting for something to turn up" like Micawber in one of Dickens' works, and indeed that expression will serve to convey an idea of the condition of the southern people generally. Until Congress decides something definite, we will not know how we stand.

FANNY COHEN TAYLOR, Taylor Residence, Savannah

This morning Dr. Ballenger came to see my maid who has been sick for several days. After he left I went to my room and darned my stockings for this week, the first time I had ever done such a thing in my life. But I suppose when she leaves me I shall always have to do so. I had better begin at once.

BREVET MAJOR GEORGE WARD NICHOLS,
Headquarters, Savannah

A highly cultivated lady said to me:

"It is terrible, sir! All my slaves have left me; my plantation is broken up. I don't know but the land will be given to my slaves. I have no money, or but little. I shall have to starve or work."

[246]

"Well, madam," I replied, "I really wouldn't advise you to starve. Supposing you do work?"

"But I never did such a thing in all my life!" she answered.

She who had always passed her summers at the North, and had lived a life of perfect ease, found her income of $20,000 a year swept away at a single blow. With the most charming innocence she protested to me, "I really fear, sir , that I shall have to submit to the disgrace of giving lessons in music."

I was rude enough to reply: "Madam, I hope so."

E. F. A., At Nel's House, Near Savannah

It begins to look as if the Yankees can do whatever they please and go wherever they wish - except to heaven; I do fervently pray the good Lord will give us rest from them there.

Monday, January 2

W. T. SHERMAN, Headquarters, Military Division of the
Mississippi, Savannah

Dearest Ellen,

The Steamer Planter arrived today, bringing N.Y. mails to
Dec. 24. I got a letter from yr. father at Washington, Hugh in
Kentucky and John Sherman all alluding to the death of our baby,
but I got nothing from you or the girls at school. I also found in the
N.Y. Herald of the 22nd a full obituary and notice of funeral
ceremonies from which I see you are up at South Bend. I have
written you twice to Lancaster, and to Minnie at Notre Dame so you
will know that I am safe again for a few days, and the northern
papers seem so full of speculations about me and my army that I
suppose you are sick of seeing the name.

The last letter I got from you at Kingston made me fear for
our baby, but I had hoped that the little fellow would weather the
ailment, but it seems he too, is lost to us, and gone to join Willy. I
cannot say that I grieve for him as I did Willy, for he was but a mere
ideal, whereas Willy was incorporated with us, and Seemed to be
designed to perpetuate our Memories. But amid the Scenes of death
and desolation through which I daily pass I cannot but become
callous to death. It is so common, so familiar that it no longer
impresses me as of old—

You on the Contrary surrounded alone by life & youth cannot take things so philosophically but are stayed by the Religious faith of a better and higher life elsewhere. I should like to have seen the baby of which all spoke so well, but I seem doomed to pass my life away so that even my children will be strangers. I did hope for some rest but all lean on me so, Grant, the President, the Army, and even the world now looks to me to strike hard & decisive blows that I cannot draw out quietly as I would and Seek rest.

Negros & whites flock to me and gaze at me as some wonderful being, and letters from Great men pour in with words of flattery & praise, but still I do more than ever crave for peace & quiet, and would gladly drop all these and gather you and my little ones in some quiet place where I could be at ease. People here talk as though the war was drawing to a close, but I know better. There remains yet a large class of Southern men who will not have Peace, and they Still have the power to do much mischief. Thomas' success in Tennessee inures to my advantage as his operations there are a part of my plan.

I know you have written to me, and I shall expect a big budget by the next N.Y. steamer.

It will not be long before I sally forth again on another dangerous & important Quixotic venture.

Love to all. Yrs. Ever

ELLEN SHERMAN, St. Mary's Academy, South Bend

Dearest Cump:

After writing you a brief letter yesterday dearest Cump I came back here to the Academy, suffering from severe headache and feel quite indisposed still this morning. The children are all well however and are as bright as little kittens. Tommy is enjoying the last few days of liberty he will have for some time. Tommy Ewing is here nearly all the time and the nuts and apples go fast. The money you sent me before I left home is all gone and more than gone - It took a good deal of it to pay up my bills and now I need not only for myself but to pay the second session for Minnie & Lizzie and to pay for Tommy when I enter him. Three hundred a month will not support us all and pay their schooling besides. I shall be happy to have a settled home when we can save the half that we spend now in changing & moving about.

Sister Angela is exceedingly kind to us all and entertains us in the most hospitable manner. Elly & Rachel are so charmed they do not want to go back to town. It is possible that I shall visit Father in Washington this winter when I shall leave my boarding house entirely and send all the children here to remain during my absence. There are several little girls as young as Elly & Rachel here. I am going tomorrow to spend the morning with Mrs. Williams, Willy's teacher at Notre Dame. That place seemed holy to me before, since Willy was there, but now that my darling baby lies there, it is indeed

[250]

sanctified ground and angels seem to dwell with the spirits of our children about the place and to speak of hope & comfort to my heart when I draw near.

My greatest hope is that I may ere long be reunited to them & never more be separated - my greatest comfort would be to know that you my dear husband were blessed with the faith which sanctified your children - that you believed in Jesus Christ through whom they are redeemed. Why can you not make your great works meritorious by offering them to God and doing them in His honor. If you do this you will then perhaps be rewarded with faith & receive for your labors and imperishable crown in the kingdom of God where our dear ones await us. If you die without the faith you leave us miserable the rest of our lives with a weight of sorrow upon the heart - which no worldly influence can dissipate. Why then not ask it of God? It can do you no harm but would afford you even in this world infinite consolation and happiness. And think what happiness it would confer upon all those who are nearest & dearest to you. The members of the Sherman family would be glad to See you a catholic because they fear to See you die without any faith.

How can you live, since Willy died, without the faith? I cannot conceive & from my heart I pity you for my own sufferings since his death has been more than I could have borne without its consolations. God sent that affliction as a lesson to us of the vanity of human glory. He took our best & fairest to Himself that our own hearts might follow. The wound was severe and is keenly tender yet

[251]

God grant it may be healed above - My blessed - my holy little ones pray for us ever until we join you in the bright home above when we shall see the face of God and learn to love Him as He deserves - Our hearts can never rest on earthly joys again after witnessing Willy's agony - and that compared with the darling baby's was almost light.

Ever faithfully yours

<u>JENNIE LEWIS</u>, Deveaux House, Savannah

The Planter sailed into the harbor trailing clouds of steam. All the men onboard waved and shouted but I could not see Papa anywhere. They started to bring off loads filled with clothes and shoes, pots and pans, foods, books, and mail. But no Papa!

All the colored crowded the shore line dressed in their best garments, ready to toss their hats in the air to salute Captain Robert Smalls and his crew. By now we all knew how he sailed right past the rebels in this ship and escaped with his family. Now, he was in charge of that very ship, a Negro man! Everyone wanted to get a look at him. Finally, a small man in a big hat stepped onto the deck, bowed and waved. A great cheer went up all along the shore. Then more men began to some into view and I stretched my neck and held my breath until finally I saw him! Papa!

I yelled to him. He could not possible hear me with all the cheers and shouts. As the men began to walk down to shore I pulled and pushed my way closer. I kept shouting Papa, and then I heard it, 'Jennie?' A short while after that he was before me and I could move another muscle. Papa stood there in his Union blue jacket and pants, with a smile as wide as the ocean and his arms stretched out to me. So much joy spread from his whole being that I could not bare it. I fell into his arms and screamed. And that is all I can remember until I woke up in another bed in another room in another house. Papa sat in a chair beside the bed.

'Oh, Papa' I cried. 'I must tell you. I must tell you something awful.'

'Dont worry yourself Jennie. Rev. Quarles spoke to me. Its all right Jennie. Im here now. Dont you tear yourself up about Caroline and her baby. They in a better place and they watching over us. One day soon we will go get your Mother. God willing, we will all live a long life of freedom. But then, we will all join our Caroline, never to part again.'

Later I learned Papa had removed me from the Generals headquarters and brought me to this house owned by Rev. Deveaux. How much had Rev. Quarles said to Papa about me and the General? Is that why he moved me away from there? Now I am gone, what will the General say?

Now was not the time to answer these questions. I held onto Papa and listened as he told me all about his life in the Navy. I fell asleep feeling something I had not felt in so long—safe in Papas arms.

Tuesday, January 3

ANONYMOUS GEORGIA CITIZEN

To General Howell Cobb:

Dear Sir,

You will excuse me for making the following suggestions upon the state of the country. Things look rather gloomy and unless something is done and that before the spring campaign opens we are undone. We want more men and where are they to come from? Some will say if the skulkers and deserters were brought up we would have men enough; but they cannot be made available. We cannot get from the militia a sufficient number to recruit our army and if we could it will not do to take all the male population out of the country. If they are, there would be nothing made to support the army and what little might be made it would be destroyed by the negroes and deserters, etc. I see but one alternative left us and that to fill up our army with negroes.

I have no doubt but they can be made as good soldiers as the population our enemies are importing from Europe. An army is a machine, and you can make anything fight if they are properly drilled. We are told however that they can not be made to fight. They have done some very good fighting for the Yanks, and I cannot see why they will not do as well for us if we will give them their freedom. If you do not put them in the field they will very soon be taken from us and made to take up arms against us. Why not then

[254]

move in the matter at once and have an army in the spring sufficient to drive the enemy back. If Georgia and South Carolina give Hardee an army of one hundred men, Sherman would not move out of Savannah, and Charleston and Augusta would be secure, our communications kept open and the state defended, or rather protected against raids. If Alabama and Mississippi would enforce Hood with one hundred thousand, we could march through Tennessee and Kentucky if Gen. Johnson was reinstated in command of that army. Then if North Carolina and Virginia would fill up Gen. Lee's ranks he would be able to drive Grant back. To say the least of this course we could fight them four years longer and by that time I think the North would be willing to make peace, and if she was not, Europe would interpose and settle matters.

Some think that our soldiers would not be willing to have negroes placed in the army. If Gen. Lee would say that it is necessary there would be but few objections. Our Congress is afraid to move unless they could be assured that the move would be popular. Six months since it would not have been, but now almost every man I see is in favor of the measure and the day is not far distant when these gentlemen will regret their want of nerve. If our Governor could know the feeling generally of the people he would assemble the Legislature and have a large army of negroes in the field, if he could under the constitution send them out as militia.

The man that leads off in this thing will be the great man of this Confederacy, for it will save us from subjugation. Now General, if you think as I do, and as a large majority of the people of Georgia, you are the very man to lead off in this thing. In the first place, you have more influence than any man in Georgia and in the second place you own a great many slaves and if you are willing to give a portion of your slaves, others could not object and would not. As far as I am concerned, I am willing to give up everything and commence the world in my old age without one cent if it will save me from Yankee rule. Anything but reconstruction or subjugation.

I feel as confident as I can of anything that if we will levy a sufficient force from our black population that it will save us from either. If the country is unwilling to fight the negroes, I am willing to propose to England and France if they will recognize us with armed intervention that we will agree to the gradual abolition of slavery. I have believed for the last two years that we would be compelled to put negroes in the army or go up the spout. I am old and have no influence. You are a man of genius, ability and influence, and if you can conscientiously lead off in this matter I believe you will make a name that will live till time will be no more.

HARPER'S WEEKLY, "The End of Rebel Logic," New York

The whole logic of the Southern system has broken down. The Southern leaders have insisted for many a year that the "peculiar institution" was also divine; and their Northern allies have lustily echoed the great and refreshing truth that, Canaan having been cursed, every colored baby was intended by divine beneficence to be sold like a sucking pig.

We have been listening now for many years to the noble doctrine that the system of slavery in our Southern States was God's appointment for the African race, and for all admixture of the European and American races with the African; that to question its benefit or beauty was to blaspheme God and his laws, and to presume to be wiser than the heavenly intelligence. Nor this alone. Not only was the system divine, but the slaves were happier than any peasantry in the world. They were comfortably cared for in sickness and age. They had no anxieties, no responsibilities. They danced to the banjo under the peaceful palmetto, and, if we only knew it, the name of happiness was Slavery in the Southern States.

Travelers from foreign lands went from plantation to plantation and found the life idyllic. Dainty ladies went from New York to pass winters with their planting friends, and returned with the rosiest romances of the felicity of Dinah and Sambo in their cunning little cabins. Every thing was lovely in the world except the dark and dreadful theory of the right of every man to himself and his own labor. Every body who did not own slaves was tolerable if he only wished that he owned some. But whoever denounced Slavery as a wrong to human nature, and an inevitable peril to the country, he was an awful monster in human form, he was the opposite of " a gentleman" he was an abolitionist.

[257]

To defend and perpetuate the divine institution it was made the head of the corner of the new nation of " the South." We were to see beyond all cavil that the only security of Liberty was slavery, the only foundation of Democracy was despotism, the only Right was Wrong. Unhappily, in the process of proving it, it becomes pretty clear that the proof will fail unless the slaves are summoned to the field. But they must be stimulated to fight, and the inspiration is to be the "boon of freedom." In other words, the structure can not be raised without knocking away the corner stone! And the whole ghastly lie from which this infamous rebellion springs stands revealed.

The rebels propose to free the slaves if they will fight. But what "boon" can freedom be to Sambo and Dinah, who are so delightfully content in the cunning cabin? The rebellion is to preserve the cabin. Why then hope to stimulate the happy peasants to fight by promising them that the system for whose protection they are to take arms, and which secures their happiness, is to be destroyed as their reward? Logic requires DAVIS and the other slave drivers to say, " Here, boys! God, you know, made you to be slaves, and we are fighting to keep you so. But the fight is a little hard. We are not altogether successful. So just take a brisk part in the fight for the perpetuity of slavery; and as you are all so happy and contented, and as it is the intention of Providence that you shall be slaves, we promise you if you will only fight bravely you shall be more slaves than ever. We will not fly in the face of Providence. Where you have

[258]

had only one child sold you shall have all your children put up on the block; and where you have been paddled and pickled between the shoulders only, you shall be whaled over the whole back. Fall in, boys, and strike home against the enemies who wish to oppose God and set you free."

If Slavery be, as the rebels and their Northern friends have so persistently assured us, the true and Christian disposition of the negro, why do DAVIS and his associates presume to outrage Christianity and thwart the divine purpose by promising the negro his liberty, if he will fight? We generally promise rewards not penalties to those whom we wish to win.

The whole debate, the proposition to give the slave who will fight the " boon of freedom," shows that the rebels know, with all the rest of mankind, that their system is inhuman and infamous. When they wish to make the slave a man they promise him his liberty, because they know that liberty is his birthright, and that they have deprived him of it. Out of their own mouths they are condemned. Their own action is the justification of every American citizen who has contended that, as Slavery was a fatal and increasing wrong, it was the necessary foe of national peace.

The rebel brethren are not harmonious upon the question. Some of the newspapers point out the absurd inconsistency of implying that Slavery can be wrong. But the official language of DAVIS is enough. If they intend to continue the war, they must arm the slaves. They know, as we do, that the slaves perfectly understand

[259]

the war. They know, as we do, that if they are armed, they will have their liberty. They make, therefore, a grace of necessity; and in the hopeless effort to save a point of shallow pride, they renounce the great object of their rebellion, and by their own act give the victory to the nation and civilization.

Wednesday, January 4

<u>W. T. SHERMAN</u>, Headquarters, Military Division of the

Mississippi, Savannah

Dearest Ellen,

I am about to Send a Steamer to Genl. Grant with dispatches and propose to send Charley if I can find him, but as usual he is out of the way and cannot be found. I have written to you and the children several times, and the newspapers keep you well advised of my whereabouts. I am now in a magnificent mansion living like a Gentleman, but Soon will be off for South Carolina and then look out for Breakers. You may count on me being here till the 15.

I have not yet had one word from you since you Knew of my having reached the Coast and only Know of the death of our little boy by, by the New York papers of Dec. 22, but was in a measure prepared for it by your letter received at Kingston. I suppose you felt his loss far more than I do because I never saw him, but all the children seemed to be so attached to him that you may be so grieved at his death you Cannot write to me.

Love to all. Yrs. Ever

<u>ELLEN SHERMAN</u>, South Bend, Indiana

Dearest Cump:

I have written you half a dozen letters none of which may reach you because I knew not exactly how to address them. I have

[261]

also written to Charley, which please say to him should he not receive my letters. I feel distressed to find from Minnie's letter just received that on Christmas day you had not heard of the darling baby's death although his precious little body had then been in its cold dark grave between two & three weeks. I had some hopes, when I left home that the journey, or rather the change of air, would be beneficial to him. Beautiful bright eyed little dove - he has left a bleak cold world at best, for the warm atmosphere of a Creators love.

Would that on our journey over we could be sure of joining him and Willy in their home of endless joy. To join them Cump, you must believe in the Saviour that redeemed them. Why set up truth and honor & principle as Gods and worship them, rather than the living God and our Saviour Christ from whom all good emanates? The faith that comforts us and sanctified our little ones in death could do you no harm, then why not ask God for it?

You sacrifice so much for the good of your fellow men on earth, why then not sacrifice something to gain the haven of rest where our darling ones await us. If you ask faith of God, He will give it to you. It would kill me to See you die without faith and prayer. Save me that sorrow in this world and in the next.

You are so crowned with earthly fame and honor and glory now, it is not necessary for me to Say anything on the subject of your achievements. What astonishes and charms the world at large does not surprise me for I knew when you were denounced that you were more capable of accomplishing great things for the country

[262]

than any man they had. Goodness like yours God rewards in this world sooner or later; would that you would perfect the character by offering all to His honor when your reward will be everlasting in the kingdom of heaven.

I am happy to know that we are soon to have a house presented to us. Philemon writes me that "the Sherman testimonial will be a grand success as it should be." Mr. Martin wrote to me requesting my preference (in confidence) for a farm in Fairfield Co. or a house in Cin: I explained to him that a residence in Cin: would be much more convenient to us with our family of daughters. But one son now - and I always feel that we will not keep him long. I grieve when I think of your bright boys taken away. Yet they were taken in mercy & in love to a Father whose love surpasses ours infinitely. In haste for this days mail ever dearest Cump your truly affectionate wife

SEAMAN GEORGE LEWIS, United States Navy, Deveaux Residence, Savannah, Georgia
To Mrs. Isabella Lewis at the Hale Farm, Decatur, Georgia
Dear Wife,

I embrace this opertunity to write you these few lines hoping they find you as the leave me, quite well. I am here in Savannah with our daughter Jennie and she is well and sends her love to you. I arrived here not four days ago, and we are staying in a nice home among the colored citizens of Savannah. I have spent time with the

General Commanding, General Sherman, and he assures me he will see my letter goes with his dispatches. We do not know the state of mails in Decatur, Isabella, but if the rails have been restored, I pray to God you will receive this letter from me.

Isabella, how I long to see you and bring you here to this fine city. It is one of accomplishment for Negroes as they have many among them who are shopkeepers and business men and learned people. Jennie and I both think highly of this place. We want to build our new life in freedom in Savannah.

Know, dear wife, that there are grate days in our future. I will come and get you as soon as I can find a way. I will not rest until we are all together again. Do hold on, Isabella. One day you will look up and you will see me coming down the lane, comeing for you. I pray the day comes soon.

Your ever devoted husband until death

W. T. SHERMAN, Major-General, Hdqrs. Military Division
of the Mississippi, In the Field, Savannah

His Excellency President Lincoln, Washington:

Dear Sir,

I am gratified at the receipt of your letter of Dec 26, at the
hand of General Logan, Especially to observe that you appreciate the
division I made of my army, and that each part was duly
proportioned to its work. The motto, "Nothing ventured, nothing
won" which you refer to is most appropriate, and should I venture
too much and happen to lose, I shall bespeak your charitable
inference. I am ready for the Great Next as soon as I can complete
certain preliminaries, and learn of Genl Grant his and your
preferences of intermediate "objectives."

With great respect, your servant,

EDWIN M. STANTON, Secretary of War, War Department,
Washington City

Lieutenant-General Grant, Fortress Monroe:

I think it would be useful if you would write to Sherman,
urging him to give facilities to the organization of colored troops. He
does not seem to appreciate the importance of this measure and
appears indifferent if not hostile.

U. S. GRANT, Lieutenant-General, Fortress Monroe, Va.

Major-General Halleck, Washington:

A special messenger from Sherman has just left here with his requisitions. Please have everything called for by Sherman forwarded without delay. He cannot move until the forage and subsistence called for is received.

U. S. GRANT, Lieutenant-General, Fort Monroe, Va.

Hon. E. M. Stanton, Secretary of War,

I wrote to Sherman some time ago to direct Foster to organize negro troops for garrison duty. Please say to Sherman that if Foster will go to work and organize colored troops, they can garrison the forts and islands, leaving all of his white troops for Savannah and the camp at Pocotaligo.

Friday, January 6

<u>PVT. HARVEY REID</u>, 22nd Wisconsin, In South Carolina, 3 miles from Savannah

The "Planter" steamer, which is now being used by our Division, is the one run out of Charleston harbor by her negro pilot, about two years ago, of which so much mention was made in the papers. The pilot, Robert Smalls, is now Captain of the steamer, and he seems well qualified for such a trust. Although he has been the recipient of flattering attentions that I never before supposed a negro head could withstand, he is as unostentatious and gentlemanly in his manners as a born nobleman. It seems odd to see our gold-laced, foppish staff officers consulting him with a deference and respect that they never would show to a white man if he happened to be beneath them in rank.

Captain Smalls was presented with half the steamer by the general rule for navel prizes and has either bought the other half or sold his half to the Government. I don't know which, as I have heard both stories.

<u>REV. G. S. BRADLEY</u>, Chaplain, 22nd Wisconsin, South Carolina Shore, Opposite Savannah

Perhaps it may be interesting to friends to know that we are now on the sacred soil of South Carolina, and it may further be interesting to know how we got here.

[267]

You probably remember that during the first year of the war, a negro pilot took possession of a small steamer in Charleston harbor, while the officers were on shore, got up steam, passed out directly under the guns of Sumpter and Moultrie, giving the proper signal, and then with a white flag flying, approached our fleet and turned over the steamer to Uncle Sam. The name of this pilot was Robert Small, and that of his boat, the Planter. The boat was appraised at $30,000, half of which, by an act of Congress, was given to this pilot, and he was also made captain of the boat. Captain Small is a mulatto, short, thick set, full face, bright, keen eyes, and withal a smart looking man.

The Planter is a boat of 375 tons, and has lately been undergoing $40,000 repairs at Philadelphia, so Captain Small informed me. The boat is one of the trimmest little steamers I have ever seen, and is kept in very fine order. Most of the crew are colored, the mate being white, also a few others.

The 22nd had the honor of being transported to South Carolina in the Planter, and all saw the man who at the time made such a stir in the papers.

We are probably the advance troops in the great campaign just about to commence. It is thought that we may remain here four or five weeks, but I should not be surprised if we start in two weeks.

One thing is certain, if we march through South Carolina, the people will fare no better than those of Georgia. Every soldier in the army feels a sort of hatred against this State, and consequently it will be pretty hard to restrain them.

JENNIE LEWIS, Deveaux Residence, Savannah

I am to be a teacher at the The Oglethorpe Colored School of Savannah. It will be open to young and old. Soon we will have our own building and spellers and books for everyone! Every day more and more eager faces line up to attend. All hungry to learn to read and write.

Papa is back on the Planter to carry the soldiers across the river. Soon he will have to leave here too. But he says this war will be over soon and we will go to Decatur and live there with Mama. I do not want to go back there but Papa says we will buy land and live a good life. I must look to that future day and pray for strength to do as Papa says.

Saturday, January 7

REV. JAMES T. LYNCH, Savannah, Georgia
New York Freedmen's Relief Association
My Dear Sirs:

I have been here for some days. There are a great many very intelligent colored persons in Savannah. We have been holding large meetings of the colored citizens. The interest evoked has been great, and the promise of good being done is bright.

We have secured from the Government the use of three large buildings:

"A Bryant's Negro Mart" (thus reads the sign over the door). It is a large three-story brick building. In this place slaves had been bought and sold for many years. We have found many "gems" such as handcuffs, whips and staples for typing, etc. Bills of sales of slaves by hundreds all giving a faithful description of the hellish business. This we are going to use for school purposes.

The Stiles house on Farm Street, formerly used as a rebel hospital, we have also secured for school purposes.

A large three-story brick building on the lot adjoining for a hospital for freedmen.

We have organized an Associated called the Savannah Educational association, composed of the pastors and members of the colored churches. There are five very large colored churches in this city, four of them will seat one thousand persons each. Three

[270]

have fine organs. That the colored people built such churches is astonishing. Hundreds of the colored people are joining the Association as honorary members.

We have examined some of the most intelligent of the colored young men and women to ascertain their qualifications for teaching and selected nine. This makes use of the ability and intelligence possessed by the colored people themselves, and gives them confidence and encouragement.

Refugees are continually coming in and filling up the city. I trust that your Association will soon have teachers here. Oh, how much books are needed! We could use right away a thousand more spelling-books, if we had them.

N. I. HOUSTON, Pastor, Minutes of the Third African Church at Savannah, Georgia

The war cloud seems to be passing away, and some of the scattered and wandering members have found their way back to the fold. Many Baptists who had left their homes in the upper part of the State, and had followed in the wake of the army marching through from Atlanta to this city, now locate themselves here in Savannah, seeking a place where they might find rest.

They have been welcomed and taken under watchful care of the church, until they become settled in the fold of Christ; and by these wandering Christian pilgrims the numbers in the congregation is considerably augmented. All who can properly account for themselves are welcome to share in the privileges and blessings of this old Zion of God until they could return to the church of their membership, some of whom are well known in the former days of peace.

These duties and the continuous service of our Lord in his house every evening but Saturday, and four meetings on the Sabbath, the praises of the God who has with a strong hand and outstretched arm delivered His people, is heard throughout the city and its suburbs.

Sunday, January 8

ELLEN SHERMAN, South Bend, Indiana

Dearest Cump:

This morning - the 8th - I had the happiness to receive yours to me of Christmas day. Your time must be so fully occupied that I fear to write you long letters. I am sorry you directed to me at Lancaster. You might have known I would be here when I had your consent to come. I was awaiting some communication from you directing me how to address my letters. Daily I looked for a dispatch from you but I recd none until long after you were in communication with the Authorities. Nor did you seem to avail yourself of the first opportunity to write to me.

I have given you in former letters the particulars of the dear baby's death. His sufferings were so protracted that I rejoiced to See his soul set free and mount to realms of bliss. Such lovely eyes - so bright, so intelligent, and so loving in expression - I have never beheld in mortal. None of my babies were as tender and as fond of me as he was; and it seemed to me I never loved one so fondly. Darling suffering little saint! If I succeed in working out my salvation how happily will eternity dawn upon me that restores him to my arms.

Willy is your fervent intercessor with our Saviour; I feel that Charley is mine. To see them suffer and die was my great sorrow - to know that they are secure from all danger and in perfect happiness is

[273]

my great consolation. I shall never be content or happy until you, like them, are a christian and thus may hope to be sanctified in death like them & with them rise in glory with the souls all the Redeemed the followers of the lowly Jesus.

Mr. Stanton has been exceedingly polite and kind in twice telegraphing to me that arrangements can be made at the Dept. at any time to Send me down to See you &c. &c. I know you do not want me to come. I feel our separation is one not only of location but also of mind.

I have written you very often. Believe me ever dearest your truly affectionate wife.

P.S. I am out of money entirely & need it for everything.

JENNIE LEWIS, Deveaux Residence, Savannah, Georgia

A message came to me this morning that set in motion the events of this day and finds me in my present state. It was from Manuel, the general's cook. 'Jennie: I request your assistance with a dinner the General is hosting tonight at the Green House. I need you here by noon. Will send a coach.'

I frowned as I read the message for I had planned to sign up students at the school all day. But if Manuel needs me, I thought, how can I say no?

Yet when I arrived at the generals headquarters, I found the Green house staffed in full. The women welcomed me with embraces and kisses. The men bowed and smiled and kissed my hand. Even Manuel was in a good mood, humming as he seasoned and stirred and sent us orders to chop and peel. I forgot to be annoyed that my plans had to change. I looked forward to the evening.

But as the time for serving supper came, I felt so tired it was hard for me to stand. I did my best. The General never looked at me but drank wine and smoked his cigar and told tales of our journey here and boasted about what was to come. 'We will leave for South Caroline in a day or two. There's no Army to stop me. Then, it's on to Richmond' he said, lifting his glass. Everyone cheered him on. More toasts and cheers followed. More empty bottles of wine. I leaned against a wall and thought of the big soft bed in the room upstairs. I longed to go back there and sleep.

But there was the dinner to get through and the cleaning up. Finally, all was done and put away. I went to the kitchen to say goodbye to Manuel. He brought me the coffee tray, set with a full pot and two cups and saucers. 'You know what to do with this' he said.

'It is so late. And I must get back to our room. Papa will wonder where I am.'

'He asked for you' said Manuel. 'You will sleep here tonight. We will take you home in the morning. Your room has been prepared.'

I sank into a chair and listened as Manuel talked. 'It was not me who requested you Jennie. It was him. He read in the papers from New York that his infant son has died. He's hit bad but the public will never know. Only me—and you.'

I felt a pull so strong but in two directions. I did miss being with him. I had not seen nor talked to him since Papa had returned. Not even to thank him for bringing Papa to me. But I could not longer be with him as I had before, not with Papa here.

Papa and I have not talked about the General at all but I feel he knows more than he lets on. I can not bring myself to tell him for the shame it will bring upon us all.

And yet, I longed to stay there, to sleep in my soft bed, to sleep with the General by my side.

I took the tray and climbed that winding staircase to the Generals room.

He was talking to a soldier. I stood back but the he saw me and waved me in.

'Ah, the coffee!' he said. He voice was loud, full of wine. He had removed his jacket and opened his shirt at the collar, and his red hair seemed to rise up like flames in the candlelight. He sent the soldier away and pulled me into the room. I placed the coffee tray on a table and turned to him. 'Here is your coffee, General. And good-night, then.' I started for the door.

'Good night? Why, Jennie, you must stay. Have a cup of coffee with me. Tell me what you have done in these past days. We are both so busy now, are we not?'

I poured the two cups and felt glad to tell him about the schools opening up around the city and the eager students in my classes. He asked a lot of questions. 'Well, Jennie. I think that is wonderful. Now, I have something for you.' He stood and walked to one of his closets. He pulled out the blue gown, the one I had worn when we first danced in Milledgeville. 'Your father left this when he moved you away. Here—it is yours to keep, you know.'

At the sight of the dress I no longer felt tired. How many nights had I worn it to bed and cried myself to sleep. Caroline had taken it in so that it fit like a second skin. The careful, even stitches across the fabric were so like the sister who made them. It was the only thing I had left that she had touched. I reached for it.

General Sherman smiled. 'Will you wear it now?'

He pulled me into his arms and kissed me, but I pulled back. 'I cant,' I said. He drew back and stared at me, dropping the dress. I stared at it crumpled on the floor. It was the finest thing I ever had but if he had begged me to take it I would not. I could not wear it again—for him. 'I must go.'

'Stay, Jennie. I need you tonight.'

'I cant.' I did not know what words to say but I kept talking. 'I know what you have done for me, for all of us who wanted to leave our lives as slaves and be free. You are a great man. But we cannot be like we were… any more. I am going to be a teacher.'

'You want to convert me now, too?' he shouted. 'I'll not be saved, damn it, Jennie.'

[277]

He held me by my shoulders as I turned toward the door. I pulled away, but he grabbed and pulled and yanked. We both heard the small snap as the chain around my neck broke and the heart pendant slipped to join the dress on the floor. I ran from the room and down the curved staircase. I stepped out into the night and started my long walk back here. After all of that I am here now, not sad, but feeling certain about things I had doubted before.

Soon, General Sherman will leave here. He will go North to end this cruel war. Then, he will return to his family, to his grieving wife with two sons dead. They will be a comfort to each other.

Papa wants to go back to Decatur. Fortune will go to his eyeland. I—will stay here. I have no more questions about it. I will live my new life of freedom as a teacher here in Savannah.

God help us all in the days and years to come.

Monday, January 9

ELLA GERTRUDE CLANTON THOMAS, Thomas House,

Milledgeville, Georgia

I confess to not being in the most enviable, cheerful mood possible. Tonight I have been cutting or clipping as the newspapers term it. I have just finished reading an interesting letter giving an account of the movements of the state line troops during Sherman's march through Georgia. Alluding to the evacuation of Savannah, he mentions that after our troops left the city, he could hear the shrieks of women caused by the stragglers—the skulkers of our army who had commenced to pillage and destroy. Some of them were shot by the citizens and others captured by the Yankees. Among the fine foreign items, I read with much interest an account of great works which are being done in Europe. "A railway through the alps"--… There they are employing their God given intellect to ennoble and elevate—to civilize their race—and we in God's name what are we doing? Striving to defend ourselves against our brethren who would butcher us—annihilate us if they could.

War is a terrible demon. It does not elevate—it debases. It does not lift heavenward—it crushes into the dust. I lose faith in humanity when I see such efforts to sink the nobler better part of man's nature in an effort to exterminate the white race at the South in order to elevate the Negro race to a position which I doubt their ability to fill—

[279]

The time will come when Southern women will be avenged--
. Let this war cease with the abolition of slavery and I wish for the
women of the North no worse fate than will befall them. Their
husbands already prepare them for the bitter cup of humiliation
which they will be compelled to drink to the dregs-- General
Kilpatrick spent a night in Waynesboro. His headquarters were at
Mrs. Dr. Carter's. He demanded that the best bed room in the house
should be prepared for himself and a good looking Negro girl whom
he had traveling with him. A seat at the table was furnished her--
The officers deferential in their manner to her while thus publicly
insulting Mrs. Carter in her own house. Lolling indolently in a
rocking chair the girl awaits the entrance of the Gen. "What not
retired yet Nellie?" is his salutation. "Not until your majesty returns"
is her reply--. Take that scene Mrs. Kilpatrick as a reward for
encouraging your husband to come amongst us.

I don't know why it is but that man Sherman has interested
me very much—perhaps it is upon the principle that all women
admire successful courage and that Gen Sherman has proven himself
to be a very brave man there can be no doubt. Our enemy as he is, I
can imagine that his wife loves him. I read that his baby six months
old had died—I could not be glad of it although his men in their
eager search after hidden treasure opened the graves of babies that
had just been buried and left the coffins on the brink of the grave.

At one time just after Sherman passed through, I wrote Mrs.
Sherman a letter which I intended having published under the head

of Personal in one of the Richmond papers—I did not send it and now that I have read of the recent death of her baby I am glad that I did not. Woman's nature is the same the world over. Northern women are colder in their temperature than our warm hearted children of the sun but I know that amongst the jubilee attendant upon her husband's "Christmas present" to Lincoln, I could send Mrs. Sherman "a New Year's gift" which would dim and make hollow and empty the mirth by which he is surrounded.

J. G. FOSTER, Major General, Commanding, Headquarters Department Of The South, Hilton Head, S. C.

Maj. Gen. H. W. Halleck, Chief of Staff, Armies of the United States:

General: I have the honor to acknowledge the receipt of your letter of the 31st ultimo in regard to the organization of all the able-bodied negroes brought in by General Sherman's army to this department for service in this department, and beg leave to express my gratification at this decision, because I need troops for garrison duty very much, and I can soon make these men available for that duty. I have several officers whose military excellence and gallantry fully entitle them to promotion to be officers in the new regiments. I anticipate no difficulty whatever in organizing these regiments and in obtaining most excellent officers. I will report the appointments, as soon as made, for confirmation by the President.

In obedience to your direction, as soon as the letter was received I submitted it to General Sherman, who desired that I might carry out the order as soon as he moved and the city was turned over to my command. Until such time he desired the services of all the negro men in the quartermaster's department in loading and unloading vessels and other preparations for a forward movement.

Very respectfully, your obedient servant

[282]

O. O. HOWARD, Major-General, Hdqrs. Department and
Army Of The Tennessee, Beaufort, S. C.

Hon. E. M. Stanton, Secretary of War:

SIR: I have allowed the corps commanders of this army to raise a colored regiment each for pioneer work. The Seventeenth Corps has succeeded in raising about 800 men. I respectfully request the same authority to appoint officers for these organizations as that received by the commanding general Department of the South. The regimental organization is superior to the ordinary pioneer force, commanded by detailed officers, and is much better in point of economy.

Respectfully

W. T. SHERMAN, Maj. Genl., Headquarters, Military
Division of the Mississippi, Savannah

Hon. S. P. Chase, Washington D.C.

My Dear Sir,

I feel very much flattered by the notice you take of me, and none the less because you overhaul me in the Negro question. I mean no unkindness to the Negro in the mere words of my hasty dispatch announcing my arrival on the Coast. The only real failures, in a military sense, I have sustained in my military administration have been the expedition of Smith and Sturgis, both resulting from their encumbering their columns with refugees. (negros) If you can understand the nature of a military column in an enemy's country, with its long train of wagons, you will see at once that a crowd of negros, men women and children, old & young, are a dangerous impediment.

On approaching Savannah I had at least 20,000 negros, clogging my roads, and eating up our subsistence. Instead of finding abundance here, I found nothing and had to depend on my wagons till I opened a way for vessels and even to this day my men have been on short rations and my horses are failing. The same number of white refugees would have been a military weakness. Now you Know that military success is what the nation wants, and it is risked by the crowds of helpless negros that flock after our armies. My negro constituents of Georgia would resent the idea of my being inimical to them, they regard me as a second Moses or Aaron. I treat them as free, and have as much trouble to protect them against the avaricious recruiting agents of New England States as against their former masters. You can hardly realize this, but it is true.

I have conducted to freedom & asylum hundreds of thousands and have aided them to obtain employment and houses. Every negro who is fit for a soldier and is willing is invariably allowed to join a Negro Regiment, but I do oppose and rightfully too, the forcing of negros as soldiers. You cannot Know the acts and devices to which base white men resort to secure negro soldiers, not to aid us to fight, but to get bounties for their own pockets, and to diminish their quotas at home.

Our Quartermaster and commissary can give employment to every negro (able bodied) whom we obtain, and he protests against my parting with them for other purposes, as it forces him to use my veteran white troops to unload vessels, and do work for which he prefers the negro. If the President prefers to minister to the one idea of negro Equality, rather than military success, which as a major involves the minor, he should remove me, for I am so constituted that I cannot honestly sacrifice the security and Success of my army to any minor cause.

Of course I have nothing to do with the Status of the Negro after war. That is the law making power, but if my opinion were consulted I would Say that the negro should be a free race, but not put on an equality with the whites. My Knowledge of them is practical, and the effect of equality is illustrated in the character of the Mixed race in Mexico and South America. Indeed it appears to me that the right of suffrage in our Country should be rather abridged than enlarged.

But these are all matters subordinate to the issues of this war, which can alone be determined by war, and it depends on good armies, of the best possible material and best disciplined, and these points engross my entire thoughts.

With sincere respect & esteem

Wednesday, January 11

<u>W. T. SHERMAN</u>, Headquarters Military Division of the
Mississippi, Savannah

Arrived today at Savannah a revenue-cutter, having on board
Simeon Draper, Esq., of New York City, the Hon. E. M. Stanton,
Secretary of War, Quartermaster-General Meigs, Adjutant-General
Townsend, and a retinue of civilians, who has come down from the
North to regulate the civil affairs of Savannah.

<u>JENNIE LEWIS</u>, Deveaux Residence, Savannah

General Sherman brought some men from Washington to our
school today. He wished to show what a wonderful school we have
gotten started. "The classes increase in size every day. They need
books, paper, pencils, chalk, and teachers. They are hungry to learn,
Sir.' Would he have known about the school but for me? Yet he
looked past me as if I were not there.

He reached down to play with the little ones, bouncing them
in his arms, letting them pull his red beard. They all loved him. All
the children do. He treats them as equals. Yet for me, he has not
even a blink. I do not know what I have done to deserve this. I
remember the first time he winked at me in public, and said my
name and helped hand out food to the colored people. I remember
how he held me and danced in a ballroom full of –colored people. I
remember the nights we sat at the campfire and talked and learned

[286]

about each others lives. He held me when I cried for Caroline and Jake. And I held him when he cried for his son, Willy. But today, with these men from Washington, he does not know me.

The general was angry when I told him I would no longer stay in his rooms, nor even come to see him there. He must still be so. Why is he angry when he always told me 'Jennie, you're free now. No one can force you to do what you dont want to do.' I dont know and I may never know. Any day now, General Sherman will pull his mighty army out of Savannah, and that will be that. He will go home a famous war hero. We will never see each other again. But can we forget the past weeks together and the parts of our lives we have given each other? We can not. He can pretend not to see me, but he will never forget me.

Papa sailed away this morning. He promised he would return with Mama 'when this cruel war is over.' He gave me a book to read 'Narrative of the Life of Frederick Douglass, An American Slave.' Imagine! A whole book about a slave who made himself free! But I find I am too tired to read a word tonight. The slights and departures of the day have made me ill.

W. T. SHERMAN, Major-General, Headquarters Military
Division of the Mississippi, In the Field Savannah
Major-General Halleck, My Dear Friend:
I received yours of January 1 about the "negro." Since Mr. Stanton got here we have talked over all matters freely, and I deeply

regret that I am threatened with that curse to all peace and comfort—popularity; but I trust to bad luck enough in the future to cure that, for I know enough of "the people" to feel that a single mistake made by some of my subordinates will tumble down my fame into infamy.

But the nigger? Why, in God's name, can't sensible men let him alone? When the people of the South tried to rule us through the negro, and became insolent, we cast them down, and on that question we are strong and unanimous. Neither cotton, the negro, nor any single interest or class should govern us.

But I fear, if you be right, that the power behind the throne is growing, somebody must meet it or we are again involved in war with another class of fanatics. Mr. Lincoln has boldly and well met the one attack, now let him meet the other.

If it be insisted that I shall so conduct my operations that the negro alone is consulted, of course I will be defeated, and then where will be Sambo?

Don't military success imply the safety of Sambo and vice versa? Of course that cock-and-bull story of my turning back negroes that Wheeler might kill them is all humbug. I turned nobody back. Jeff. C. Davis did at Ebenezer Creek forbid certain plantation slaves—old men, women, and children—to follow his column; but they would come along and he took up his pontoon bridge, not because he wanted to leave them, but because he wanted his bridge.

He and Slocum both tell me that they don't believe Wheeler killed one of them. Slocum's column (30,000) reports 17,000 negroes. Now, with 1,200 wagons and the necessary impedimenta of an army, overloaded with two-thirds negroes, five-sixths of whom are helpless, and a large proportion of them babies and small children, had I encountered an enemy of respectable strength defeat would have been certain.

Tell the President that in such an event, defeat would have cost him ten thousand times the effort to overcome that it now will meet this new and growing pressure.

I know the fact that all natural emotions swing as the pendulum. These southrons pulled Sambo's pendulum so far over that the danger is it will on its return jump off its pivot. There are certain people who will find fault, and they can always get the pretext; but, thank God, I am not running for an office, and am not concerned because the rising generation will believe that I burned 500 niggers at one pop in Atlanta, or any such nonsense. I profess to be the best kind of a friend to Sambo, and think that on such a question Sambo should be consulted.

They gather round me in crowds, and I can't find out whether I am Moses or Aaron, or which of the prophets; but surely I am rated as one of the congregation, and it is hard to tell in what sense I am most appreciated by Sambo—in saving him from his master, or the new master that threatens him with a new species of slavery. I mean State recruiting agents. Poor negro—Lo, the poor Indian! Of course, sensible men understand such humbug, but some power must be

[289]

invested in our Government to check these wild oscillations of public opinion.

The South deserves all she has got for her injustice to the negro, but that is no reason why we should go to the other extreme.

I do and will do the best I can for negroes, and feel sure that the problem is solving itself slowly and naturally. It needs nothing more than our fostering care. I thank you for the kind hint and will heed it so far as mere appearances go, but, not being dependent on votes, I can afford to act, as far as my influence goes, as a fly wheel instead of a mainspring.

With respect, &c., yours

Thursday, January 12

MINUTES OF AN INTERVIEW BETWEEN THE COLORED MINISTERS AND CHURCH OFFICERS AT SAVANNAH WITH THE SECRETARY OF WAR AND MAJOR-GEN. SHERMAN, Headquarters Of Maj.-Gen. Sherman, Savannah—8 P.M.

On the evening of Thursday, the 12th day of January, 1865, the following persons of African descent met by appointment to hold an interview with Edwin M. Stanton, Secretary of War, and Major-Gen. Sherman, to have a conference upon matters relating to the freedmen of the State of Georgia, to-wit:

One: William J. Campbell, aged 51 years, born in Savannah, slave until 1849, and then liberated by will of his mistress, Mrs. May Maxwell. For ten years pastor of the 1st Baptist Church of Savannah, numbering about 1,800 members. Average congregation, 1,900. The church property belonging to the congregation. Trustees white. Worth $18,000.

Two: John Cox, aged fifty-eight years, born in Savannah; slave until 1849, when he bought his freedom for $1,100. Pastor of the 2d African Baptist Church. In the ministry fifteen years. Congregation 1,222 persons. Church property worth $10,000, belonging to the congregation.

Three: Ulysses L. Houston, aged forty-one years, born in Grahamsville, S.C.; slave until the Union army entered Savannah.

[291]

Owned by Moses Henderson, Savannah, and pastor of Third African Baptist Church. Congregation numbering 400. Church property worth $5,000; belongs to congregation. In the ministry about eight years.

Four: William Bentley, aged 72 years, born in Savannah, slave until 25 years of age, when his master, John Waters, emancipated him by will. Pastor of Andrew's Chapel, Methodist Episcopal Church—only one of that denomination in Savannah; congregation numbering 360 members; church property worth about $20,000, and is owned by the congregation; been in the ministry about twenty years; a member of Georgia Conference.

Five: Charles Bradwell, aged 40 years, born in Liberty County, Ga.; slave until 1851; emancipated by will of his master, J. L. Bradwell. Local preacher in charge of the Methodist Episcopal congregation (Andrew's Chapel) in the absence of the minister; in the ministry 10 years.

Six: William Gaines, aged 41 years; born in Wills Co., Ga. Slave until the Union forces freed him. Owned by Robert Toombs, formerly United States Senator, and his brother, Gabriel Toombs, local preacher of the M.E. Church (Andrew's Chapel.) In the ministry 16 years.

Seven: James Hill, aged 52 years; born in Bryan Co., Ga. Slave up to the time the Union army came in. Owned by H. F. Willings, of Savannah. In the ministry 16 years.

Eight: Glasgon Taylor, aged 72 years, born in Wilkes County, Ga. Slave until the Union army came; owned by A. P. Wetter. Is a local preacher of the M.E. Church (Andrew's Chapel.) In the ministry 35 years.

Nine: Garrison Frazier, aged 67 years, born in Granville County, N.C. Slave until eight years ago, when he bought himself and wife, paying $1,000 in gold and silver. Is an ordained minister in the Baptist Church, but, his health failing, has now charge of no congregation. Has been in the ministry 35 years.

Ten: James Mills, aged 56 years, born in Savannah; free-born, and is a licensed preacher of the first Baptist Church. Has been eight years in the ministry.

Eleven: Abraham Burke, aged 48 years, born in Bryan County, Ga. Slave until 20 years ago, when he bought himself for $800. Has been in the ministry about 10 years.

Twelve: Arthur Wardell, aged 44 years, born in Liberty County, Ga. Slave until freed by the Union army. Owned by A. A. Solomons, Savannah, and is a licensed minister in the Baptist Church. Has been in the ministry 6 years.

Thirteen: Alexander Harris, aged 47 years, born in Savannah; free born. Licensed minister of Third African Baptist Church. Licensed about one month ago.

Fourteen: Andrew Neal, aged 61 years, born in Savannah, slave until the Union army liberated him. Owned by Mr. Wm.

Gibbons, and has been deacon in the Third Baptist Church for 10 years.

Fifteen: Jas. Porter, aged 39 years, born in Charleston, South Carolina; free-born, his mother having purchased her freedom. Is lay-reader and president of the board of wardens and vestry of St. Stephen's Protestant Episcopal Colored Church in Savannah. Has been in communion 9 years. The congregation numbers about 200 persons. The church property is worth about $10,000, and is owned by the congregation.

Sixteen: Adolphus Delmotte, aged 28 years, born in Savannah; free born. Is a licensed minister of the Missionary Baptist Church of Milledgeville. Congregation numbering about 300 or 400 persons. Has been in the ministry about two years.

Seventeen: Jacob Godfrey, aged 57 years, born in Marion, S.C. Slave until the Union army freed him; owned by James E. Godfrey—Methodist preacher now in the Rebel army. Is a class-leader and steward of Andrew's Chapel since 1836.

Eighteen: John Johnson, aged 51 years, born in Bryan County, Georgia. Slave up to the time the Union army came here; owned by W. W. Lincoln of Savannah. Is class-leader and treasurer of Andrew's Chapel for sixteen years.

Nineteen: Robt. N. Taylor, aged 51 years, born in Wilkes Co., Ga. Slave to the time the Union army came. Was owned by Augustus P. Welter, Savannah, and is class-leader in Andrew's Chapel for nine years.

[294]

Twenty: James. Lynch, aged 26 years, born in Baltimore, Md.; free-born. Is presiding elder of the M.E. Church and missionary to the department of the South. Has been seven years in the ministry and two years in the South.

Garrison Frazier being chosen by the persons present to express their common sentiments upon the matters of inquiry, makes answers to inquiries as follows:

First: State what your understanding is in regard to the acts of Congress and President Lincoln's [Emancipation] proclamation, touching the condition of the colored people in the Rebel States.

Answer—So far as I understand President Lincoln's proclamation to the Rebellious States, it is, that if they would lay down their arms and submit to the laws of the United States before the first of January, 1863, all should be well; but if they did not, then all the slaves in the Rebel States should be free henceforth and forever. That is what I understood.

Second—State what you understand by Slavery and the freedom that was to be given by the President's proclamation.

Answer—Slavery is, receiving by irresistible power the work of another man, and not by his consent. The freedom, as I understand it, promised by the proclamation, is taking us from under the yoke of bondage, and placing us where we could reap the fruit of our own labor, take care of ourselves and assist the Government in maintaining our freedom.

Third: State in what manner you think you can take care of yourselves, and how can you best assist the Government in maintaining your freedom.

Answer: The way we can best take care of ourselves is to have land, and turn it and till it by our own labor—that is, by the labor of the women and children and old men; and we can soon maintain ourselves and have something to spare. And to assist the Government, the young men should enlist in the service of the Government, and serve in such manner as they may be wanted. (The Rebels told us that they piled them up and made batteries of them, and sold them to Cuba; but we don't believe that.) We want to be placed on land until we are able to buy it and make it our own.

Fourth: State in what manner you would rather live—whether scattered among the whites or in colonies by yourselves.

Answer: I would prefer to live by ourselves, for there is a prejudice against us in the South that will take years to get over; but I do not know that I can answer for my brethren. [Mr. Lynch says he thinks they should not be separated, but live together. All the other persons present, being questioned one by one, answer that they agree with Brother Frazier.]

Fifth: Do you think that there is intelligence enough among the slaves of the South to maintain themselves under the Government of the United States and the equal protection of its laws, and maintain good and peaceable relations among yourselves and with your neighbors?

[296]

Answer—I think there is sufficient intelligence among us to do so.

Sixth—State what is the feeling of the black population of the South toward the Government of the United States; what is the understanding in respect to the present war—its causes and object, and their disposition to aid either side. State fully your views.

Answer—I think you will find there are thousands that are willing to make any sacrifice to assist the Government of the United States, while there are also many that are not willing to take up arms. I do not suppose there are a dozen men that are opposed to the Government. I understand, as to the war, that the South is the aggressor. President Lincoln was elected President by a majority of the United States, which guaranteed him the right of holding the office and exercising that right over the whole United States. The South, without knowing what he would do, rebelled. The war was commenced by the Rebels before he came into office. The object of the war was not at first to give the slaves their freedom, but the sole object of the war was at first to bring the rebellious States back into the Union and their loyalty to the laws of the United States. Afterward, knowing the value set on the slaves by the Rebels, the President thought that his proclamation would stimulate them to lay down their arms, reduce them to obedience, and help to bring back the Rebel States; and their not doing so has now made the freedom of the slaves a part of the war. It is my opinion that there is not a man in this city that could be started to help the Rebels one inch, for that would be suicide. There were two black men left with the Rebels because they had taken an active part for the Rebels, and thought something might befall them if they stayed behind; but there is not another man. If the prayers that have gone up for the Union army could be read out, you would not get through them these two weeks.

Seventh: State whether the sentiments you now express are those only of the colored people in the city; or do they extend to the colored population through the country? and what are your means of knowing the sentiments of those living in the country?

Answer: I think the sentiments are the same among the colored people of the State. My opinion is formed by personal communication in the course of my ministry, and also from the thousands that followed the Union army, leaving their homes and undergoing suffering. I did not think there would be so many; the number surpassed my expectation.

Eighth: If the Rebel leaders were to arm the slaves, what would be its effect?

Answer: I think they would fight as long as they were before the bayonet, and just as soon as soon as they could get away, they would desert, in my opinion.

Ninth: What, in your opinion, is the feeling of the colored people about enlisting and serving as soldiers of the United States? and what kind of military service do they prefer?

Answer: A large number have gone as soldiers to Port Royal [S.C.] to be drilled and put in the service; and I think there are thousands of the young men that would enlist. There is something about them that perhaps is wrong. They have suffered so long from the Rebels that they want to shoulder the musket. Others want to go into the Quartermaster's or Commissary's service.

Tenth: Do you understand the mode of enlistments of colored persons in the Rebel States by State agents under the Act of Congress? If yea, state what your understanding is.

Answer: My understanding is, that colored persons enlisted by State agents are enlisted as substitutes, and give credit to the States, and do not swell the army, because every black man enlisted by a State agent leaves a white man at home; and, also, that larger bounties are given or promised by State agents than are given by the States. The great object should be to push through this Rebellion the shortest way, and there seems to be something wanting in the enlistment by State agents, for it don't strengthen the army, but takes one away for every colored man enlisted.

Eleventh: State what, in your opinion, is the best way to enlist colored men for soldiers.

Answer: I think, sir, that all compulsory operations should be put a stop to. The ministers would talk to them, and the young men would enlist. It is my opinion that it would be far better for the State agents to stay at home, and the enlistments to be made for the United States under the direction of Gen. Sherman.

[299]

In the absence of Gen. Sherman, the following question was asked:

Twelfth: State what is the feeling of the colored people in regard to Gen. Sherman; and how far do they regard his sentiments and actions as friendly to their rights and interests, or otherwise?

Answer: We looked upon Gen. Sherman prior to his arrival as a man in the Providence of God specially set apart to accomplish this work, and we unanimously feel inexpressible gratitude to him, looking upon him as a man that should be honored for the faithful performance of his duty. Some of us called upon him immediately upon his arrival, and it is probable he would not meet the Secretary with more courtesy than he met us. His conduct and deportment toward us characterized him as a friend and a gentleman. We have confidence in Gen. Sherman, and think that what concerns us could not be under better hands. This is our opinion now from the short acquaintance and interest we have had. (Mr. Lynch states that with his limited acquaintance with Gen. Sherman, he is unwilling to express an opinion. All others present declare their agreement with Mr. Frazier about Gen. Sherman.)

Friday, January 13

<u>BREVET MAJOR GEORGE WARD NICHOLS</u>, Savannah

A memorable interview has taken place here between the Secretary of War and the colored clergymen of the city. These good men represented almost every religious denomination. I was present during a portion of the interview, which occurred at General Sherman's headquarters, and I shall never forget the impressive spectacle. Mr. Stanton sat at a table, asking questions and making notes of the replies; now and then putting down his pen and adjusting his spectacles in a surprised way, as if he could not comprehend how these men came to possess such a clear consciousness of the merits of the questions involved in the war. Their replies were so shrewd, so wise, so comprehensive, that, as Mr. Stanton afterward observed, they understood and could state the principles of this question "as well as any member of the Cabinet."

General Sherman stood near the fireplace, occasionally walking to and fro, or making some pregnant suggestion, which would call forth new thoughts or start another train of remark.

In one corner of the room, watching with curious and interested gaze this singular interview, stood General Townsond, a gentleman who has for many years fulfilled with rare justness and courtesy the onerous duties of Adjutant General of the United States Army.

The black clergymen, fifteen or twenty in number, were grouped about the room, sitting and standing. With all due respect for the clerical profession, I doubt if twenty white ministers of the Gospel could have been called together so suddenly out of one of our Northern cities (certainly not in the South) who could represent so much common sense and intelligence as these men. Nor would an average score of clergymen present an array of nobler heads. In an artistic sense, the negroes would certainly have the advantage of color.

This conference lasted until the small hours of the morning, when the visitors were sent home with words of kindness and counsel.

It is surprising to all of us to see how admirably the negroes of the city behave, in view of their knowledge that our coming sets them at liberty from the control of their masters. They take no advantage of their freedom in any way in their conduct to those who ill treated them in former days, except that they leave them for the sake of obtaining remunerative employment. They put on no "airs," as the Southern people term it, but are uniformly quiet and respectful. One of them said to me:

"We don't wish to do any thing wrong. We know you came here to set us free; we expect you to tell us what to do, and we shall act in accordance with that. Some of these masters have treated us shamefully, whipped, and imprisoned, and sold us about; but we don't wish to be revenged on them. The Bible says that we must

[302]

forgive our enemies. They have been our enemies, and we forgive them. Thank God! we are slaves no longer."

It is shameful that the negro, even in a state of freedom, can not escape the cupidity and persecution of the white man. Since we have been here, negro men have rushed frightened to General Sherman's headquarters begging for protection from the "land-sharks," who, it appears, have seized all the able-bodied negroes they could lay their hands upon, and locked them up until they could be mustered into the service. The wretches who perpetrate this outrage take the names of these men and the evidence of their enlistment to the North, and sell them as substitutes for the army. General Sherman was exceedingly angry, and at once gave orders to have the negroes released, threatened the recruiting agents with severe punishment if violence was again used, and assured the negroes that they were free to go where they liked for work, and that they could become soldiers if they choose, but that they should not be forced into the army.

W. T. SHERMAN, Headquarters Military Division of the Mississippi, Savannah

Mr. Stanton talked to me a great deal about the negroes, the former slaves, and I told him of many interesting incidents, illustrating their simple character and faith in our arms and progress. He inquired particularly about General Jeff. C. Davis, who, he said, was a Democrat, and hostile to the negro. I assured him that General

Davis was an excellent soldier, and I did not believe he had any hostility to the negro; that in our army we had no negro soldiers, and, as a rule, we preferred white soldiers, but that we employed a large force of them as servants, teamster, and pioneers, who had rendered admirable service.

He then showed me a newspaper account of General Davis taking up his pontoon-bridge across Ebenezer Creek, leaving sleeping negro men, women, and children, on the other side, to be slaughtered by Wheeler's cavalry. I had heard such a rumor, and advised Mr. Stanton, before becoming prejudiced, to allow me to send for General Davis, which he did, and General Davis explained the matter to his entire satisfaction. The truth was, that, as we approached the seaboard, the freedmen in droves, old and young, followed the several columns to reach a place of safety. It so happened that General Davis's route into Savannah followed what was known as the "River-road," and he had to make constant use of his pontoon-train—the head of his column reaching some deep, impassable creek before the rear was fairly over another. He had occasionally to use the pontoons both day and night. On the occasion referred to, the bridge was taken up from Ebenezer Creek while some of the camp-followers remained asleep on the farther side, and these were picked up by Wheeler's cavalry. Some of them, in their fright, were drowned in trying to swim over, and others may have been cruelly killed by Wheeler's men, but this was a mere supposition.

At all events, the same thing might have resulted to General Howard, or to any other of the many most humane commanders who filled the army. General Jeff. C. Davis was strictly a soldier, and doubtless hated to have his wagons and columns encumbered by these poor negroes, for whom we all feel sympathy, but a sympathy of a different sort from that of Mr. Stanton, which is not of pure humanity, but of politics.

The negro question is beginning to loom up among the political eventualities of the day, and many foresee that not only will the slaves secure their freedom, but that they will also have votes.

Saturday, January 14

<u>CAPT. DAVID P. CONYNGHAM</u>, War Correspondent,

Observations in Savannah

Some northern philanthropists are for extending the franchise to the emancipated negroes. If they do so, be assured they are only throwing so many votes into the hands of the planter, to enable him to reestablish the power of the land-ocracy, and restore the political status of the south.

Many colored folks, no doubt, understand the importance of the franchise; but with four fifths of them it will be as it was with the old nigger, who, when asked would he not take an oath to support the Constitution, replied, scratching his woolly pate, "By de gor, massa, me hab no dejection to support her; times dredful hard, massa; hab 'nuff to do to support the ole 'oman and de children, I s'pect."

FREEDMEN in Savannah

"It's de white man's turn ter labor now. Whites will no longer own all the land, fur the Gouvernment is gwine ter give ev'ry nigger forty acre of lan and a mule."

"Shut yer mouth, Amos. The Gouvernment ain't for giving no land to we.'

"Well it sure looks like the Gouvernment would give us part of our Maser's lan 'cause ev'rything he had or owned the Slaves made it for him."

"That the gospel truth, Amos."

"Shore it is. They oughten to give us land and de vote too!"

Sunday, January 15

CAPT. GEORGE W. PEPPER, Headquarters, 14th Corps,

Savannah, Georgia

I attended a meeting of colored people in the Baptist Church today. The building was packed to its utmost capacity, and hundreds stood during the whole evening, while hundreds of others came and went away, being unable to find even a place to stand. The meeting was opened by one of the brethren in a prayer of great pathos and rare power. He paused in the midst of his supplications and offered up a thrilling supplication for the great army that had delivered them. In a strain of rude but hearty eloquence, he thanked God that the black people were free, and forever free. The whole congregation here gave vent to their joyous emotions, in bursts of: Glory to God! Hallelujah! Praise his name!

The following hymn was read and sang with wonderful power:

Blow ye the trumpet, blow, The gladly solemn sound,

Let all the nations know The year of jubilee has come.

The effect of this stirring poetry on the assembly was thrilling. The elder, who read the hymn, when he came to the words: The year of jubilee is come! was so overwhelmed with emotion, that it was impossible for him to proceed, The audience caught the magical influence, and then a scene ensued which baffles

[308]

description. All classes, black and white, old slave owners, and the soldiers of the army were alike affected.

That staunch patriot and eloquent minister, Mansfield French, well known in Ohio, as the friend of the negro, was the principal speaker. He called the attention of the emancipated to the duties and responsibilities devolving upon them in their present position. He recommended them to cultivate habits of honesty, purity, thrift and enterprise; admonishing them of the necessity of industry on their part; advising them to love their old masters, and not cherish feelings of revenge.

At every mention of the Union, and Liberty, and the names of Lincoln and Sherman, the walls almost trembled beneath the thunder which followed. When the orator declared the re-election of Mr. Lincoln as the guarantee of their freedom for all time, the vast gathering rose to their feet, and with shouts and tears, returned thanks to Almighty God. Never did the painter find a nobler sight for his pencil than the spontaneous uprising of that liberated people. What a lofty ambition for one man to be the emancipator of the oppressed!

History, who keeps a record of events, will hand down the name of Abraham Lincoln to posterity on her brightest page. Our hearts yearn to thee, noble patriot. We are lifted up in wonder and admiration; when we see thy cheerful endurance, thy uncomplaining spirit; we respect and honor thee. Brother French electrified the multitude by earnest outbursts of glowing patriotism, which was received with cheer upon cheer. But it is useless to attempt to convey any adequate idea of the great meeting held in the Baptist Church. The colored population of Savannah send greeting, a solid, enthusiastic greeting to their brethren in other States and cities throughout the length and breadth of the land, and ere long, we trust and expect similar meetings will be held everywhere.

JENNIE LEWIS, Deveaux Residence, Savannah

General Rufus Saxton read the Presidents proclamation at the meeting tonight. I will always remember standing outside Second African Baptist Church on this windy, cold night, with thousands of Negroes warming the night with cheers, hugs, crying and laughing, and shouts of joy when he read the words 'thenceforward, and forever free'. Our hearts swelled, our voices rose into the night. I looked up to see Papa crying and I dare not ask whether they were tears of joy or of sadness, for as glad as we are, we are only half of our family.

But there we stood, Papa and I, and so many who made this journey to this place. I thought, the whole world will know us because of this moment. For ever now, people will know that we came to this holy city, on this holy night, to shout to the world, after hundreds of years of being silence as we were sold away and worked to death and beaten and stolen from, after lifetimes of bowing our heads, we now hold them up to the sky and shout to the world,

Thenceforward and Forever Free! And I know that is the moment I felt the first flutter of life within me.

Monday, January 16

L. M. DAYTON, Assistant Adjutant-General, By order of
MAJOR-GENERAL W. T. SHERMAN, Headquarters Military
Division Of The Mississippi, Savannah, Georgia,
SPECIAL FIELD ORDERS, No. 15

1. The islands from Charleston south, the abandoned rice-
fields along the rivers for thirty miles back from the sea, and the
country bordering the St. John's River, Florida, are reserved and set
apart for the settlement of the negroes now made free by the acts of
war and the proclamation of the President of the United States.

2. At Beaufort, Hilton Head, Savannah, Fernandina, St.
Augustine, and Jacksonville, the blacks may remain in their chosen
or accustomed vocations; but on the islands, and in the settlements
hereafter to be established, no white person whatever, unless military
officers and soldiers detailed for duty, will be permitted to reside;
and the sole and exclusive management of affairs will be left to the
freed people themselves, subject only to the United States military
authority, and the acts of Congress. By the laws of war, and orders of
the President of the United States, the negro is free, and must be
dealt with as such. He cannot be subjected to conscription, or forced
military service, save by the written orders of the highest military
authority of the department, under such regulations as the President
or Congress may prescribe. Domestic servants, blacksmiths,
carpenters, and other mechanics, will be free to select their own

work and residence, but the young and able-bodied negroes must be encouraged to enlist as soldiery in the service of the United States, to contribute their share toward maintaining their own freedom, and securing their rights as citizens of the United States. Negroes so enlisted will be organized into companies, battalions, and regiments, under the orders of the United States military authorities, and will be paid, fed, and clothed; according to law. The bounties paid on enlistment may, with the consent of the recruit, go to assist his family and settlement in procuring agricultural implements, seed, tools, boots, clothing, and other articles necessary for their livelihood.

3. Whenever three respectable negroes, heads of families, shall desire to settle on land, and shall have selected for that purpose an island or a locality clearly defined within the limits above designated, the Inspector of Settlements and Plantations will himself, or, by such subordinate officer as he may appoint, give them a license to settle such island or district, and afford them such assistance as he can to enable them to establish a peaceable agricultural settlement. The three parties named will subdivide the land, under the supervision of the inspector, among themselves, and such others as may choose to settle near them, so that each family shall have a plot of not more than forty acres of tillable ground....

Tuesday, January 17

W. T. SHERMAN, Headquarters Military Division of the

Mississippi,

In the Field Savannah

Dearest Ellen,

Mr. Stanton has been here and is cured of that Negro nonsense which arises not from a love of the negro but a desire to Dodge Service. Mr. Chase & others have written to me to modify my opinions but you Know I cannot for if I attempt the part of hypocrite it could break out at each Sentence. I want soldiers made of the best bone & muscle in the land and won't attempt military feats with doubtful materials. I have said that Slavery is dead and the Negro free and want him treated as free & not hunted & badgered to make a soldier of when his family is left back on the Plantations. I am right & won't Change.

As to myself don't distress as I have been and Still am. You may rest assured I have given death a fair study, and fear it but little. I fear somewhat your mind will settle into the "Religio Melancholia," which be assured is not of divine inspiration, but rather a morbid state not natural or healthful.

It may be some days yet before I dive again beneath the Surface to turn up again in Some mysterious place. I have a clear perception of the move, but take it for granted that Lee will not let

[314]

me walk over the track without making me sustain some loss. Of course my course will be north.

ELLEN SHERMAN, South Bend, Indiana

Dear Cump,

I have not written to you for nearly a week, dearest Cump, nor have I heard from you for more than that length of time. For several days past I have been exceedingly unwell. Until this moment I thought it no use to send letters to you now but I have just seen in the papers a notice that your Staff leave Louisville tomorrow to join you via Savannah. I have not had a letter from you since you heard from me. I wrote you very often but I fear my letters did not reach you.

Mr. Hunter Mr. Talmadge & Mr. Brasee are the Committee that has put the idea in motion of presenting you a homestead, political office, &c. I have not yet heard the result of the meeting which was held in Columbus on the 11th inst.

May God continue his mercy to you - ever your truly affectionate wife

JENNIE LEWIS, Deveaux Residence, Savannah

The young ladies in town—black and white—are in a state of great excitement. General Sherman's army is sailing away from here, but Negro soldiers are pouring into the city, filling the streets with marching bands and drills. They look so grand in there Union

[315]

blue. We are all glad to see them. They will be welcome in every Negro home.

The Army is leaving but the general is still here. If he will see me once more. I have news for him that he may want to know before he leaves Savannah – and me – for good.

Wednesday, January 18

<u>PVT. THEODORE UPSON</u>, 100 Indiana, Onboard ship

We are on a transport. We have had some fun. We have seen several Negro Regiments arriving here. They make pretty good looking soldiers but our boys dont think much of them. They still say this is a White Mans War.

<u>MAJ. JAMES A. CONNOLLY</u>, 123rd Illinois Infantry, In the Field, Pocotaligo,
South Carolina

I have received yours of January 6th, and that is the second letter I have had from you since reaching this city. I have no idea whether you get my letters or not; I hope you do though for I know too well what it is to be waiting and watching and hoping for letters, while days and weeks roll away without bringing any tidings from home.

I enclose a copy of a letter which I wrote to the Member of Congress elect from my district in Illinois, in regard to the manner in which General treated fugitive negroes during our late campaign. I also gave General Baird a copy of the letter, and he sent it to New York, and he told me a few days ago that the substance of it has been published in the New York Tribune.

He also told me that the substance of the letter was sent to Stanton, Secretary of War, and that a few days ago, when Stanton came down here, he brought it with him and called on General Davis to answer the statements of the letter in writing. My name is not connected with it here, and I don't want it to be, unless the matter comes before the military committee of the Senate, and then I don't care, for I know all the officers whose names I have mentioned will corroborate my statements of fact.

I shall leave Savannah very favorably impressed with it as a city, but I don't care how soon we get over into South Carolina, for I want to see the long deferred chastisement begin. If we don't purify South Carolina it will be because we can't get a light.

Your husband

Thursday, January 19

MAJOR HENRY HITCHCOCK, Assistant Adjutant
General, Headquarters, in the Field,
near Savannah, Georgia

But for bad weather, we should have left Savannah at least two days ago, by land. As it is, a steady and heavy rain compelled delay. Probably I shall not have another opportunity for the present of writing to you, as we shall be departing by steamer for Beaufort and beyond any day now, and will be then out of the reach of mails for the time. Impatient as I am on all other accounts to be moving again, I confess I rejoice a little in secret over the storm which I am sure will delay us long enough for the "Arago" mails,--as it did; and in them came your letter of 7th inst.

As to where we are going, or what we are going to do, that will all appear in due time. Nobody knows the details except Gen. Sherman himself; very few know even the general outlines, though my position is such that I am one of those; and you may be assured that neither the rebels nor the newspaper men know anything about it—and value what you see in the papers accordingly. This campaign cannot but be even more important in its bearings on the war than the last; it will very likely not be as much of a mere "pic-nic," because we may not go into so desirable or rich a country,--nor will it, in all probability, be as apparently remarkable because the novelty is worn off.

But we have the same genius to drive us,--an even more "demoralized" enemy to meet, and the same good and loving Father to watch over us. And I assure you I will be heartily glad to be moving again. I did not enter the service to "loaf" anyway.

CAPTAIN JAMES M. RANDALL, 21st Wisconsin, In camp, near Pocotaligo,
South Carolina

The *Savannah Republican* published a letter written by Gen. Sherman to the people of Georgia. He said that the people of the state had only to lay down their arms, elect members to Congress, together with U.S. Senators, send them to take their seats at Washington D.C. and then the state of Georgia will have resumed her functions in the Union. All differences then could be settled by the courts. I give this as Gen. Sherman's opinion. The fact is however that before reconstruction is an accomplished fact, the state of Georgia will be obliged to ratify some changes in the constitution in regard to slavery, negro suffrage, Confederate war debt, etc.

Friday, January 20

E.F.A., Savannah, Ga.

I never in all my life knew such furious rains as we had last night; it seemed as if the heavens themselves were falling upon us. I am afraid God will suffer some terrible retribution to fall upon us for letting this war happen. Oh, what a horrible thing war is when stripped of all its "pomp and circumstance"!

ANNA MARIE COOK, Cook House, Milledgeville, Georgia

Our country is in a deplorable condition. Men fear a war of races, and indeed it seems impossible for the white man to submit to negro rule. Men look ominously at one another and wonder what the times will bring.

DOLLY S. L. BURGE, Burge Plantation, near Covington, Georgia

The state of our country is very gloomy. General Sherman's army has devastated Georgia and will no doubt do the same to South Carolina. Well, if it will only hasten the conclusion of this war, I am satisfied. There has been something very strange in the whole affair to me, and I can attribute it to nothing but the hand of Providence working out some problem that has not yet been revealed to us poor, erring mortals. At the beginning of the struggle the minds of men,

[321]

their wills, their self-control, seemed to be all taken from them in a passionate antagonism to the coming-in President, Abraham Lincoln.

Our leaders, to whom the people looked for wisdom, led us into this, perhaps the greatest error of the age. "We will not have this man to rule over us!" was their cry. For years it has been stirring in the hearts of Southern politicians that the North was enriched and built up by Southern labor and wealth. Men's pockets were always appealed to and appealed to so constantly that an antagonism was excited which it has been impossible to allay. They did not believe that the North would fight. Said Robert Toombs: "I will drink every drop of blood they will shed." Oh, blinded men! Rivers deep and strong have been shed, and where are we now? - a ruined, subjugated people! What will be our future? is the question which now rests heavily upon the hearts of all.

MARY ANN HALE, Hale Farm, Decatur, Georgia

This morning I saw Mr. Pate, the depot agent at Decatur, coming toward me. "Oh, Mr. Pate, have you heard anything in the last week?"

"Yes, and it is very hard."

I did not have to ask another question. I knew it all, and am dumb with grief. The thought that I will never see my darling brother again paralyzes me. I see him in the mirror of my soul, in all the periods of his existence. The beautiful little baby boy, looking at me the first time out of his heavenly blue eyes, and his second look, as if not satisfied with the first, followed by the suggestion of a smile. Ah, that smile! It has never failed me through successive years and varying scenes. The boyhood and youth—honest, truthful and generous to a fault—and the noble, genial boyhood, had all developed within my recollection, and I loved him with an intensity bordering on idolatry. My heart cries and I refuse to be comforted.

"Killed on the battle-field, thirty steps from the breastworks at Franklin, Tennessee, November 30th 1864."

Oh, the weight of this grief that is crushing me! Had the serpents which attacked Laocoon, and crushed him to death by their dreadful strength, reached out and embraced me in their complicated folds, I could not have writhed in greater agony. I do not believe it was God's will that my brother should die, and I can not say to that Holy Being, "Thy will be done." In some way, I feel a complicity in his death—a sort of personal responsibility. When my brother wrote to me from Texas that, having voted for secession, he believed it to be his duty to face the danger involved by that step, and fight for the principles of self-government vouchsafed by the Constitution of the United States, I said nothing in reply to discourage him, but rather indicated that if I were eligible I should enter the contest. These, and such as these were the harrowing reflections which accused me of personal responsibility for the demon of war entering our household and carrying off the hope and prop of a widowed mother.

My country is prostrate and bleeding from many such lacerations.

Saturday, January 21

GEORGIA SOUTHERN WATCHMAN, "The Desolation of War"

A correspondent of the Indianapolis Journal paints the following picture of Northern Georgia:

As you wind through the forest, ravine and open country from Resaca to Dalton, the utter loneliness, the want of human life, strikes one with a feeling of desolation. The fences are gone, the houses are deserted, the bubbling spring on the road side has no happy child drinking or paddling in its water. No sheep graze in the fields, no cattle browse in the woods, not even the crowing of a cock is heard. The bee hive is deserted by its once busy tenants, and the ruined mill is still. So startling is the utter silence, that even when the wild bird of the forest carols a note, you look around surprised that amid such loneliness any living being should be happy. This is the result of war.

RICHMOND, VIRGINIA WHIG, "The Refugees from Atlanta Yearning for Home"

Among no class of refugees whom we have met since the war, says the Augusta Register, do we find the same excessive longing for home as we find among the citizens of Atlanta. Old men and women, girls and children, are all longing to return to the desolated scenes to which their local attachments cling. Even as the

[324]

Jews long for Jerusalem so they yearn for their homes. They are willing to go back to the charred and blackened walls of Atlanta, and live during the winter in tents, for the sake of being among the dear old scenes of home.

There are the scenes that are dear to them as the apple of their eye; the hearthstones where the family circle communed, the sanctuaries where they worshiped, the old familiar streets once thronged with familiar faces, all, all are dear to them still and their anxiety, is now on tiptoe to go back to those scenes, even though their businesses are in ruins, their sanctuaries demolished, and the streets strewn with the ruins of their homes. It is home to them. All other lands are as strange places to them, and they feel as strangers among those with whom they are sojourning. They long for home— home, the dearest spot of earth to them.

We hope the day is near when their wishes may be gratified. But ah! it will be a sad pleasure after all. The sweet return will be mingled with much bitter when they see the work of the desolator.

Sunday, January 22

CAPT. GEORGE W. PEPPER, Aide-de-Camp, Headquarters
14th Corps, in the field,
near Savannah, Georgia

THE REVIEW OF THE MARCH

A wonderful march has been made, and most substantial successes achieved. Considered as a spectacle, the march of General Sherman's Army has surpassed in some respects, all marches in history. This great and unexampled expedition has added another laurel to the brilliant record of the armies of the Military Division of the Mississippi, and justified the hopes of its most ardent friends. The conception and execution of this stupendous military movement is the crowning glory of Sherman's brilliant career, and places his name high on the roll of fame, as the most consummate General of the nation. The immense army, composed of the following Corps: the 14th, 15th, 17th, and 20th, commanded severally by Gens. Davis, Osterhaus, Blair, and Slocum--the whole Corps D'Armee, under the immediate supervision of Gen. Sherman.

The whole distance traveled is estimated at about two hundred and seventy miles, the march occupying four weeks. This must be regarded as a rapid movement, when the great size of the army, the length of its wagon-trains, the rivers and swamps traversed, and the work of destruction accomplished are all considered. The face of the country is level, and, near the coast,

[326]

marshy; the soil is sandy and the timber chiefly pine. Sweet potatoes, corn and cotton are grown in abundance; and in the neighborhood of the coast, rice and sugar-cane. Often did we bivouac or encamp in vast forests of tall upright pines, perfectly free from undergrowth, carpeted with green, fragrant grass, and vocal with birds, even in December. During the march, we have been favored with pleasant weather, and usually dry roads. On some days the sun was almost uncomfortably warm.

The smaller planters live in cheaper and less ostentatious dwellings than persons of the same means at the North. At a distance, the master's mansion is sometimes hardly distinguishable from the cottages of his slaves. About three-fourths of the families fled at our approach, leaving home and farm in the care of their negroes; and in such instances the buildings and their contents seldom escaped the torch of straggling troopers. Strict orders restrained, though they did not entirely prevent, arson and pillage of dwellings. Foraging parties scoured the country daily, bringing into camp at night pork, beef, and sweet potatoes in abundance, piled upon ox-carts or army wagons. In the morning the carts were usually burned, and the oxen added to our drove of beeves. The wholesale destruction which attended our progress was painful to behold, unless considered in its true light, namely, as a means of crippling the enemy's resources.

Hundreds of able-bodied negroes were collected, and armed with pick, shovel, and pan, are now doing Uncle Samuel good service. Thousands of good horses, mules and oxen were also brought in to replace poor and worn-out animals. Grist and saw mills, and cotton gins were burned wherever found, and millions in value of baled cotton consigned to the flames. From Atlanta eastward to Covington, from Gordon to Savannah, and from Millen northward toward Augusta, the railways were laid in ruins.

In addition to the skilled negroes, thousands of miserable looking men and women, negroes and the lower class of whites, flocked to our ranks, telling tales of distress, and uttering savage imprecations on the authors of the rebellion. It was enough to puzzle a saint, or to bother Job. They resembled the images of a frightful dream, rather than living men, women and children. In fact, the poor whites of this section are as ignorant, filthy and wretched as can be found anywhere in the world. They are the dirtiest people I ever saw. The hands and faces of many of them were positively loathsome and thick with dirt. This indifference to cleanliness may be ascribed in part to the war; but, I am persuaded that they never had great love for soap or water at any time. Throughout the whole route there seemed to be much destitution and misery.

The state of the habitations of the poor in many parts of Georgia is a libel on the humanity of their more wealthy superiors. A fine dressed lawn, surrounded with miserable cabins and hovels of the poor, nothing can reflect more discredit on the character of the dominant class, than such a contrast.

In accounting for this horrible condition of affairs, it is just and fair to ascribe it all to the mercenary slaveholders. They are haughty, improvident, intemperate and full of hate to the poor whites and blacks. One word as to the origin of this fell hate. Among the multitudes of profundities which distinguish the pages of Tacitus, there is not one more sagacious or pertinent to the present case, than his declaration that "men hate those whom they have injured." This is the utmost stretch of philosophy on the point--it reaches the bottom at once. The quenchless hatred of the slaveholders to the blacks is founded solely in their boundless injuries toward them. The fires of their Pandemonium hate are always fed by the remembered cruelties they have perpetrated and do still perpetrate on millions of the helpless.

I will only add that the Union itself had better work hard to avoid inflicting our own brand of injury on the Negro, even those of us who intend to do good.

HARPER'S WEEKLY, "Sherman's Freedmen,"

Every great military success upon our side brings equally great responsibilities. None of them is more obvious, none more pressing, than the condition of the freedmen in the States which we occupy, or who flock to our lines. Their coming is natural and inevitable. Even the opponents of what is called the emancipation policy have always agreed that the march of our armies would free the slaves. It is more accurate to say they freed themselves by coming boldly into our lines toward an uncertain destination. Those opponents are men, and they know very well that they themselves would rather take the chances of liberty than the certainties of slavery. It was hoped, it was known, that Sherman's great march would bring thousands of slaves with it. It has done so. Did we think, also, how we should be ready to receive them?

After Sherman reached Savannah he sent this message to General Saxton at Beaufort, with a ship-load of negroes: "Please find inclosed seven hundred contrabands, the first installment of fifteen thousand. Many of them are from far up in Georgia, and a long, weary, and sorrowful tramp they have had. Many of them with little children have not brought a thing with them, and have most miserable covering. Bales of clothing could be disposed of among them."

On Christmas Day the agent of the National Freedmen's Relief Association at Beaufort was called upon to prepare for these seven hundred, mostly old men, women, and children, who would arrive within an hour. Half of them had come from Macon, Atlanta, and even Chattanooga. They were intelligent and healthy, but footsore and wary. They were utterly without blankets, stockings, and shoes. Among the seven hundred there were not fifty pots or kettles for cooking, no axes, and few coverings for the head. The agents of the Association at once set vigorously to work, and had the unfortunates housed in a disused commissary building through the rainy night that followed.

[330]

The next morning four hundred were sent off properly guarded, and were encamped upon the island of Port Royal, to be scattered among the plantations as soon as possible. What little superfluous stores were in General Saxton's hands were distributed among them. But the agent reports that there are no stockings, no children's clothing, no cloth for shirts or petticoats, no needles or thread to make them. The blankets are almost gone. Through exposure two hundred of the four hundred are sick; and before his report could reach the officers of the association in New York, the agent says that from three to five thousand more, equally destitute, will arrive to join his suffering colony.

The story is its own appeal. These people are thrown upon our care. We can not avoid it if we would. The most needed supplies are cooking utensils, axes, large and heavy shoes, wool socks and stockings, heavy pantaloons, petticoats, children's dresses of all kinds, blankets, thread, and needles. Money may be sent to Joseph B. Collins, Treasurer, 40 Wall Street; goods and clothing to C. C. Leigh, 1 Mercer Street, New York.

Sunday, January 22

<u>W. T. SHERMAN</u>, In the field, Savannah, Georgia

Dearest Ellen,

Today I embark for Hilton Head. We should have left days ago but the rains have left this entire country under water. It is estimated that there are about twenty thousand inhabitants in Savannah, all of whom have participated more or less in this war, and have no special claims to our favor. But I regard the war as rapidly drawing to a close, and it is becoming a political question as to what was to be done with the people of the South, both white and black, when the war is over.

My aim is, to whip the rebels, to humble their pride, to follow them to their inmost recesses, and make them fear and dread us. "Fear of the Lord is the beginning of wisdom." I do not want them to cast in our teeth what General Hood did in Atlanta, that we had to call on their slaves to help us to subdue them. But, as regards kindness to the race, encouraging them to patience and forbearance, procuring them food and clothing, and providing them with land whereon to labor, I assert that no army ever did more for that race than this one I have commanded through Georgia. I have done enough.

If you ever hear anybody use my name in correction with a political office, tell them you know me well enough to assure them that I would be offended by such association. I would rather be an engineer of a railroad, than President of the United States, or any political officer. Of military titles I have now the maximum, and it makes no difference whether that be Major-General or Marshal. It means the same thing. I have commanded one hundred thousand men in battle, and on the march, successfully and without confusion, and that is enough for reputation.

Next, I want rest and peace, and they can only be had through war. You will hear of me, but not from me for some time.

Affectionately your husband

JENNIE LEWIS, Deveaux Residence, Savannah, Georgia,

Dear Baby,

No doubt about it now. We're all free. And everybody knows it now. Even the white folks.

You will be the first baby in our family born free in this country. You and a whole lot of other babies between soldiers and young women. Miss Jane Deveaux calls you all Jubilee Babies, and she says you will never be slaves.

Long before this cruel war started, Miss Jane Deveaux taught Negro children to read without the white folks knowing a thing. It is because of Miss Jane that so many Negroes in Savannah can read and write with the best of skill. She taught in the very room where we now meet, me and the other young mothers to be. We meet every morning, and the first thing Miss Jane checks is how we're feeling. "You have a special place in history. You have nothing to be ashamed of. You will raise a generation of leaders who will continue to lead us to the Promised Land."

Miss Jane is teaching us how to care for our babies. "Your condition is all part of God's plan," she says. 'It is His plan that we be free. It is his plan that you be the best mothers you can be to these Jubliee Babies. And for that, you must have a good education.'

All of the negroes in Savannah feel the same way. Ten new schools for colored children have already opened around the city. So many groups and clubs and committees have come along in just a few weeks. Colored folks are meeting and talking and planning what we will do now that we all are free. Miss Jane says soon there will be a Teacher's College, where all of us soon-to-be mothers can go. 'You can take your classes at night, and study in the daytime while your babies are sleeping. The women of Savannah will care for the children all evening long, for no charge at all. You can go to college. You can work as teachers, and you can support yourselves and your babies.'

Because of what is going on now, you will go to school. You will learn everything there is to learn. You can be a soldier like your father. You can have a family and never have children sold away. You will do ~~grate~~ great things! I never thought such a future was possible just three months ago. It was not my plan, so it must be God's.

When I feel the sharp longing for my dear Caroline and little Jake, when I think of the many hundreds gone along with them in the waters of Ebenezer Creek, I place my hand on my growing belly and let your beating heart comfort me. It is because of you Baby that I survived that awful night.

Outside my window, I hear the drumbeat as the soldiers march through town. The Colored Soldiers singing along with the newly freed citizens lining the streets:

Glory! Glory! Hallelujah! Glory! Glory! Hallelujah! Glory! Glory! Hallelujah! Our God is marching on.

[335]

As great as our future is, I must also tell you about the past. You must ~~no~~ know what it means to be free. One day I will tell you about the Freedom Road that brought us to this place. And about the man who delivered us here-- your father.

The white people called him the devil. The black people said he was sent from God. I knew him for only a short time but he was a kind and generous man. He loved his children, and he would love you if he could.

I will hold onto the locket that arrived this morning, the broken chain mended, and the note from General Sherman: *'Dearest, Jennie. Please accept this locket and my highest regards and deep affection. I hope you will wear it and think of me, and I hope to see you again in this life--when this cruel war is over. W. T. Sherman.'*

If you are a girl I will name you Caroline. If you are a boy—I will name you William. William Tecumseh Lewis. I will tell you about a great man and a great journey to end slavery and bring us all to freedom. You will know who your father is. You will know how you came to be a Jubilee Baby.

With all my love, I am your mother to be—and I am free.

THE SOURCES

Andrews, Matthew Page, Compiler. *The Women of the South in War Times*. Baltimore: The Norman, Remington Co., 1927

Berry, Carrie. *Diary*.

http://americancivilwar.com/women/carrie_berry.html

Blassingame, John W. *Slave Testimony*. Baton Rouge: Louisiana State UP, 1977.

Bradley, Rev. G. S. The Star Corps; or, Notes of an Army Chaplain, During Sherman's Famous "March to the Sea." Milwaukee: Jermain & Brightman, 1865.

Burge, Dolly Sumner Lunt. *A Woman's Wartime Journal*. New York: The Century Co., 1918.

Burr, Virginia, ed. *The Secret Eye, The Journal of Ella Gertrude Clanton Thomas 1848-1889*. Chapel Hill: The Univ. of North Carolina Press, 1990.

Byrne, Frank L. ed. *Uncommon Soldiers. Harvey Reid and the 22nd Wisconsin March With Sherman.* Knoxville: The University of Tennessee Press, 2001.

Campbell, Randolph and Donald Pickens. "'My Dear Husband:' A Texas Slave's Love Letter." The Journal of Negro History. 65:4 (Autumn 1980) 361.364.

Candler, Allen Daniel, ed. *Confederate Records of the State of Georgia*. "Correspondence of Governor Joseph E. Brown." State Printer, 1909-1911.

Carroll, Andrew. *War Letters*.

Connolly, Maj. James A. *Three Years in the Army of the Cumberland*. Bloomington: Indiana UP, 1959.

Conyngham, Capt. David P. *Sherman's March Through the South*. New York: Sheldon and Company, 1865.

Davis, Burke. *Sherman's March*. New York: Vintage Books, 1980.

Gay, Mary Ann Harris. Life in Dixie During the War.

Georgia Writers Project. *Drums and Shadows: Survival Studies Among the Georgia Coastal Negroes*. Athens: The University of Georgia Press, 1940.

Hoehling, A. A. *Last Train From Atlanta*. New York: Bonanza Books, XX.

Jones, Charles C. Jr. The Siege of Savannah in December, 1864, and the Confederate Operations in Georgia and The Third Military District of South Carolina During General Sherman's March From Atlanta to the Sea. Albany, NY: Joel Munsell, 1874.

Jones, Katharine M. *When Sherman Came: Southern Women and the "Great March."* Indianapolis: The Bobbs-Merrill Co., Inc., 1964.

Lenoir Family Papers. Personal Correspondence, 1861-1865: Electronic Edition. University of North Carolina at Chapel Hill, 2000. http://docsouth.unc.edu/imls/lenoir/lenoir.html

Liwick, Leon F. *Been in the Storm So Long*. New York: Alfred A. Knopf, 1979.

Miles, Jim. *To The Sea*. Nashville: Cumberland House, 2002.

Official Records of the War of the Rebellion, Chapter LVL.

Orr, James. *The Civil War Diary of James Laughlin Orr*.
http://www.crossmyt.com/hc/gen/civwdiar.html #lifeinfo

Pepper, Capt. George W. Personal Recollections Of Sherman's Campaigns In Georgia And The Carolinas. Zanesville, Ohio: Published By Hugh Dunne, 1866.

Phillips, Ulrich B., ed. "The correspondence of Robert Toombs, Alexander H. Stephens, and Howell Cobb." *Annual report of the American Historical Association* 2 (1911): Volwiler, A. T. "Letters from a Civil War Officer." *The Mississippi Valley Historical Review*. 14 (Mar. 1928): 508-529.

Perdue, Robert E. *The Negro in Savannah. 1865-1900*. New York: Exposition Press, 1973.

Platter, Cornelius C. *Platter Diary, 1864 – 1865*. Digital Library of Georgia, Materials from the Hargrett Library.

"S-TC," Villanova University, Box 11, Folder 2. April 13, 1874 letter from Ellie Sherman to William T. Sherman.

Savannah Republican. Editorial. December 21, 1864.
http://www.cviog.uga.edu/Projects/gainfo/ SavRepub.htm

Sherman, Ellen. Letters.
http://www.archives.nd.edu/findaids/ead/index/fulltext/cshr9_40.htm

Sherman, William Tecumseh. Memoirs. Online, Project Gutenberg.

Simpson, Brooks D. and Jean V. Berlin, eds. *Sherman's Civil War: Selected Correspondence of William T. Sherman, 1860-1865.* Chapel Hill: University of North Carolina Press, 1999.

U.S. War Department. *The War of the Rebellion: A Compilation of the Official Records of the Union and Confederate Armies.* Washington: U.S. Government Printing Office, 1893, reprinted by The National Historical Society, 1971).

Sterling, Dorothy ed. *The Trouble They Seen: Black People Tell the Story of Reconstruction.* Garden City, NY: Doubleday & Company, Inc. 1976.

Swint, Henry L. ed. *Dear Ones At Home: Letters from Contraband Camps.* Nashville: Vanderbilt UP, 1966.

Wills, Charles W. *Army Life of an Illinois Soldier.* Carbondale, IL: Southern Illinois UP, 1996.

Winkler, Major Fredrick C. *Civil War Letters of Major Fredrick C. Winkler, 1864.* http://www.russscott.com/~rscott/26thwis/26pgwk64.htm.

ABOUT THE AUTHOR

J. A. Barnes is a writer, teacher, wife and full-time Mom Again to two of her grandchildren. If it weren't for these two children, she would have become a lawyer and would never have written this novel. She may never finish another one. However, this story compelled her to completion. The thousands of nameless ex-slaves who left the fields and big houses of slavery to take their freedom on the road inspired many subsequent marches for freedom, and inspired the author to tell their stories in these pages, to recreate their journey from slavery to freedom along the Great March from Atlanta to the Sea. Barnes has written several books for young readers--*The Baby Grand, the Moon in July and Me; Promise Me the Moon; Amistad, the Junior Novel*—and several award winning plays. She considers *Sherman's Fifth Corps* her least marketable, yet most beloved project to date.